THE Rules OF BEING Friends

NEW YORK TIMES BESTSELLING AUTHOR
JESSICA SORENSEN

The Rules of Being Friends

The Art of Being Friends
Book 2

Jessica Sorensen

Formatted with Vellum

Chapter 1
Raven

The first time I realized my uncle Ben was a total nutjob was about a week after I moved in with him and my aunt. He had mostly ignored me until then, although my aunt and cousin were pretty verbal about how much they loathed the new edition to their "perfect" family.

Before I moved in with them, I'd met my aunt, uncle, and cousin a whopping two times. Once I was at my dad's parents' funeral after they had died in a car crash. My uncle and my dad were the only children they had, which left them only having each other. According to my dad, though, he never got along with my uncle. He never embellished on the specifics, but I figured he wasn't a fan of my dad being a thief and a conman, since my uncle was—and is—a cop.

The second time my uncle made an appearance in my life was a couple of weeks before my parents were killed. He just showed up at our house, something my mom was really upset about. I can't remember much about what happened while he was there, but my memory has always been pretty shitty.

I can always remember having gaps in my memories; tiny holes that I could never fill. I once asked my mom about it when I was younger and couldn't remember how I got home after school.

She feels my forehead for a fever then looks at me worriedly. "You don't feel warm, but maybe we should take you to a doctor, just in case."

I shake my head. "No, I hate doctors."

She crouches down in front of me. "Now, Raven, remember what we talked about. Doctors help us. There's no reason to fear them."

I know she's probably right. My mom usually is. But every time I even think about going to see a man or woman wearing one of those creepy white coats, I feel like I'm going to throw up—

"Raven! Are you up yet?" My aunt pounds on my shut bedroom door, startling me.

I've been awake since before the sun came up, mostly because my side hurts and also because I've been overanalyzing everything that happened yesterday—

"Raven!" my aunt shouts again. "Wake up! You're taking the damn bus today, and it gets here in twenty minutes."

I sigh heavily. "Okay."

She pauses. "You're not going to argue about this?"

"Nope." Because I don't plan on riding the bus.

Harlow told me yesterday that I could ride with her, so I'm going to. Then again, Hunter, Jax, and Zay sort of implied that I could ride with them, too ... I think anyway. Honestly, I'm confused at this point if I have a ride to school or not.

Sighing, I sit up and scoot to the edge of the bed. "Crap, what am I going to do?" I mumble to myself. "I mean, I could just text one of them and see, but ..." *What if this is all a prank?*

No matter how nice the guys and Harlow have been to me, that worry plagues my mind. And I can't help thinking of all the times in the past when I've been pranked by people pretending to be my friend only so they can humiliate me.

"Well, hurry up," my aunt snaps, "or you'll miss the bus. And I'm not driving you to school if you miss it. Dixie May's car arrived last night, so I have no reason to go there." She grows quiet then, and I assume she's left.

I get up to leave my room and use the restroom so I can get ready quickly, so you know, I won't miss the bus, because yeah, I'm a big old chicken and can't bring myself to text anyone. And when I open the door, my aunt is still standing there.

Her blonde hair is pulled into a messy bun, and she's wearing a pair of yoga pants and a long-sleeved shirt—her usual morning look.

She eyes me over suspiciously. "Why are you being so cooperative about this?"

I elevate my brows. "Do you *want* me to argue with you?"

"No," she snaps. "But it's unlike you to be so agreeable."

"Yeah, well, I'm tired," I mumble. Exhausted really. Of her. Of my uncle and Dixie May. Of having to live in this house.

"Probably because you've been doing too many drugs," she sneers. "Just like your mother."

My blood burns underneath my flesh. My mother wasn't a

drug addict. And even if she were, my aunt wouldn't know since she didn't know my mother.

My lips part, and I'm probably about to spit out words that'll get another word carved into my flesh, but my uncle interrupts me.

He steps out of the room across from mine and into the hallway. He's dressed in his uniform, buttoning the top button of his shirt.

"Honey, remember what we talked about," he says to my aunt.

"Right." My aunt's lips twist into a malicious grin as she looks at me. "The bus gets here in twenty minutes. If you miss it, you can walk." She tosses me a smirk then spins around and walks toward my uncle. When she reaches him, she places a kiss on his cheek, but he doesn't even so much as glance at her, his eyes fixed on me like a hawk.

Well, this is new. Usually, my uncle only acknowledges my presence when he's punishing me.

"Breakfast will be ready in ten minutes," my aunt tells him then whispers, "Last night was amazing." She gives him this lustful look that makes me want to puke then struts off toward the stairs.

God, they're so messed up. Both of them. I mean, what did he do? Touch himself after cutting me then go fuck her?

"Why are you looking at me like that?" My uncle approaches me as he readjusts his belt.

"I'm not looking at you." I step back into my room and move to shut the door.

He slams his hand against the door and holds it open. "You

better start being more respectful toward me. I've got a whole list of words waiting to be carved into that pretty little flesh of yours."

So many words burn at the tip of my tongue, but I swallow them down, too tired and too sore to get into it with him this morning. Besides, if I decide to help Jax, Zay, and Hunter spy on him, maybe I can get some sort of revenge. That sounds nice. Although, I'm still a bit wary that what they told me last night is real.

"Yeah, that's what I thought." He grins, but a trace of disappointment reflects in his eyes. Still, he seems pretty damn chipper as he turns around and whistles while walking away.

Flipping the middle finger at his back, I close the door. Then I grab a pillow, press it against my face, and scream. I scream until my lungs are about to burst, until my chest aches. I scream until I have nothing in me. But I can't seem to get rid of *everything*, so I do something I haven't done in a while. I go over to my dresser drawer, take out a razor blade I keep in there, and make a small cut on my side. I breath of relief flickers through me as the wound weeps and the pain inside me seeps out. I know it's fucked up, after my uncle cut me last night, but I am fucked up. To be honest, I've done this for a long time, before I even moved in with my aunt and uncle. I started doing it after and incident with this guy…

I make another small cut before that memory tries to surface. Once I feel good and dead inside, I put the razor away, clean up the cut, and start getting ready for school.

I decide on a black, short-sleeved shirt, with shorts, fishnet tights, and clunky boots. Then I put on a choker, my leather jacket, tie a plaid jacket around my waist, and call it good. I don't even bother doing my hair, just combing it to the side with my fingers. Then I dab on my usual minimal makeup—kohl eyeliner and lip gloss.

I wander over to my computer chair, pick up my bag, and dig out a joint, deciding to take a hit or two before I head out to the bus stop. Hopefully, that'll keep me chill during the bus ride to school.

As I'm heading over to the window, I receive a text.

Harlow: Hey! So, I was going to give you a ride to school, but I have a doctor's appointment this morning, so I can't. But don't worry! I messaged Hunter, and he said he can pick you up!

Okay, so I do have a ride to school. And while Harlow is super nice, and I want to hang out with her, I also am sort of glad Hunter is picking me up so I can talk to him more about this whole ... spy thing or whatever the crap it is that they want me to help them with.

Me: No worries. Are you sure Hunter doesn't mind, though?

Harlow: Ha, does he mind? Trust me, new BFF, he totally wants to give you a ride.

Me: Okay, cool. Thanks for that.

Harlow: No worries. Tomorrow, though, I'll pick you up!

I'm about to put my phone away, feeling slightly better, when I receive another message.

Hunter: Hey, so Harlow told me you needed a ride to school.

Me: Yeah, she text me and said you'd give me a ride, but you don't have to. I can ride the bus.

Hunter: No way! You're riding with us.

Us?

As in Jax, Zay, and him. I'm assuming, anyway. Not that they're totally bad. Jax seems nice anyway. Zay ... I'm still on the fence about.

Me: Are you sure? I don't want to make you drive out of your way or something.

Hunter: It's not a big deal. Besides, we're already almost to your house.

Okay then, I guess I'm riding to school with them.

But now I feel nervous for a whole new set of reasons.

I lock my bedroom door, open the window, and duck my head out. It's cold as balls outside, so I need to make this quick. I pop the end of the joint between my lips, light up, and suck in a deep inhale.

Smoke laces in front of my face as I sit down on the windowsill, holding the joint outside while staring out at the scenery. The house I now call home is located in a small neighborhood of about ten houses, each spaced apart by at least five acres, so the chances of someone spotting me are pretty low. Just below my window is an inclined roof to the porch, and just in front of that is the dirt driveway lined with trees.

Just last night, I was out in those trees with Hunter, Zay, and Jax. They were nicer to me than anyone has been for a while. And then Hunter kissed me on the cheek which was so fucking weird but not necessarily in a bad way. Still, I can't help thinking about how I swear I know him. How, though?

Hunter.

Hunter.

Hunter.

Just who the hell are you?

I'm taking my third hit when I spot a car cruising down the driveway, leaving a trail of dust in the air. And not just any car, but the prettiest Chevelle I've ever seen.

My dad used to be into cars. Up until he died, he drove a 1969 GTO Judge that was this really pretty light-blue color. This car is a similar shade but has a black hood. I'm not positive about the year, but I'd guess either a '68 or '69.

But seriously, whose car is that?

I watch as it pulls up to the house and parks next to my uncle's patrol vehicle. No one gets out right away, but my bet is one of my uncle's new police buddies. Or maybe a neighbor. But then the passenger door opens and Jax climbs out.

So, apparently, this is one of their cars.

"Jesus, they have a Camaro and a GTO," I mumble as I observe Jax. "Those lucky motherfuckers."

Jax is dressed in a black shirt with a matching hoodie and jeans. Leather bands ornament his wrists, his facial piercing glint in the sunlight, and his inky black hair hangs in his eyes. He doesn't notice me as he stares at the lower section of the house. Then he turns toward the car, makes a signal with his fingers, and Hunter climbs out of the passenger side from the back seat.

He's wearing an all-black outfit, too, but his pants have pockets on the sides and a chain dangles from his belt loop. He's also sporting a short-sleeved shirt and has a knitted cap on his head, strands of his blond hair dangling out from it. Even from up here, he still looks too gorgeous to be real.

I shift my gaze across them and to the driver's seat as I take another hit. The windows are too tinted to see inside, but I'm betting Zay is sitting there—

My phone rings.

I startle then move to answer it, noting that Hunter has his phone pressed to his ear.

Sure enough, *Hunter* flashes across my screen.

"Hello?" I answer.

"Hey, so we're outside your house, waiting on your pretty little ass to come out," Hunter says in a cheerful tone, and I can see the smile on his face from all the way up here. "One of us can knock if you need us to. Not sure how strict your aunt and uncle are."

Part of me wonders if he's just asking to ask or if he's trying to get more info about my aunt and uncle from me.

"I can just come down," I tell him. "But why're you and Jax just standing outside the car?"

"How did you know that ...?" He trails off, his gaze straying to me. Then his smile widens. "Aw, are you admiring the view? Or just playing spy again?"

"Neither. But I am rolling my eyes at your cheesy view remark," I quip.

He chuckles. "So damn cute."

My heart does this dumbs fluttering thing, and I immediately tell it to shut the fuck up.

"And that's me rolling my eyes again. But, for reals, why are you guys just standing out there?"

"Well, for starters, we're waiting for you," he replies amusedly.

"Right." My stoner mind is making me an idiot.

I put out the joint on the side of the house.

"And also, Jax and I are having a little bit of a disagreement," Hunter adds.

"And that requires you to stand outside the car?" I duck back inside and put the joint up. Then I shut the window and douse myself with some perfume.

"Well, the disagreement is who gets to sit in the back seat with you," he explains. "I think we're about to have a rock, paper, scissors throw down."

"That you're going to lose," Jax remarks in the background.

"So, what? The loser has to sit in the back seat with me?" I ask as I collect my bag.

He gives a short pause. "Nah, the winner does." Another pause. "Hey, Raven, I know you said you're new to this whole friendship thing, but we do want to be your friend. And friends don't okay rock, paper, scissors because they *don't* want to sit in the back seat with you. It works in the totally opposite way."

For a moment, I sort of just stand there, trying to process his words. Then I try to be cool and say nonchalantly, "Okay," like it's no big deal that he's saying all this stuff about wanting to be my friend.

But deep down, it is a big deal. And I feel nervous. While I try to be nonchalant most of the time, having friends is a whole new territory for me. I just hope I don't mess it up.

And I hope it's actually real.

Chapter 2
Raven

When I make it downstairs, I notice the house is pretty quiet. I figure my uncle must've left for work and Dixie May must've already left for school. But, as I'm passing the kitchen, I hear my uncle murmuring to someone on the phone.

"No, I understand," he hisses. "No, I've tried that, but ... Look, I told you last night that it probably wouldn't work. Yeah, I guess I can try that, but ... I don't know ... Does doing drugs interfere with that sort of stuff ...? No, I have everything under control. That's not going to happen ... No one will find out ... No, she doesn't remember what happened."

That makes me pause.

Is he talking about me and the death of my parents?

I'm not sure, and I don't get any more info because he says goodbye and ends the call.

Still, I can't help thinking about how the guys want me to

help them figure out why my uncle, aunt, cousin, and me are off the grid. Is my uncle aware of this? Did he do it? How?

Sighing, I hurry toward the front door. As I pass the living room, I spot my aunt sitting on the sofa with her face pressed against the window.

Is she staring at the guys?

What a creeper.

I reach for the doorknob to the front door, hoping I can just sneak out without her noticing.

She lets out this wistful sigh and says, "God, to be young again and have potential lovers showing up at your door. I miss it."

I'm not sure if she's talking to me or not, or what the hell she's talking about, but instead of saying something, I hurry out the front door and into the freezing cold air.

Damn, it's cold here. It wasn't this cold yesterday. I probably shouldn't have worn shorts, but I'm not about to go back inside to change. So, I suck it up and march forward, only to grind to a halt again.

Dixie May is standing in front of Hunter, all decked out in a dress and high heels, her hair curled. She's chatting animatedly and, while I can't see her face, I'm sure she's giving her flirty smile.

Hunter is listening to her with this weird look on his face that I can't decipher, and Jax is staring at the dirt with his hands stuffed into his pocket.

For a second, flashbacks of all the times Dixie May humiliated me in front of people flash through my mind.

I'll admit, I almost bolt back into the house, but Hunter spots me, and I swear relief washes over his features.

"There's my new BFF." He hurries away from Dixie May and toward me with a bounce in his step—the dude is so bouncy. When he reaches me, he wraps his arms around me and hugs me, startling the heck out of me. "Oh my God, please get me away from her," he whispers in my ear.

I laugh, but the noise sounds a bit strained due to the fact that Hunter has his arms wrapped around my midsection where the cut is.

He abruptly pulls back and worry creases his features. "What's wrong?"

"Nothing," I lie, gripping his shoulders stiffly.

He frowns. "Are you sure?"

I nod and make myself to relax. "Yeah, just not thrilled that I have to deal with my cousin this morning."

"That makes two of us," Hunter agrees as Jax steps up beside us.

"Can we please get the hell out of here?" he whispers, casting a look over his shoulder at Dixie May, who's staring at us with her jaw practically hanging to her knees. "Before her yapping melts all of my brain cells."

When I giggle, Jax reveals the tiniest of smiles.

Hunter smiles, too. "Yeah, let's get out of here." Then he drapes an arm around my shoulders, which feels super weird. Not in a bad way, but in an unfamiliar way. I wish I could completely enjoy it, but that voice of doubt is whispering softly in the back of my mind. *What if this is all a prank?*

That doubt fades a little as Dixie May continues to stare at the three of us in shock. When we near her, she manages to collect herself, sneaking one glare at me before smiling at Hunter.

"I didn't know you guys knew my cousin," she says, chewing on her bottom lip.

Hunter stops in front of her and, since his arm is around me, I have to stop with him. "That's weird," he says. "Why did you think we were at your house then?"

Her smile fleetingly falters. "Oh, I don't know. I just thought maybe you were ..." She struggles for an answer then straightens her shoulders. "I just thought I'd come out and say what's up. You know, introduce myself, since I didn't get to yesterday." She smiles sweetly at him.

"Yeah, well, we're here to pick up Raven." With his fingers, he lightly skims the side of my arm.

"Oh." Dixie May frowns.

Insert crickets to fill up the awkward silence.

"Okay, well, bye." Hunter throws her a dismissive wave then guides me toward the car. Jax has already climbed into the back seat, so I guess he won their rock, paper, scissors throw down.

Once we reach the car, Hunter removes his arm from my shoulders and gestures for me to climb into the back. I do so, sliding in beside Jax.

Zay is texting on his phone and doesn't glance up at me. He's sitting in the driver's seat, so I'm assuming this beautiful car is his. Like yesterday, he has on a black hoodie with the hood pulled over the top of his head. His hands are resting on top of the steering wheel, so I can see that his knuckles are a bit scraped up. The wounds look fresh.

I wonder what happened.

As Hunter hops in and shuts the door, Zay puts his phone away. "That took way longer than I wanted it to."

"Yeah, I know." Hunter blows out the loudest exhale. "Dude, that was so damn awkward. Seriously, she wouldn't stop talking to me, and I didn't even say a word."

"Even more awkward than getting chased through the parking lot by that Katy chick?" I joke, buckling my seat belt.

Jax snorts a laugh, and Zay flicks a glance at me from over his shoulder before throwing the car into reverse and backing down the driveway. Dixie May is heading back inside but keeps casting glances over her shoulder at the car, as if half-expecting the guys to come back and give her a ride.

Hunter twists around in the seat to look at me with a playful smile on his face. "That thing with Katy wasn't awkward for me since I was the one being chased. Not doing the chasing."

"Liar," I mock. "You totally looked *so* uncomfortable."

"I did not." He rests his chin on the back of the seat. "I was completely calm."

"Bullshit. You basically threw me in your car so you could escape her," I tease, sitting back.

"He threw you in the car ... huh?" Confusion creases Jax's face. "Okay, he didn't tell us about that part."

"That's because she's exaggerating." Hunter smirks at me while reaching for his seat belt.

"I am not. But whatever. We can pretend if it makes you feel better." I flash him a toothy grin.

He struggles not to smile, but then he turns serious, and I

think, *Okay, here it is. He's gonna ask me if I'm in or out with their whole spy, or whatever it is they are, thing.*

"I have to ask you something very important," he says. "And I need you to answer me truthfully, okay?"

"Um ... okay." I glance at Jax to see if he looks as serious as Hunter, but he's just rolling his eyes.

Puzzled, I return my attention back to Hunter, who's carrying my gaze intensely.

"I need to know what your favorite breakfast food is."

I blink. "What? How is that important?"

A smile curves across his lips. "Every person should know what their BFF's favorite breakfast food is."

"Dude, you're weird," I state with a trace of a smile on my lips.

His brow cocks upward. "I think we already established that yesterday. Remember? We both agreed that we're both weird, and that we're perfect for each other."

Zay lets out an exasperated sigh as he steers out onto the road. "Quit flirting with her, man, and get to the point."

Flirting?

"There's a point to this?" I question, causing Hunter to jut out his lip and Jax to chuckle.

"There's a point. Hunter just isn't good at making them." Zay gives me a quick glance from over his shoulder. "What he was supposed to ask is if you're in or not."

"You mean, with helping you spy on my uncle and find out why we're off the grid?" I double-check.

He nods, measuring my reaction closely.

I pause, but only for a second. To be honest, while I've been pretending to think on their offer, I've wanted to say yes since the moment it was proposed to me. "Yeah, I'm in."

"You sure?" A challenge dances in his eyes.

Maybe it should scare me away. I mean, Katy told me all that stuff about the guys yesterday, about how scary they are, and how Zay is into some really weird sexual stuff and never kisses anyone on the lips, not that that should matter to me ... But anyway, her warning should make me cautious, yet it doesn't. Besides, after witnessing Katy chase after Hunter yesterday, I don't think I'm going to take to heart anything she told me. Plus, I want to know why my family and I are off the grid, too, which means I need to help the guys get to the truth. I also want to know why Hunter is off the grid, but I'm not sure if I'm ready to ask that. That would mean telling him why I looked into him in the first place. And how weird would that sound? *Hey, I had a dream last night that I think you were in, but I couldn't quite tell because we were kids. Then I got weird and searched your name online.*

Yeah, I'm so not doing that yet.

"Yep, I'm in," I tell Zay with confidence. "Although, I still don't get why Hunter asked me what my favorite breakfast food is."

"Because we're picking up breakfast on our way to school." Jax props his boot-clad foot onto his knee. "That was just Hunter's weird way of asking if you want anything."

"Hey, at least I asked," Hunter points out while giving Zay the side-eye. "This guy over here would've just assumed she didn't."

"Technically, you're assuming she even wants to go," Zay

says. "And by her agreeing to help us, she's agreeing to pick up breakfast with us because we need to talk about some things before we get started on this."

While they're bantering, I check the time on my phone. "Honestly, as lovely as breakfast sounds"—not that I can afford to eat anywhere—"doesn't school start in like fifteen minutes?"

Hunter's lips kick up into a smirk. "Afraid you're going to be tardy, pretty Raven?"

Great, he's given me a nickname. And while it's a nice nickname, it's completely unfitting.

"No," I reply. "But unlike you, I can't charm the receptionist into giving me a pass. And pretty Raven? Seriously?"

"What?" He gives me an innocent look. "I think it's fitting."

I try not to blush, but holy shit, it's difficult.

"No, it's not. So, if you've gotta call me something besides Raven, think of something better."

"Hmm ..." He rubs his lips together as he pulls the knit cap off his head, strands of blond hair sticking up everywhere. "I'll try, but once I get something stuck in my head, it's usually stuck there. Hence the term *stuck*."

When I playfully narrow my eyes at him, he grins then turns around in the seat. "And I can get you out of being tardy."

"How?"

"You just leave that to me," he replies vaguely. "I just need to know if you're okay with getting some breakfast at the cost of being a little bit late for school."

I lift a shoulder. "I'm cool with being late as long as I don't get detention."

He gives me a thumbs-up. Then he starts texting on his phone.

Zay seems pretty content on driving in total silence, something that's a little weird. Why can't he turn on the radio or something? Talk about awkward.

"You never did say what your favorite breakfast food was." Jax leans over and quietly says to me so abruptly that I jolt in the seat. "You okay?" he asks with a crease between his brow.

"Yeah. I'm just being a spaz; that's all." I rewind over what he asked me ... Oh yeah, my favorite breakfast food ... "It's French toast. I haven't had it in forever, though." Since my parents died. Not that my aunt doesn't cook French toast. I'm just usually not invited to family meals and have to cook my own food. So, you know, frozen pizzas and crap like that.

He smiles. "That's my favorite, too. And this place we're going to has the best French toast ever."

I smile back, but on the inside, something dawns on me again. I have no money. The story of my life.

I'd love to get a job and everything, but I can't drive, and my aunt and uncle won't taxi me around. And since there's no public transportation here, I'm pretty much screwed on the job thing.

"I'll definitely have to try it, then." Sometime, when I have money.

Smiling, Jax opens his mouth to say something else, but my phone pings, causing him to pause. Confused, because who the heck would be texting me so early, or at all, I dig out my phone from my pocket.

Jax looks at my phone with his brows raised. "That's your phone?"

I nod. "I know it's super outdated."

"Outdated is a total understatement," Hunter says while texting on his phone. He saw my phone yesterday when he tried to help me track down that unknown number, so why didn't he say anything then? "You seriously need a new one."

"Hey, it works," I point out. "That's all that really matters."

"We need to get her a new one," Jax states. "If she's going to help us out, that one isn't going to fly in some circumstances."

I gape at him. "What circumstances would this phone not work in? It gets texts and calls. What else does it need to do? It's a phone."

He offers me a sympathetic look that I don't quite fully understand. "We need to be able to make sure we can send files to and from each other safely without anyone being able to hack into our phones and see them. It requires a phone that can hold a pretty large program, and I'm guessing that"—he gestures at the phone—"doesn't have much storage space."

He's completely right, but still ...

"I get it. Well, sort of ... I'm still kind of confused what I'm going to be doing for you guys ... Anyway, this is the only phone I have, and I can't afford a new one right now, so ..." I shrug, like *what're you gonna do?*

"No one's asking you to buy yourself a new phone," Zay says as he makes a turn onto the main road that leads to the center of town where all the shops, food places, and stores are. "We'll buy you one."

I shake my head. "No, you won't."

Zay throws me a hard look that would probably scare a lot of people. I'm not one of those people, though. "That wasn't a request," he tells me firmly. "You work for us now, so we will get you a new phone."

My lips part in protest, because I don't want anyone to buy me anything. It makes me feel like I'm a charity case or something. Before I can say anything, though, Hunter speaks first.

"She did this to me yesterday at lunch, too," he tells Zay as he sets his phone down on his lap. "I bought her lunch, and she made this big deal about it."

"I didn't ask you to buy me lunch," I protest, hugging myself. I can feel it—the embarrassment and discomfort stirring inside me.

"He didn't mean anything by it," Jax tells me, as if sensing what's going on inside my head. "He was making a joke. Just a bad one."

"My jokes aren't bad," Hunter insists, turning around in the seat. He has a smile on his face, but when he looks at my expression, the smile plummets. "Aw, shit. I didn't mean anything by that. I promise I was just joking. And it was definitely a very bad joke."

Zay peers over his shoulder at me, and I suddenly feel like the freak everyone thinks I am.

Here they are, being super nice to me, and I'm getting all defensive over dumb things.

"It's fine." I lower my gaze and start picking at my chipped fingernail polish. "I just don't like feeling like a charity case, and when people buy me stuff, I kind of feel that way. But I'm totally overreacting." I sigh softly. "Sorry."

When they say nothing, I want to shrink inside myself. Awesome. My first day with real friends and I've already messed it up.

I feel fingers brush my jawline, causing me to jolt a little and glance up.

Hunter withdraws his hand from my face and offers me the kindest smile ever. "You don't need to apologize. You didn't do anything wrong, baby."

"I'm being weird," I point out, "about silly things."

He dazzles me with a grin. "If anyone is an expert on being weird, it's me. And I think you know that by now, since you called me weird yesterday at least ten times."

"True." I exhale quietly, telling myself to calm down.

"We're all pretty weird," Jax adds, drawing my attention to him. A faint smile touches his lips. "Zay's the worst. Seriously, he's a freak."

"For sure," Hunter agrees with a grin.

When I look at Hunter, he winks at me, causing me to smile.

Zay doesn't seem as amused. "Great, here we go. Let's make fun of Zay to impress the new girl. Story of my damn life."

I elevate a brow at Hunter. "Do you guys spend a lot of time trying to impress new girls?"

"Nope." Hunter grows serious then. Well, serious for him. "To be completely honest, you're the first person we've ever brought into our group."

While Katy had mentioned the guys never let anyone into

their group, this still surprises me, mostly because I just assumed Katy was being batshit crazy.

My brows pull together. "You've never hung out with anyone else? Ever?"

He shakes his head. "Not really. I mean, we go to parties and shit like that, and talk with people, but that's it."

"It's kind of one of our rules." Jax shoves up the sleeves of his hoodie. "We don't bring anyone else into our group."

"We kind of have trust issues," Hunter tells me without a drop of humor in his tone.

He's being completely serious, and it makes me wonder why. Why don't they befriend anyone else?

What I really want to know, though, is why they decided to befriend me. I could ask them, but I think I've acted like a weirdo enough for the morning.

"Jesus, look at the line," Zay remarks as he steers into the parking lot of a drive-thru diner.

It looks old-school with a marquee and neon signs in the windows. These types of places usually have pretty good food, at least from what I can remember from back in the day when my parents were alive and I went out to eat all the time. Zay is right, though; the line of cars to the drive-thru goes almost all the way back into the entrance of the parking lot.

Zay pulls the car up to the end of the line but doesn't put the car in park yet. "Maybe we should pick someplace else."

"No way," Hunter tells him. "This is our first time getting breakfast with pretty Raven, and this is the best place in town."

"It's fine if we go someplace else," I chime in. "I'm not even

23

that hungry." A total lie. I can't afford breakfast, but I'm not about to go back to that conversation with them.

Hunter gives me a suspicious look, as if he knows exactly what I'm thinking. "Is that the real reason?"

"Yeah," I reply without missing a beat.

He sighs then looks at Jax. Jax looks back at him, and they exchange an unreadable look. Then Hunter looks at Zay, who looks at him.

Um ... What in the world is happening? Are they talking telepathically or something?

Then Zay subtly nods and puts the car in park while Hunter twists all the way in the seat to look at me.

"We want to make you a deal, okay?" he says. "And I want you to really think about it before you answer. Can you do that for me, pretty Raven?"

That is the second time he's called me that in one minute, and I want to comment on it, but his question has me sort of weirded out.

I slowly nod, confusion whirling through me. "Okay."

He smiles softly at me as he rests his arms on the back of the seat. "So, here's the thing. Clearly, you're a little low on cash, right?"

I nod.

"And we're not, so we're thinking, since you're going to be helping us gather information on your uncle and aunt, instead of you just doing it as a favor for us, you can let us pay you with cash when you need it and new phones, breakfast, lunch, dinner —whatever you need while you're working for us, we'll get it for you. You know, like a job ... sort of." He gives a short pause.

"How does that sound?"

Deep down, in the unguarded parts of me, it sounds nice. But in the outside shell of me, I feel unsettled about the idea of relying on someone at all. I have to rely on my aunt and uncle for things I wish I didn't, and with every single thing they do for me, they make a point to show how big of a deal it is. I hate that feeling—being in debt to someone, of not being able to take care of myself, of being a burden to someone.

"It's not *sort of* like a job." Zay rotates around in the seat and looks directly at me. "It *is* a job. You get money and things in exchange for working for us. And it's not going to be easy work."

Jax presses him with a firm look. "Don't scare her, man."

Zay doesn't even so much as glance at him, the corners of his lips kicking up into a slight smirk. "Yeah, I'm pretty sure she doesn't scare that easily."

I throw his smirk right back at him. "If you're referring to your tizzy tantrum of seating arrangements yesterday, then no, I wasn't scared."

His gaze burrows into me. "See? I'm right. And it's a good thing, too, considering our line of work can get intense." He rotates back around in the seat as the line moves.

"So, I guess we're eating here then," Jax says as Zay drives forward with the line as it moves.

"As long as Hunter gets us all out of detention," Zay replies as he stops with the line.

"You know I'm good for that." Hunter fiddles with the leather band on his wrist. "But we need to make sure this one's on board." He looks at me. So do Zay and Hunter.

It's kind of a lot to take in, all three of them looking at me.

And I know they're not just asking me if I'm good to be a little late for school. They want to know if I accept their job offer. I want to. Boy, do I want to. I've wanted to work and earn money for a very long time. I just don't want this to be a favor to me.

"You promise you'll make me work my butt off?" I double-check. "I have to feel like I'm earning my keep or it's going to bother me."

Hunter grins deviously. "I can definitely make sure you work your pretty ass off."

Zay nudges him in the side. "Easy with the flirting."

I can feel my cheeks warming.

Hunter gives him an innocent look. "I wasn't flirting. I was just answering her question."

"You're always flirting," Jax mutters from beside me while staring out the window.

Hunter flicks a look in his direction, but Jax remains focused on the window.

"So, do we have a deal?" Zay interrupts, meeting my gaze in the rearview mirror.

I hesitate. Do I do it? Do I accept this job and just cross my fingers that they won't act like I owe them afterward? I'm not sure.

Then, as if fate decided to bitch-smack me in the face, I receive a text message, and it reminds me of the one I received earlier that I never checked, you know, the one that got this whole conversation about money started.

I quickly glance at it, wondering if it's Harlow. Nope. One message is from my aunt and another is from Dixie May.

Aunt: You'll be locked out of the house when you

get home. I have to go to the city for the day, and I'm not going to just leave the door unlocked just because you need a place to stay. I won't be home until late, and Dixie May will be home at about seven or so because she has cheerleader tryouts. You'll have to hang out on the front porch until someone can let you in.

Me: Can't you just leave me a key underneath the mat?

Aunt: Like I'm going to just let you be inside our house by yourself. You'll probably steal everything.

Her words throw me off a bit. Does she know about the drugs I stole from my uncle? Because I always assumed she wasn't even aware *he* was stealing them.

Not knowing what else to do, I reply with a: **Fine**. Then I move on to the next message.

Dixie May: You must think you're so special, but I promise you I'm going to get you back for embarrassing me in front of those guys this morning. Just you wait. I'm going to get you when you least expect it.

Jokes on her since I always expect that from her.

"Raven?"

Hunter's questioning tone brings my attention back to him.

He's looking at me expectantly, and I'm not sure why.

I pull an apologetic face. "Um ... Sorry, I wasn't listening. What did you say?"

His brows crease, his gaze flitting from the phone in my hand to me. "I asked if you were in or not."

Oh. Yeah. Right. The job offer.

After reading those texts, I want to now more than ever. I want to end having to rely on that family so, so much. And these guys, they seem nice enough. At least nicer than my aunt, uncle, and bratty cousin. So, crossing my fingers that I won't regret this decision, I nod. "Yeah, I'm in."

Chapter 3
Raven

Even though the guys are buying me breakfast, I keep my food items to a bare minimum, not wanting to take advantage of the situation. I order French toast; that's it. But then Hunter orders an extra coffee, and Jax orders an extra hash brown, and then they both try to give me the extras.

"Dudes, seriously?" I set the box with my French toast down on my lap. "Again?"

"Yes, again." Hunter urges me to take the extra coffee he's holding. "If you'd just order a full meal, I wouldn't have to get extras."

"Did you ever think that maybe I just wanted French toast?" I ask as Zay pulls out of the parking lot and onto the road. He has a breakfast sandwich in one hand and is steering the car with his other. "And to be honest, I'm not even used to eating this much food."

I didn't really mean anything by what I said, but apparently, they take it as me not getting enough food in general. At least, that's what I'm assuming from the look of pity that crosses both Hunter's and Jax's expressions.

"I didn't mean it like that," I stress. "I get enough food." To be honest, I do spend a lot of time feeling hungry.

Hunter sighs. "Just take the coffee, pretty Raven, or it'll go to waste."

Now I'm the one to sigh but take the coffee from him anyway. "Thanks."

"You're welcome." His smile broadens. "See? That wasn't so hard, was it?"

I hesitate then shake my head, even though it kind of was.

"Good. And now it'll be easier to accept Jax's extra hash brown," Hunter tells me then looks at Jax.

I turn to Jax and take the hash brown he's holding out to me. "Thanks."

He smiles then opens the box that's on his lap, causing the wonderful scent of cinnamon-y French toast to waft through the air.

I open my own box of food and breathe in the scent. "That smells so good."

"I wasn't kidding when I said it's the best French toast you'll ever have," Jax tells me as he opens the container with the syrup in it. Then he douses his French toast and hands it to me.

"I don't know." I pour syrup onto my French toast. "My dad made some really good French toast."

As soon as I say the words aloud, I bite down on my tongue. It's a little out of character for me to speak about my dad so openly, and I'm not sure if Jax or Zay know my parents are dead. How much do they know about me? I mean, they're spies or something like that, so if they wanted to, they could find out a lot about me.

Crap, what if they know my entire story? Then again, if they did, they probably wouldn't be here with me, so ...

I focus on taking a bite of my French toast and, holy mother-ships, it's like the best distraction ever.

"Oh my God," I moan as the deliciousness engulfs my tastebuds.

No one really says anything, but they all look at me.

I glance at the three of them with my brows furrowed. "What?"

Jax rubs his lips together, his gaze flicking from my mouth to my eyes.

Thinking I must have syrup on my face, I grab a napkin and wipe at it, but it doesn't seem like anything is on it.

Jax clears his throat while scratching his jawline. "I take it from that moan that you like it?"

I nod, more puzzlement webbing through me. "Yeah, it's yummy. Definitely one of the best I've ever had."

Smiling, he stuffs a bite of his French toast into his mouth, but I do catch him trading a quick look with Hunter.

For the next few minutes, everyone remains quiet as we eat our breakfast while making the drive to school. When Zay finishes his and tosses the wrapper into the bag, he breaks the silence to get into business-y stuff.

"So, what I'm thinking is," he starts as he turns onto a road that leads to the school, "Raven can find out a time when the house will be empty, and then she can let us inside so we can do a little bit of snooping around. Maybe set up a few cameras."

"You're gonna set up cameras in my house?" I ask as I cut into the French toast.

Zay casts a glance over his shoulder at me. "You gotta problem with that?"

I shrug. "That all depends. I mean, there's not going to be any in my room or the bathroom, right?"

Zay grumbles, "No. We're not perverts."

I crinkle my nose. "I didn't really mean it that way, but I guess it does sort of sound like I'm implying that, doesn't it?"

He looks at me again with a drop of surprise in his eyes, like he didn't quite expect me to not argue. "Yeah, it did." He redirects his attention to the window. "And to answer your question, we're just going to put them in the living room and kitchen. That way, we don't risk seeing anything we don't want to see."

"Good idea," I state this lightly, but the truth is that I more than agree with him. I couldn't imagine one of them seeing what my uncle did to me last night. "And if you want to get into the house without anyone being home, today is probably the perfect day since my aunt is going to be gone all day 'cause she's going into the city to do some shopping. And my uncle has to work. Although, the house will be locked, so I'm not sure how we can get in."

Hunter and Zay trade an amused look while Jax presses back a smile.

"What's so funny?" I ask then stuff another bite of French toast into my mouth.

"Nothing," Hunter says, but gives me this smile, like he thinks I'm amusingly clueless. "It's just cute that you think that's a problem for us."

My suspicious gaze glides across the three of them. "So, you guys want to break in?"

"Well, technically, we won't be breaking in since you'll be with us and you live there." Hunter takes a sip of his coffee then licks a drop off his pierced lip. "And we won't really break anything. We'll just pick the lock."

I snort a laugh and nearly choke on my French toast. "I hate to break it to you, dude, but if my aunt or uncle caught me going into the house while they were gone and had locked me out, they'll have me arrested," I say between coughs.

Hunter arches a questioning brow. "By your uncle?"

I nod. "Yep. He's not a fan of mine." Just talking about my uncle makes those damn scars on my side throb.

"We assumed so since you agreed to help us so easily," Zay says as he pulls into the school parking lot.

It's fairly empty since school has already started, but there are a few lollygaggers hanging out near their cars. One group in particular draws my attention, because they sort of remind me of Zay, Jax, and Hunter—all decked out in dark clothes and standing around a massive SUV with tinted windows. There are five guys total, and three girls with them.

"Who are they?" I wonder as Zay parks just across from them.

"Who?" Hunter asks then shoves nearly half a hash brown into his mouth.

I point at the group of people who are all staring at Zay's car now. "The fancy Goth people all staring in this direction."

Zay shoves the shifter into park and silences the engine. "That would be one of our many enemies."

"Oh." I guess that makes sense, seeing as how they're all glaring at Zay's car now.

Hunter's eyes glitter with amusement. "You don't seem very surprised we have a lot of enemies."

"Well, considering what Katy told me about you guys, I'm not," I tell him. "Plus, with how big of a douchebag Zay was to me yesterday about sitting in his seat, I kind of assumed he probably makes a lot more enemies than friends."

Zay throws me an unimpressed look as he removes the keys from the ignition. "You know, usually when people talk to me like you do, I teach them a lesson."

I smirk at him. "Yeah, but I doubt you're going to since you want my help."

He stares at me with a somewhat curious look, like he's not sure what to do with me, while dragging his teeth along his bottom lip.

"You know what I think?" he finally says but doesn't wait for me to answer. "I think you're going to cause a lot of trouble for us."

"You don't need to worry about that," I inform him. "I can handle myself."

He rolls his eyes.

"I can," I insist, kind of getting annoyed that he seems to doubt me. "I've taken care of myself for a very long time." *Ever since my parents died.* I resist the urge to swallow hard at that thought and keep up my badass attitude. "Do you know how many times I've gotten in trouble for kicking someone's ass?"

"Probably a lot. And I'm not doubting that you used to be able to take care of yourself." Zay looks me directly in the eyes. "However, you weren't in Honeyton then." With that, he turns around, shoves open the door, and gets out.

"What does Honeyton have to do with anything?" I ask, starting to collect my trash and stuff it into the bag my food came in.

Hunter begins balling up the wrappers to the three breakfast sandwiches he ate. "Honeyton is ... well, it's not like your average town."

My brows knit. "What do you mean by that exactly?"

He hesitates, and I get this churning feeling in my stomach, but I'm not even sure why.

"Because Honeyton is way more dangerous than any other town in the country," Jax says as he grabs the bags of trash. "And people here are ..."

"Wealthy and power hungry," Hunter finishes for him. "Which makes for a bad combination. And the low population and isolation of the town only makes it more dangerous, because it allows these people to do what they want and get away with it. It's part of the reason why these people are having us look into your uncle, so they know what kind of person he is and if he can be bought off."

"Yeah, you said something like that yesterday, but I guess I just didn't realize the whole town was corrupt."

"Not the entire town," Jax mumbles as he stuffs his phone into his pocket. "But a lot of it."

My head is spinning in confusion.

Hunter must read it all over my face because he adds, "You don't need to be scared. You're safe with us, pretty Raven." He smiles at me, but it looks a bit forced. Then he shoves open the door, climbs out, and flips the seat forward to let me out. Zay does the same on the driver's side, scooting the seat forward to let Jax out.

I climb out and sling the handle of my backpack onto my shoulder while holding the bag of trash in my other hand. Hunter takes the trash from me and tosses into a nearby trash can. Then he returns to my side and nods for me to follow him toward the school.

As I start walking with him, with Jax and Zay behind us, I'll admit it feels a bit weird. Not just because I'm walking into school with people, but because I'm not super stoned and don't have my earbuds in.

It's not too bad, though. At least, it isn't at first. But then one of the guys standing around the SUV calls out, "Who's the new girl?"

I stiffen, even though it seems like such a simple question. But it's like a nervous tick linked to all those years of being bullied, I think.

"None of your goddamn business, Porter," Zay calls out in a tone that would probably send a chill up most people's spine, but this Porter dude just grins.

He pushes away from the SUV that he was leaning against and starts toward us, his thick boots scuffing against the pavement. He has short, dark hair that's a bit longer on the top and brushed back, and a few metal piercings ornament his brow and lips. To be honest, he looks like he could be friends with Hunter, Zay, and Jax, but Zay already told me he was an enemy of theirs, something that's made fairly clear as they all give him dirty looks as he approaches us.

Then they slow to a stop, tension rippling from their bodies.

Porter appears unfazed, an easy smile spreading across his face. "Relax," he says as he stops in front of us. "I just came over here to introduce myself." His gaze lands on me then as he sticks out his hand. "I'm Porter Averlyson. My father owns all the car dealerships in Honeyton."

Hunter lets out a soft, disdainful laugh while Jax rolls his eyes. Zay, however, appears to be even more irritated.

"Nobody here gives a shit who your father is."

"I wasn't talking to you," he says to Zay while grinning at me. "I was talking to this sexy girl whose name I still don't know."

I'm partly annoyed at this dude and partly suspicious, not just because he seems to be attempting to be nice to me, but also because it seems like he's using the act of being nice to irritate the guys. Why, I'm not sure, but that suspicion is enough for me not to shake his hand. Besides, who shakes hands anymore?

"Well?" Porter says while looking at me expectantly.

"Well, what?" I ask him in a bored tone.

Jax laughs softly from behind me while Hunter rubs his hand across his mouth, I think to conceal a smile. Zay just crosses his arms, a ghost of a smirk playing at his lips.

"Guess she's not interested in introductions with you, so why don't you go back to your friends and save yourself from more humiliation?" Zay tells him with a smirk.

For a flash of an instant, Porter's smile falters, anger flickering in his eyes as he glances at Zay. Then he recovers, his grin returning as he looks at me. "I'm going to figure your name out, beautiful girl. Because, when I want something, I won't stop until I get it." He winks at me in a way that causes my heart to skip a beat, and not in a good way.

"Did he just threaten me?" I ask as Porter spins back around and returns to his friends, who are all looking at him like they have no idea what's going on.

"No ... I think it was more of a threat to us," Hunter mumbles with a frown.

Zay's gaze is glued to Porter. "It definitely was."

The corners of Porter's lips twitch when he notices Zay looking at him.

"He wants to get his ass kicked," Zay says in a low tone. He stares at Porter for a beat longer before turning and striding by us, heading for the school.

Sighing, Jax hurries after him with his books tucked under one arm. "Great, here comes the drama," he utters.

Hunter gives me an apologetic look. "Sorry about that."

"You don't need to be sorry," I tell him as we start across the parking lot again, the wind nipping at my arms. "You guys didn't do anything. And honestly, I'm not even really sure what just happened."

I sneak a glance over my shoulder at Porter. He's leaning against the back of the SUV with his foot propped up on the bumper. His friends have gone back to their conversation, but Porter is staring right at me so that, when I look at him, our gazes briefly lock. The corner of his lips kick up into a half-smirk that causes my confusion to double, and I look away as my brows dip.

"What just happened is that one of our enemies made a statement," Hunter explains as he retrieves his phone out of his pocket.

"What sort of statement?" I wonder.

He reads something on the screen then pockets the phone, his blue-eyed gaze landing on me. "That you're free game."

"What the heck?" I hiss. "Free game for what?"

He sucks on his lip ring with a contemplative look on his face. "You're new, and you're spending time with us, yet you're not officially part of our group yet. At least, that's how Porter sees it, which means he's going to go after you."

Great. I knew this whole not-being-bullied-in-this-new-town thing wasn't going to happen, even though I desperately wanted it to.

"Should I be worried?" I ask. "I mean, I've been bullied before, but there are different levels of it, you know."

A bit of sympathy flickers in his eyes but quickly dissipates when he frowns. "I didn't mean he was going to bully you. I meant he was going to try to *claim* you."

I scrunch my nose. "Claim me for what?"

He shakes his head with his teeth sunk into his bottom lip. "You're so fucking innocently cute. I seriously don't know what to do with it."

I blast him with a dirty look. "I'm not innocent or cute, dude."

He wavers, scrubbing his hand across his jawline. "You're definitely cute. And as for the innocence thing, you may not be it with some things, but I think you're definitely innocent when it comes to guys."

Now I just feel like a dumbass, mostly because what he's saying is true. And I don't like how much he can see of me.

"I'm going to get to class," I mumble then quicken my pace.

He rushes after me, lightly touching my arm as we reach the curb. "I'm sorry if I upset you," he tells me, gently pulling me to a stop.

I spin around to face him, the wind slowly kicking up and blowing leaves into the air and making strands of his hair dance around his face.

He's so pretty.

I quickly shake the thought from my head. *Stop being weird, Raven.*

"You don't need to be sorry." I fold my arms around myself. "I just need to get to class."

He offers me a small smile. "I know, but I just want to make sure you're not mad at me. I don't think you're naïve or anything. In fact, I think you're extremely smart. I just ..." He hesitates. "Look, all I meant by Porter trying to claim you is that he's probably going to try to get you to go out with him."

I snort a laugh. "You're kidding, right?"

A quizzical line forms between his brows. "Why would I kid about something like that?"

I shrug. "Because there's no way that guy would want to date me."

"Why would you think that?" he wonders. "I mean, I don't want you to date him, but I'm curious to know why you think the possibility of him wanting to date you is so crazy."

I shift my weight and shrug. "Because he's an FH."

His mouth quirks upward. "And you're not?"

"*No*," I annunciate the word.

He eyes me over curiously. "You really believe that, don't you?"

"It doesn't really matter to me whether or not I'm an FH," I say, avoiding the question, "because I don't care if I am or not."

"And now you're avoiding the question."

What is he? A fucking' mind reader or something?

"I'm not an FH. And I don't care if I am."

He steps toward me. "Yeah, you are one. But it's okay if you don't want to agree with me yet. I'm not going to force you to do anything you don't want to do." He takes another step toward me and tucks a strand of my hair behind my ear, causing flutters of confusion to dance through me. "And being an FH doesn't need to matter to you, but as your BFF, I do need to tell you that you are fucking beautiful and totally beyond fuckable. I thought that from the second I saw you in the office." He smiles at me, and this strange sense of familiarity washes over me.

I can't help thinking about that dream I had about the blond-haired boy and how he sort of reminded me of Hunter. But it was just a dream. And even if it wasn't, it doesn't mean that the blond-haired boy was him.

Then I realize what he just said to me, and my cheeks start to warm. I don't know what the hell to do with it. I hardly ever get embarrassed anymore, but right now, I'm definitely veering toward that direction.

I'm about to bail, run off like a freak, go around the school and smoke until I can't feel the warmth on my cheeks anymore, but again, I swear Hunter knows what I'm thinking because he says, "Let's get you to class, okay?"

I nod, relief washing through me.

He smiles at me, and I smile back, feeling a bit better.

I wish the feeling could last, but as we head inside, I take one last glimpse over my shoulder and any relief I felt fizzles when I find that Porter is still staring at me, this time with a huge grin on his face.

Chapter 4
Raven

Jax and Zay are waiting for us when Hunter and I enter the school. Jax is leaning against the wall near the display cases, but he straightens when we walk in. Zay is on his phone, reading what I assume is either a really intense article or a text from someone he's not a fan of, judging by his expression. The hallways are empty, something I appreciate. Of course, about a second later, I became aware that I'm still going to have to walk into first period late. And since this school is on a block schedule, it's a class I've never been to before.

"Give me a second, and I'll get us all excused for being late," Hunter tells us then turns to me. "What class do you have first period?"

"Let me see." I dig my schedule out of my pocket and look at it. "English."

Hunter leans over my shoulder to look at my schedule. "Well, the good news is you have it with Jax."

That makes me relax a smidgeon. At least I won't have to walk in late to class alone.

"And Jax is a poet," Hunter informs me. "So, if you suck at English, he can help you."

"Actually, I like English," I say. "Books are awesome."

That gets Jax to smile. He remains quiet, though. I think he might be the most soft-spoken of the three. Or maybe he's just mysterious ... I don't know, but I find myself curious about the guy with the beautiful smile.

"I'll be right back," Hunter says then spins on his heels and saunters into the office.

As the door slowly swings shut, I hear the receptionist say, "Mr. Hathingford, don't even try to get me to write I pass for you. I told you yesterday ..." Her voice fades as the door softly clicks shut.

"I'm worried he's not going to be able to get us out of detention." I tear my gaze off the office door. "I was in the office yesterday, and the receptionist told him no more passes."

Jax just smiles. Even the edges of Zay's lips tug upward, his gaze remaining glued to his phone.

"He'll be able to pull it off," Jax says with his hands stuffed in his pockets. "If there's one thing Hunter is good at, it's charming people into getting what he wants."

"Something I thought you already caught onto." Zay shoves his phone into his pocket and looks at me with his intense eyes. "I mean, he did it with you, right?"

"Don't be an asshole," Jax says to him.

"I'm not being an asshole. Just stating a fact," he tells Jax but keeps his gaze fastened on me.

"Why're you looking at me like that?" I question. "Do you want me to agree with that or something?"

A challenge dances in his eyes. "If it's the truth, then yes."

"Okay. Then, yes, I agree," I say. An arrogant grin starts to curl at his lips when I add, "That you are being an asshole."

His smile dissolves, and Jax bites back a laugh. Zay gives him a dirty look, but Jax disregards it and sticks his fist out in my direction.

"Nice one," he says to me.

I tap my fist against his, unable to stop a small smile from tugging at my lips.

Zay stares at me, not really glaring, but it's not a friendly look, either. It's almost like he can't decide what to do with me, and it's frustrating the hell out of him.

Story of my damn life.

Zay slowly steps toward me.

"Zay," Jax says with a warning in his tone.

Katy had mentioned that people feared him, but I question if that's exaggerated. *Maybe I'm about to find out.*

"You're not afraid of me, are you?" he asks, assessing me with intrigue.

"No, but I'm not afraid of much." How could I be when fear has been my life for years now? I've felt so much fear for so long that it's just one of those things that live inside me, but I don't fully feel it anymore.

"Yeah, I got that already. I'm not sure if that's a good thing or not, though," he states, his gaze continuing to dissect me. He remains that way for a few slamming heartbeats before stepping back. "Meet us at my car at lunch. We're going to head over to your house." Then he turns and strides away down the hallway, making a turn around the corner.

I release a breath I wasn't aware I was holding then turn to Jax. "Is he always so intense?"

Jax nods. "Pretty much. Don't worry, though; he likes you."

"And you came to that assumption because ...?" I lift my brows in doubt.

He smiles amusedly. "Well, for starters, he let you into our group, something that hasn't happened in ... a while." For a moment, I swear I see panic in his eyes, but he quickly erases it. "Plus, he never lets anyone talk so defiantly toward him without losing his shit."

"He's lost his shit with me."

"Sort of, I guess."

His nonchalant attitude makes me wonder what Zay normally does to people who smart off to him.

"Don't worry; it's a good thing that he likes you," Jax tells me, misreading my expression. "You want someone like Zay to have your back."

He's possibly right. And I guess, in a way, Zay and I are alike, mostly with our toughness. I've just never had a group of friends that I knew would have my back, so my confidence is a bit lower, I think.

"What about you?" I wonder.

"Yeah, I like you, too," he says without missing a beat, almost as if he does it absentmindedly.

I press my lips together to stop myself from giggling at his statement. "Well, that's not what I meant, but I'm glad you do."

Now he's the one to press his lips together. Then he looks

away and I think, *Holy crap, he might be a bit embarrassed.* And I decide right then and there that cute, quiet guys are absolutely adorable when they get embarrassed. Then I decide to let him off the hook, even though I kind of like how cute he looks right now.

"What I mean was: are you as scary as Zay is?" I say. "Well, to other people anyway."

He lets out a quiet exhale then looks at me, fiddling with his brow piercing. "What do you think?"

I consider what he said while eyeing him over. "I think you're like the quiet, calculating type. Like you're not as in-your-face as Zay, but only because you like to plot your revenge."

Amusement sparkles in his eyes. "That's how you see me, huh?"

I shrug. "Maybe. Or maybe you're just shy."

That gets him to laugh. "Yeah, hell no. I'm just not a fan of talking to people unless it's worth my time."

His remark makes me think about how he's standing here talking to me, but I really doubt he meant it like that. Then he smiles again, and I wonder if maybe he did.

We're still smiling at each other, like a couple of idiots, when Hunter strolls out of the office. He has a cocky grin on his face and is carrying a few pink slips of paper. "See? Told you I could pull it off." His smile stays on his face but puzzlement fills his eyes as his gaze bounces back and forth between Jax and me. "Okay, what'd I miss?"

I angle my head to the side. "Nothing really. Why?"

He stops beside me and assesses me. "Then why are you and Jax smiling at each other like a couple of weirdoes?"

"If smiling makes you a weirdo, then you're the biggest weirdo ever," I quip with a cheeky grin.

Hunter grins. "Touché, BFF."

I giggle, and he gives me this amused smile. I'm about to ask him what's up when his brows pucker as his gaze sweeps the hallway.

"Where's Zay?" he asks, his gazing landing back on Jax.

"He went to class," Jax tells him with a shrug. "I'm not sure what he's going to do about being late, but I figure that's his problem."

Hunter pulls a face. "Yeah, I'm gonna go give him the pass. The last thing we need is for him to be stuck in detention while we're working a case."

He hands Jax and me a pink slip then looks at me. "You can meet us at lunch, right?"

I nod. "Zay already basically told me I had to."

"He can be bossy, can't he?" Hunter asks, and then he becomes serious. "You don't have to listen to everything he tells you to do. I mean, I don't think you're the kind of girl who would, but I also know Zay will use you working for us as an excuse to boss you around, but you shouldn't let him."

"I wasn't planning on it," I assure him. "But I don't mind meeting you guys for lunch. I don't have any other plans anyway."

Smiling, he reaches out and lightly tugs a strand of my hair. "Good. I'm glad I get to have lunch with my BFF." He starts to back away as he adds, "And I can try to work a little bit on tracking down that person sending you harassing texts."

With everything going on this morning, I almost forgot to bring that up to him.

"Okay, thanks," I tell him. "They texted me again last night, so I was going to ask you if you could."

He pauses. "Really?"

I nod.

"Okay, I'll look at those texts at lunch, too." Then he spins on his heels and basically skips down the hallway.

It takes a second for his last words to register, and then I feel sick. He wants to look at those messages? The ones that implied I killed my parents? What if he wants to know the entire story?

"You okay?" Jax asks.

The sound of his voice startles me, and when I glance at him, worry is written all over his face.

"I'm fine," I lie. "I'm just not a fan of having to walk into class late."

He rakes his fingers through his hair. "Me neither, but at least we get to do it together, right?" He offers me a small smile that alleviates a drop of my worry.

But then a whole new set of worries rises. What if, when the guys find out what I may have done in my past, they ditch me? Sure, I barely know them, and I'm more used to not having friends than having them, but I kind of like this—having someone to drive to school with, eat breakfast with, walk into class late with, share smiles with, and tease me in a playful way. I don't want to want it, because letting yourself want something means you're opening yourself up to the risk of losing it.

Concern creases Jax's pretty features again. "Are you sure you're okay?"

I do my best to make myself chill the hell out so I don't come off as a total nutjob. "Yeah, sorry," I tell him. "I really don't like drawing attention to myself and being the new girl who walks late into class is going to do that."

He stares at me with hesitation written all over his face, and I feel like he wants to say something but is holding back. Then he sighs. "We should get to class."

I nod in agreement, crossing my fingers that we can slip in undetected. But nope, we don't even come close to doing so. In fact, we don't even manage to make it down the hallway without getting spotted.

As we round the corner, a girl around my age is leaning against a locker. She has long, blonde hair and is staring off into space with her arms crossed and aggressively chewing her gum.

"Shit," Jax curses, skidding to a halt and stiffening at the sight of her.

I glance from him to her then back to him. His expression says it all.

"Let me guess, old girlfriend?"

"Yeah ..." He massages the back of his neck, his gaze flitting between her and me. "Do you mind if we take the long way? I'd rather not deal with her right now."

I shrug. "Sure. We're already late anyway."

He smiles with gratitude then spins around, but as he does, the girl spots us. She immediately stops chewing her gum and straightens.

"Um ... We've been spotted," I hiss under my breath.

I expect Jax to sigh and twist back around, but he snags

ahold of my hand and tows me with him as he basically sprints away from her.

As we round back around the corner, I sneak a peek back at the girl. She's watching us walk away with a hurt expression on her face, and I kind of feel sorry for her. Although, I don't know the story of how they broke up, so perhaps I shouldn't.

Jax continues to hold my hand as he steers me down a hallway that wraps around in the other direction. It's kind of strange that he's holding my hand. I've spent years not being touched by anyone ... well, in a welcoming nice way. But yesterday, Hunter grabbed my hand and now Jax is holding my hand. Honestly, I don't even think he realizes it.

"Was it a bad breakup?" I finally ask when about a minute of silence trickles by.

"What ...?" He blinks at me. "Oh ... yeah ..." He lets out a quiet exhale. "Honestly, at this point, I should be over it. It's been about two years. And I am over it. I just ..." He huffs out a frustrated breath as he rakes his fingers through his hair with his free hand. "It was just a really bad breakup and seeing her reminds me of everything that happened." He lowers his hand to his side and meets my gaze.

"You don't need to explain it to me. I get that breakups can be hard. Or, well, I don't get it personally since I've never dated anyone before, but I know enough to know that they have to be hard." Jesus, can I ramble anymore? Seriously, what is wrong with me this morning?

His lips part in shock. "You've never dated anyone before? *Ever?*"

Why, oh why, do I have to open my mouth sometimes? Le sigh.

I shake my head. "Nope."

His gaze skims across his face. "How ?"

Huh? "How what?"

"How can you have never dated anyone?"

I shrug, feeling a bit squirrely. This conversation is getting way too personal for me. "I don't know. I guess maybe because I've just always been sort of a social outcast." *You know, because my evil villain of a cousin tells everyone that I'm a murderer.*

"I just ..." His confusion doubles. "I just don't get it. I mean, you're easy to talk to, amusing, and beautiful; how can you have never dated anyone?"

Okay, now I'm going into full-on squirm mode. I don't do well with compliments and, to be honest, I almost just want to take off, because I feel like I'm about to shed this layer of skin and all my secrets will be totally exposed.

"I'm sorry if I'm making you uncomfortable," he says.

"You're fine," I assure him. "I just don't do well with compliments and stuff."

"I get that," he tells me understandingly then squeezes my hand. "I'll try to be a better friend and stop complimenting you." The corners of his lips twitch as he attempts to lighten the mood.

I can't help smiling just a bit.

Of course, that smile falters as he pulls me to a stop in front of a closed classroom door.

"Let me guess ... This is our class?" I ask with a heavy sigh.

He gives my hand another squeeze before letting go. "Yep. If you want to hide behind me, you can."

"I think that might make it worse." Sucking in an inhale, I square my shoulders. "No, I got this."

And for a moment, I do. That is, until we walk into the classroom and everyone turns to look at us, including Dixie May. When she sees me, her eyes narrow and a smirk twists at her lips.

"*You're so going down,*" she mouths. "*Payback is a bitch.*"

I'm not sure what she's planning, but I'll admit, as much as I don't want to be afraid of her, I also don't want to lose my new friends.

What if she does something to ruin that? Can I handle it?

Chapter 5
Raven

Despite Dixie May's threat, walking into the classroom isn't too awful. The teacher doesn't make a big deal about there being a new student, and I get to sit in the desk beside Jax's at the back of the classroom. But I'm twitchy during class, and not just because of Dixie May. No, everyone keeps staring at me. And when I say staring, I mean full-on gawking.

During a brief break where the teacher has us working on an assignment—a poem of all things—I lean over and whisper to Jax, "Do you guys really not get that many new people here or something?"

He's scribbling something down but pauses and glances up at me. He seems a little out of it, like he's just coming out of a daze or something.

"What ...?" He trails off, scanning the room. A frown touches his lips as he glances back at me. "Yeah, so I didn't want to freak you out in the hallway, but I kind of figured this would happen. Not just because you're the new girl, and you ... well, all those things I said about you that I promised I wouldn't say anymore." A slight smile touches his lips, but then it fades as he heaves a sigh. "I'm guessing part of the staring probably has to do with the fact that you walked into class with me."

My brow curves upward. "Why?"

He shrugs, tapping his pencil against the desk, his leg bouncing up and down restlessly, causing the chain dangling from his belt loop to jingle. "People aren't really used to seeing me, Hunter, or Zay hang out with anyone outside our circle. At least, not while we're in school. So, I have a feeling you're gonna have people interested in you because of that. Then add in the fact that you're the new girl who's ... Well, you know what I think of you ... But yeah ..." He clears his throat, his knee bouncing even more.

I'm uncertain how I feel about what he just told me, but if he's right, then I guess I'll have to figure out a way to get used to it. Or just get more stoned in the morning.

"You're nervous?" I state, not wanting to talk about me anymore.

He glances at me in puzzlement. "Huh?"

I give a pressing glance at his bouncing knee. "You're nervous."

His leg stops moving. "It's not that I'm nervous. I'm just not a fan of people watching me, either. I like to try to blend in with the shadows." He gives a swift glance around the classroom and, unlike when I look around, everyone hurries to avoid his gaze.

"Well, at least they stop looking at *you* when you make eye contact with them." I grimace. "When I tried to do that, they either smirk or just openly gawk."

His lips kick up into a half-smile. "That's because they're afraid of me."

"Right." I make mocking spooky fingers, and he laughs. "To be honest, I don't really find you guys that scary."

His smile is all sorts of amusement. "That's because we like you. If we didn't, we'd make sure you feared us."

I rest my elbow on the desk and slant closer to him. "By doing what exactly?"

He chuckles. "I'm not sure, since I have a feeling it'd take a lot to scare you."

I point the end of the pencil at him. "You're right, Jax ... Hey, I don't even know you're last name, dude." Although Katy had mentioned it yesterday, it was so brief that I don't remember it.

He winks at me. "That's because it's a secret."

I roll my eyes then lean over and look at the top of his paper where he's written his name. "Jaxon Capperellie ..." My smile falters a little when I spot the word *raven* written in the middle of the inked words staining the page.

He hurriedly moves the paper away from me so I can no longer see it, and for a moment, I think I've made him upset, like maybe he's writing the poem about me. But that just sort of makes me feel vain.

Seriously, Raven, you think he's writing a poem about you? Don't be an idiot.

"I never let anyone read my poems," he explains with a smile. "And no one calls me Jaxon."

I arch a brow at him. "Even the teacher doesn't get to read

your poem? Because this is an assignment, dude. How are you going to get credit?"

He rolls his eyes but continues to smile. "I don't let anyone read them *but* the teacher, smartass."

I can't help but laugh. My laughter fades, though, when the teacher calls us out for talking. Luckily, he approaches our desks and quietly scolds us instead of calling us out in front of everyone.

"Jaxon, while I appreciate you befriending Ravenlee, I would appreciate it if you worked on the assignment during class and set a good example for her," he says to Jax.

I smash my lips together, trying not to smile. But it's kind of funny that he thinks I need a good example, like I haven't learned yet that I'm not supposed to talk in class.

"Sorry, Mr. Johnson," Jax apologizes.

"It's fine. Just make sure to get this poem done."

Mr. Johnson turns to me. "Do you need any help with the assignment?"

I shake my head. "No, I'm okay."

"Okay then, let's get to work." He walks down the aisle, returning to the desk.

"Sorry, *Jaxon*, for getting you in trouble," I whisper under my breath while flashing him a smile. "You really should be a better example, though."

He narrows his eyes at me, but it's a playful move. "Jaxon, huh? So that's how it's gonna be? Okay then, *Ravenlee*, two can play this game."

I roll my eyes, and he smirks at me. Normally, I'd worry if someone was smirking at me like that, but I don't know ...

As scary as people think Jax is, I just don't see it. Like, at all. And that feeling only magnifies as we return to our poems and I watch him write from out of the corner of my eye.

He's extremely intense when he writes, all hunched over, his gaze fixed on the paper that his hand swiftly moves across, staining the pages with ink. Part of me wants to know what he's writing about, but the other part kind of just enjoys watching him. But *le sigh*, unfortunately, I need to work on my own assignment.

Tearing my gaze off Jax, I stare down at my own paper. And stare. And stare. And stare.

I stare so hard my eyes start to hurt. *Gah*, I'm going to fail the assignment.

Finally, I set down the pencil and reach up to rub my eyes. The instant I do, someone walks by my desk and drops a piece of paper onto it. At first, I think it was an accident, so I pick it up and open my mouth to call out to the person who dropped it. But the person—a blond-haired guy who's wearing a letterman jacket —is already sitting down in his desk, right beside Dixie May, who's smirking at me with the end of her pencil touching her lips.

Gritting my teeth, I unfold the paper.

Murderer.
You'll get what you deserve one day.

It's not in Dixie May's handwriting, which means she told someone about my past.

I crumble the paper up, balling it so tightly in my hand that my fingernails pierce my palms.

"You okay?" Jax's voice rises over the rage throbbing inside my head.

I blink at him and find him staring at me with concern overflowing his eyes.

Did he see the paper? Does he know now what I could be?

"I'm fine," I lie, releasing the paper from my death grip.

His gaze zeros in on the balled-up paper then skates back to me. "Are you sure?"

I nod, stuffing the paper into my jacket pocket. "I'm just stressing about this assignment. I can't write for shit."

I don't think he totally believes me but doesn't press. "Try to write about how you feel. That's always a good start."

I force a smile. "Okay."

He frowns, the worry in his eyes remaining.

Worried he might decide to press me more, I focus my attention on the paper and force the pencil to move across the page so I can at least look like I'm doing something. I try to do what Jaxon suggested and write about my emotions, but all I feel is rage, and pain, and shame.

Self-loathing.

Brokenness.

Fear.

I hate the latter, but I can't get it out of me. I don't want to lose my new friends. I hate admitting that, but I don't.

I don't want to be alone anymore.

And I know I'm not anything special. I know there are a ton of people out there in the world who feel like me. What I don't get is why people like Dixie May want to make these people miserable.

My hand moves across the paper ...

There once was a girl made of starlight and pearls.
She shone bright in the smog-covered world.
But that light was too bright for some to bear.
So, every day, they'd throw their flames of grim and hate,
And burn and mark the girl who shone so brightly.
Then they'd stand back and watch her burn.

By the time girl went home, she was covered in burns.
And when she looked in the mirror, it was all she saw ...
The dimness of her light, the burns, the pain,
And it made her own eyes burn.

So she scrubbed at the marks.
She scrubbed until her fingers bled and ached.
Until they burned.
Until everything burned.

And the smudges and marks, they started to fade.

The Rules of Being Friends

And some of her shine faded along with it.
Or maybe her eyes were just too burnt to see it anymore.

Chapter 6
Raven

Despite Dixie May threatening me and that dude dropping a note on my desk, first period ends up not being a total bust. I got to know Jax a little bit, and I managed to complete an assignment that was complicated for me.

By the time the bell rings, I don't feel too awful as I gather my books and stuff them into my bag, including that stupid note. Jax gathers his stuff, too. Then, instead of leaving, he waits for me.

"Well?" he asks once I've gotten my stuff collected.

"Well what?" I ask.

"I saw you writing," he says. "The emotion thing work for you?"

"Actually, it did," I tell him as we make our way toward the door. "Thanks for the tip, oh epic writer." I do a little bow.

He chuckles. "I'm not an epic writer. I just like to write." We pause for a group of girls walking out of the classroom, and then we exit, too. "It's therapeutic for me." He tucks the pen he's holding behind his ear, and I find myself pressing back a smile.

Not a writer, huh? 'Cause he sure does look the part.

The hallway is fairly crowded, but that's normal for high schools between classes. What isn't normal is how much staring is being aimed in our direction. Sure, I've gotten stared at before, mostly because Dixie May spread the awesome story of my past. But I've never gotten gawked at this much, and the staring is more in confusion instead of mocking. It kind of doesn't make sense, since that note someone dropped on my desk clearly means she's told people.

"So, is everyone staring right now 'cause I'm walking with you?" I whisper to him with my gaze sweeping the hallway.

Jax is texting on his phone and distractedly glances up. Then he grimaces. "Probably." He stuffs his phone into his back pocket. "Sorry about this. I can tell it makes you uncomfortable." He dithers, chewing on his lip as he studies me. "If you want, we can give you your space. Personally, I don't want to do that, but I get it if this is too much." He gives a subtle nod at a group of girls sneaking peeks in our direction.

I could say yes. For all I know, this little friendship will be over soon anyway, once the guys learn everything about me. But again, the idea of going back to being alone doesn't sit well with me.

"Nah, it's fine," I assure him.

He visibly relaxes. "Good."

I playfully nudge him in the shoulder. "You wanna be my friend, Jaxon?"

He shakes his head, struggling not to smile. "You're lucky I do, or I'd have to teach you a lesson about calling me Jaxon."

I can't help thinking about what Katy said to me yesterday, about Jax being a scary mothereffer or whatever. Besides a few subtle remarks here and there that could be a little bit uneasy, I just can't picture him being scary.

Why do these rumors get started? Are they just rumors? Or is there truth to it?

"What's your next class?" Jax asks, drawing me from my thoughts.

I dig my schedule out of my pocket. "Math. Blah."

"Math definitely sucks." He leans over to look at my schedule, getting so close that this hair tickles my cheek.

He smells good, like cologne and mint.

An arm suddenly loops through mine as someone steps up beside me. "What're we doing?"

I immediately tense, preparing myself to have to relive the incident of being in the janitor's closet. Then my head snaps to the side to see who's got me, and the tension unravels from my body.

Hunter is beside me, all cheery and full of smiles, like he usually is.

"We're going to class," I tell him as we continue to wander down the hallway with his arm looped through mine.

Jax is walking close beside me on the other side of me, and I feel safe wedged between the two of them. Although, Hunter's appearance has made the staring increase.

"Or, well, I am," I tell him. "I don't think anyone has math with me, do they?"

"Unfortunately not," Jax says as he moves his books into his other hand.

Sighing, I tuck my schedule into my back pocket, secretly wishing I didn't have to go to class alone. Then I roll my eyes at myself. Since when can't I handle going to class alone? I've done it a ton of times before.

"What teacher?" Hunter asks me as he swings us around a couple making out against their lockers.

Well, at least that's two people not staring at us.

"Mr. J." Jax's shoulder lightly touches mine as he moves closer to me to dodge around a cheerleader. Once he gets around her, he keeps his shoulder resting against mine.

And that's how I get walked to class with Hunter's arm looped through mine and Jax's shoulder attached to mine. It's a nice way to get walked to class, and by the time we arrive, I'm feeling pretty decent.

After Hunter unloops his arm from mine, he faces me. "Text any of us if you need anything at all, okay?"

I nod, trying to conceal my nerves of walking into class alone.

Get over this, Raven. You're a big girl.

So, mustering every ounce of courage I have, I walk through the door, hoping everything will be fine. And it is for a while. That is ... until I receive a text. One single text, but it's enough to ruin my entire day.

Unknown: I see you, Ravenlee, and I know what you did. But, do they?

Chapter 7
Raven

By the time lunch rolls around, I'm in a sullen mood. And worried. Not just because of the text, but because I'm worried that, when Hunter tries to work on tracking down the sender, he'll see the text and might ask questions. Or that this person sending the text will somehow tell them since I took the last message they sent as a subtle threat to do that.

I guess that's the one good thing about me being off the grid or whatever. Sure, the guys said they found some vague stuff, but I doubt they know the whole story, like how I was accused of murdering my parents, of the state I was found in that day, of my time in the psychiatric ward. After Hunter looks at the texts, though, he might ask. And then what? I just lie or tell them the truth and cross my fingers they don't look at me like I'm the freak that I am?

Murderer.

Loser.

Disappointment.

To add to the craptasticness, my side is beginning to hurt like a real bitch. I do my best to disregard the pain as third period comes to an end and I make my way out of the classroom to go get lunch. Or, well, play spy.

When I exit the room, I see a familiar face. Blonde hair, blue eyes, basically the female version of Hunter.

"Hey." Harlow waves at me as she practically skips over to me.

I'm starting to think the skipping thing is a family trait, since Hunter does it, too.

She's got her hair in a high ponytail, is wearing the coolest plaid sneakers, and she has a huge smile on her face.

"So, how's your second day going?" she asks as we start down the hallway with her hands tucked into the back pockets.

"Not too bad." At least, it's not if you don't count the note I got in first period and the text. But, to be honest, this is definitely not the worst day I've ever had. In fact, all that is pretty mild. "Well, except for I got a headache in math."

"Almost everyone gets a headache in math," she says. "Mr. J. is so monotonous."

"He really is," I agree. "I swear I even saw him fall asleep for a second while he was giving his own lecture."

"Oh, he did that once already." She laughs. "Literally, he let out this snort then woke himself up. It was so funny."

I laugh. "Really?

"Yep." She grins. "Anyway, I wanted to apologize for not giving you a ride to school. I totally spaced off this appointment I had."

"You're fine," I assure her as we head in what I hope is the direction of my locker—I'm still trying to get my bearings here. "You didn't owe me a ride or anything."

"I know, but I told you I would, so now I feel bad. Next time, I won't blow you off, I swear." She brushes a wisp of hair out of her eyes. "So, totally off the subject, but I heard a rumor about you today."

Tension zaps through my body, and I nearly trip over my own feet. "What? What'd you hear?"

She gives me a sneaky smile. "That the one and only Jaxon Capperellie was super friendly with you this morning. He even walked you to class, which is kind of weird 'cause I thought you and my brother had a thing going."

I can't tell you how relieved I am to hear her say that. For a second, I thought she was going to tell me she heard I was a murderer.

"Both of them have been nice to me, but we're just friends." Sort of. Honestly, I don't know what we are. Colleagues? Yeah, I can't tell her that. "Jax didn't walk me to class, though. He had the same class as me, so we walked in together."

"It's still weird."

"Why?"

"Because Jax barely speaks to anyone besides Hunter and Zay, let alone go to class with someone."

I wish I could tell her that the only reason he's hanging out with me is because I agreed to help them spy on my aunt and uncle, but I'm unsure if she's supposed to know that. Probably.

"Well, to be fair, I think he only did it because we rode to school together, and we had the same class first period, so he offered to show me where it was." I slow to a stop at my locker, giving myself a pat on the back for being able to find it.

She slants against the locker beside mine with her arms crossed. "It's still super weird. In fact, I think the last time he even paid attention to a girl was Lana."

I spin the combination to my locker. "Who's Lana?"

"The only girl he's ever dated. They broke up a while ago, and he hasn't dated anyone since. I think everyone assumed he was still in love with her. Now, though ..."

This Lana girl must be the same girl in the hallway that Jax ran from, I'm guessing. "Now, though, what?"

She gives me an insinuating look, but it takes me a moment to catch on.

"Wait—do people think Jax and I are dating?" I ask, taken aback.

"Not everyone," she stresses. "But I've heard a couple of people talking about it."

I open my locker. "Just because we went to class together?"

She lifts her shoulder. "Call it the perks of a small town. And being friends with my brother and his friends."

"Yeah, about that ..." I put my bag into my locker then shut it. "What's the deal with Hunter, Zay, and Jax? I mean, Katy basically corners me yesterday to tell me they're scary, but they don't seem scary to me. In fact, they've been nice. And everyone stared at us this morning when I walked down the hallway with Hunter and Jax."

"Well, personally, I don't find them scary, but they've done some stuff that's given them a reputation. It's for a good reason." She presses her lips together, almost seeming frightened.

"What is it?" I wonder.

She rubs her lips together, contemplating. "Has Hunter or Jax told you much about this town and the families who run it?"

"Families who run it?" *What?*

"So, I'm gonna assume that's a no." She bends down to tie her sneaker. At least, I think that's what she's doing. "Let's not talk about this anymore while we're standing out in the open, okay?" she whispers as she ties her shoe. "However, if you want to hang out at lunch or after school, I can totally give you the rundown of this hellhole that you now call home. That way, you'll be able to survive."

I want to ask her, *Survive what?* but she seems pretty adamant about shutting that conversation right now, so I let it drop.

She stands up and dusts off her hands. "So, you wanna leave campus and get some lunch?"

I want to. I like Harlow, and it'd be nice to hang out with her, but I'm helping the guys, and I really do want to help them, mostly so I can get some answers for myself.

I'm about to tell her I can't when Jax walks up to us. He still has that pen tucked behind his ear, which I find amusing, and he's also carrying a small wooden box.

"Hey, Low," he greets then looks at me, his eyes all warm, again making me question what this shy, sweet guy could've possibly done to make everyone afraid of him. "You ready to go to lunch?"

I start to nod then look at Harlow. "Sorry, I was about to tell you that I told Jax, Hunter, and Zay that I'd go to lunch with them today."

"It's cool," she says, but I can tell she's a bit hurt, and I feel bad. "You want a ride home from school?"

I start to nod when Jax interrupts.

"Actually," he says with hesitancy, "I was going to take you to get a new phone after school."

"Oh." I can feel Harlow's gaze burrowing into me.

"You're buying her a new phone?" she asks with a trace of amusement. "Interesting."

"Hers is really old," Jax explains, looking at her confusedly. "But why did you say it like that?"

"Like what?" Harlow replies innocently.

Jax does not seem impressed, narrowing his gaze on her. "Don't play dumb with me, Low."

She tosses a sassy grin in his direction. "You don't scare me, *Jaxon*. I can still remember that shy little boy who cried because he accidentally killed a butterfly."

He shakes his head and mumbles, "That's not why I was crying."

I'd probably find it funny and kind of adorable that he cried over something like that, but I'm getting the strangest sense of déjà vu.

The little boy holds the butterfly in his hand, crying. "I killed it."

"It's okay," I say, crouching down beside him. "Butterflies have multiple lives."

He sniffs as he glances up at me. "You promise?"

I nod, even though I don't know for sure. But it seems possible. Butterflies are magical, right? That's what my mom told me. And magical things live forever.

He stops crying, but sadness continues to reflect from his eyes.
"I don't want you to die."

"Earth to Raven." Harlow waves her hand in front of my face.

I jerk back and blink. "Huh?"

She examines me with concern. So does Jax.

"Are you okay?" Harlow asks with a questioning look on her face.

I nod, an uneven breath slowly easing from my lips. "I think I'm just tired. I slept like shit last night."

That appears to satisfy her. Jax, however, doesn't seem to buy it, his gaze basically burning a hole into the side of my head.

"We should get going"—he shifts the box to underneath his arm—"before Zay has a shit-fit."

"Zay always has a shit-fit," Harlow remarks. "But yeah, I'll let you go." She starts to back away then pauses. "You remember that thing I texted you about them yesterday? That club thing?"

I nod, attempting to focus past the bizarre déjà vu still plaguing me. *But seriously, what was that?* "Yeah. Why? What's up?"

"Well, I want to talk to you about it more," she explains. "However, since my brother and his friends seem to think they get to claim your entire schedule, I wanted to pen in some time with you Saturday night."

"To go clubbing?" I check to make sure that I'm understanding her correctly.

"Sort of." Her gaze glides to Jax then back to me. "I'll text you more info tonight, okay?"

I nod, and then we wave goodbye as she heads off toward the cafeteria while Jax and I start toward the exit.

My thoughts instantly go back to those images. I don't know why they appeared other than maybe my imagination is working overtime. Still, I can't help but think about all the time I've forgotten memories.

Do I know Jax from a long time ago?

And then there was that dream I had that I thought Hunter was in ...

"So, about this club she wants you to go to," Jax interrupts my thoughts as he opens the door for me. "Did Low mention what it was called?"

I take a discreet breath and force myself to focus on the conversation, shaking my head as I step outside. "No, but even if she did, I don't think I'm supposed to tell you," I tell him with a teasing smile, hugging my arms around myself as the cool breeze touches my arms.

He steps out and lets the door shut, looking completely serious. "You need to be careful about the places you go in town, especially with you hanging around with us. If you run into one of our enemies, it could get bad if you're by yourself."

"You make it sound like you're in the mob or something." I start to laugh, but the noise fizzles when he doesn't even so much as crack a smile. "Are you in the mob?"

He briefly hesitates. "No."

"You hesitated," I say slowly.

He hesitates again, strands of his hair blowing away from his face, giving me a good look at his eyes, which I'm noticing look shadowed, haunted.

"We're not really in the mob," he finally says. "We're just ... I don't know ..." He sighs. "Can I talk to you more about this when we're in the car where no one can overhear the conversation?"

He sounds just like Harlow, and I'm left wondering what the hell is going on in this town.

I nod, shivering from the wind. "Sure, but you kind of have me worried."

"You don't need to be worried. You're with us, so you'll be protected." He offers me a small smile, and I want to return it, but *protected*? Protected from what?

Then his gaze drops to my arms, and he frowns. "Are you cold?

"A little," I admit. "It was a lot warmer where we moved from. I wore shorts around this time of year all the time, so I didn't think much of it, but I'm definitely regretting my clothing choice right now."

"Yeah, Honeyton gets cold earlier than a lot of places," he says, setting the box down on the ground. "And we have snow like nine months out of the year." He slips off the zip-up hoodie.

My eyes widen. "*Nine months*? Holy shit."

He nods then moves to place the hoodie on my shoulders.

My shock of the wintery weather here is mild in comparison to what he just did. No guy has ever done something like this for me. Like ever. No one has, really.

"I don't really need your hoodie," I tell him. "I can tough it out until we get to the car."

"No way. You're not used to the cold, and I am." He tugs down the sleeves of his shirt then leans over and picks up the box.

Yeah, scary my ass.

"Well, thanks." I slip my arms through the sleeves, and then, to add to his sweetness, he zips it up for me.

The fabric smells like his cologne, and I discreetly breathe it in.

"So, when does it start snowing then?" I ask as we make our way across the campus yard and to the car. Unlike my old school, hardly anyone is eating lunch outside, but it's also probably like forty degrees tops right now.

Jax's gaze flicks up the cloudy sky. "To be honest, it could easily snow right now."

I look up at the sky. "It's not cold enough for snow, is it?"

"Temperatures can drop quickly here," he explains, lowering his gaze, and so do I.

"This town is fucking weird," I remark as the wind stings my cheeks.

"That it is." He reaches over and draws the hood of his jacket over my head. "It'll keep your face warm."

"Thanks." I lightly bump my shoulder against his. "You know, you're making me doubt this whole scary thing more and more, Jaxon."

He just laughs and shakes his head, slipping his hands into his pockets. We reach the car then. Zay is leaning against the bumper, texting on his phone, and Hunter is standing on the passenger side with the door open and has his arms resting on top of it. I think he's dazing off since he's just staring across the parking lot at nothing in particular. Zay spots us first and pushes away from the bumper, putting his phone away.

"About damn time." He crosses his arms. "What the hell took you so long?" He looks at both of us when he says this.

Hunter glances at us, and his brows pucker as his gaze sweeps up and down me. "Are you wearing Jax's jacket?"

I nod. "I was cold."

He angles his head to the side as he curiously looks at Jax. Whatever the meaning behind the look, Jax shifts his weight, uneasiness flowing off of him.

What the heck? Is it really that big of a deal that I'm wearing his jacket?

"I can give it back." I begin to unzip it, but Hunter promptly shakes his head.

"No, keep it on if you're cold," he insists as he walks up to me. "It's not a big deal. I was just being weird." Then he brushes his thumb along my lips. "We wouldn't want those pretty lips of yours to get frozen."

"Jesus," Zay mutters under his breath.

"The jacket's not going to help protect my lips," I stress with a roll of my eyes.

"You know what? You're right." Hunter grins cleverly. "I better kiss those pretty lips and make sure they stay nice and warm."

Zay lets out a groan.

So do I. "Dude, BBFs do not use cheesy lines on their BFFs, remember?" Although, part of me wants to see what it'd be like to kiss him.

Hunter grins. "You never said that before."

"Well, I'm saying it now."

"Hmm ..." He rubs his jawline. "I'll do my best, but no

promises." With that, he spins around and heads to go hop into the car.

I glance to Jax. "Is he always like that?"

"Sort of, I guess." He gives a short pause. "Usually, he has a short attention span and would be moving on by now."

"I've only known him for two days," I point out.

"I know," he says. "That's a long time for him."

I'm unsure what to make of what he said, and question if Hunter will get bored of me soon. Sure, the flirting kind of makes me squirmy, but I also secretly like that he jokes about me being his BFF. I've never had one before, and I kind of want one. Although, I'm sure we have a long way to go before that actually happens.

Trying not to stress too much about that, I head to get into the car. Jax moves with me, walking close. So close that his hand keeps brushing against my lower back. Or maybe he's doing that on purpose? Why would he, though? I don't know.

Zay is the first to get into the car, hopping into the driver's seat. When I climb into the back, I scoot all the way over so that Jax can have room. But he doesn't get in right away, standing just outside the car with Hunter. They're talking about something quietly enough that I can't hear.

Zay shakes his head in annoyance then he rotates around in the seat to look at me. "You know, you're going to cause a lot of trouble for me."

I point at myself. "*Me*? What the hell did I do except offer to help you out?"

He looks at me, his grey eyes dissecting me. I notice he has a scar across his brow.

I wonder what happened.

"You really have no idea, do you?" he finally says.

"I'm not clueless," I reply. But for reals, I have no idea what he's talking about. I'm not about to divulge that, especially to Zay.

He rubs his lips together. "Okay."

"I'm not," I say defensively.

"And I said okay." Although the arrogant sparkle in his eyes completely contradicts what he's saying.

My jaw ticks in annoyance as he twists fully around in the seat. Then he draws the hood of his hoodie over his head and something snags my attention—his hands. Or, well, his knuckles are raw, as if he scraped them badly and recently. And whatever he did, he must do a lot because beneath the rawness are elevated scars.

I rest my arms on the back of the seat. "What happened to your hands?"

He raises his knuckles. "What? This?"

I nod.

A cruel smile curves across his face. "I beat the shit out of someone last night."

"Really?" I ask with intrigue.

"What do you think?" He almost seems to be mocking me.

I shrug. "I don't know. You seem like the kind of guy who might've spent the night beating up people."

He assesses me. "And that doesn't scare you?"

I snort a laugh. "Hell no. My dad used to do stuff like that all the time."

As soon as the words leave my lips, I bite down on my

tongue. Why do I keep speaking about my father so openly with them?

Guilt begins to twist in my gut.

Murderer.

"What did your dad do for a living?" Zay wonders.

I shrug. "I don't know."

He frowns. "You don't know?"

I shake my head, not liking the direction of this conversation. "I already told you I kind of have amnesia."

"Yeah, but I thought that it was just that you couldn't remember a traumatic moment in your life."

"It mostly is, but there are holes that go way back to early in my childhood."

His forehead creases. "Does anyone know what caused it?"

"No. But no one's really looked into it, either."

"Weird," he mutters.

"For sure. But it is what it is."

"You don't want to know what you forgot?"

"Sometimes I do," I admit. "But sometimes I think that perhaps I forgot for a reason, you know. And whatever those forgotten memories are, maybe they were really awful."

He nods like he understands, but how could he unless he's had amnesia, too?

"So, where are we going first?" Hunter asks as he slides into the back seat with me and Jax gets in the passenger side.

Zay immediately turns back around in the seat and revs up the engine. "We need to stop by the house to grab some cameras and stuff. We can get food there."

Hunter scrunches up his nose as he reaches for his seat belt. "We don't really have much in the fridge, man."

"And whose fault is that?" Zay shoves the shifter into drive and backs out of the parking space.

"Jax's, obviously," Hunter says with hilarity ringing in his tone.

"No, it was *your* turn to do the shopping," Zay continues to scold him as he drives out of the parking lot and onto the road.

Hunter reclines in the seat. "Well, I don't know why it was. Jax has the best pushing carts skills."

I snort a laugh then throw my hand across my mouth.

Hunter grins, so pleased with himself.

"He's not funny," Zay grumbles as he shifts gears.

"He kind of is, though," I say with a shrug.

Grinning, Hunter stretches his arm along the back of the seat and around my shoulders. "You are, by far, the best BFF I've ever had."

"Even better than them." I nod at Jax and Zay.

He nods, attempting to appear serious, but his lips are twitching to turn upward. "They're just my Fs."

My brow curves upward. "Fs, as in, they're your forevers? Because that sounds more intimate than best friends forever."

Hunter busts up laughing, his eyes crinkling around the corner.

"Good God, there are two of them," Zay mumbles, shaking his head.

Jax glances at us and, while he's not fully smiling, his eyes glitter a little, so I think he finds me funny.

"Jax thinks she's funny, too," Hunter tells Zay. "So, you're outnumbered, dude."

Zay stays quiet, but his grip on the wheel tightens.

"I think you made him mad," I whisper to Hunter.

"Nah, that's just how Zay is," he says with a dismissive wave of his hand.

Zay shifts the gears again, and the engine roars as the gears lower. I think maybe he's slowing down, but instead, he presses on the gas and switches lanes, flooring it around a slow-moving minivan. He goes faster than necessary, I think playing with his car. It's how my dad used to drive, like he was racing all the time. And he did race sometimes.

"Do you drag race this?" I ask Zay, even though he still seems kind of grumpy.

When he gets in front of the minivan, he speeds up even more, definitely speeding through town.

His gaze remains on the road as he pushes on the clutch and shifts gears again. "Yeah ... Why?"

"Just wondering," I reply. "My dad used to, and you drive a lot like he did."

And again, I'm talking about my dad. What's my deal today?

He flicks a glance over his shoulder. "What'd he drive?"

"Well, he owned a GTO, but he also had a lot of different ones, like a Firebird," I tell him. "He fixed them up and sold them as a hobby, so he had a lot of different ones. Never a Chevelle, though. I know he wanted one. He just ... never got one."
'Cause he died.

Maybe because of me.

"You're into cars then?" Hunter asks, shifting closer to me in the seat.

"Yeah," I tell him. "I used to go on these rides with my dad for hours. It was fun. I've never actually driven anything, so who knows? Maybe I'll hate driving."

Hunter straightens while Zay looks at me with surprise in his eyes. Even Jax looks a little surprised.

"You've never driven *ever*?" Zay asks in shock.

I shake my head. "Nope. I've never had the opportunity."

"Your aunt or uncle didn't try to teach you?" Zay questions.

"No." The bite in my tone is obvious, and I can tell they notice.

Zay raises his brows then faces forward. "Someone's gonna have to teach her to drive."

"I'll do it," Hunter offers, and my stomach somersaults with excitement.

They're going to teach me how to drive? Okay, I'm not one for accepting offers to help me, but I'll take this one!

"No way," Jax says, turning in the seat and resting his arm on the back of it so he can look at Hunter. "You've gotten into, like, five accidents."

"Those were mild fender benders," Hunter stresses, but he has sort of a *whoopsie* face on.

"No, they weren't," Jax says then skates his gaze to me. "I'll teach you. I'm the best driver here."

"That's not even close to the truth," Zay says as he speeds up the car.

"Fine, I'm the safest driver here," he revises, glancing at him. "And I'll be the most patient with her."

Zay must agree since he doesn't argue. Or he just doesn't want to teach me.

"What're you going to teach her in?" Hunter questions. "Your truck? Because I can barely drive that beast of a thing."

"I think we already established you can't drive for shit," Jax tells him, eliciting a dirty look from Hunter. Jax ignores it. "It'll be good for her to learn on it. I can take her to the mud pit, so it'll be easy."

"It's a clutch," Hunter points out, like that should mean something.

"Yeah, so? She should learn how to drive a clutch." Jax pauses. "Stop trying to look for excuses here." He looks at me then. "You okay with learning how to drive in my truck?"

I nod eagerly. "I'd be okay with learning how to drive in anything."

"Even a minivan?" Hunter asks me.

I nod. "Even a minivan."

"My truck's way better than a minivan," Jax assures me with a smile. "I'll take you tomorrow if you want."

Again, I nod eagerly, probably looking like a freak, but in this moment, I don't care. "I want."

Jax's smile widens, and Hunter chuckles, the annoyance leaving his expression.

"You're not a little bit excited about this, are you?" Hunter teases me.

"I'm way excited," I answer, even though his question wasn't serious.

"Really? Huh? I couldn't tell." Chuckling, he urges me closer with his arm that's draped around my shoulders.

"I've just wanted to learn how to drive since I was five and took my first drive with my dad," I explain. "I just never thought it'd happen."

The atmosphere shifts then, a heaviness clouding over.

"Why won't your aunt or uncle teach you?" Hunter asks cautiously.

I lift a shoulder, fidgeting with the leather bands on my wrists that hide some of my scars; scars I once put there myself. "I don't know … They just don't like me that much." I shrug again. "I am kind of a pain in the ass." Not that that's an excuse for anything they do to me, especially my uncle.

That man is a messed-up psycho. Deep down, I know this, and I could tell them, but then I'd have to explain why. And what would I say? He carves my flesh up with words that match the self-hatred I often feel toward myself? Nope, those are never words I can utter aloud, because it'll poison everything.

Silence stretches by.

"Is that the reason you're helping us?" Zay steers into a neighborhood lined with nice, two-story homes.

"Partly," I say. "I do want to find out why we're off the grid."

Zay slows down the car then and pulls into a driveway that belongs to a two-story home that has black shutters, a small front porch, and a two-car garage.

"This is where you guys live?" I ask, straightening in the seat.

"Yeah?" Hunter sits up with me, his eyes skimming across my expression. "Not what you were expecting?"

I shake my head as I gape at the house. "No, not at all."

Hunter removes his arm from around my shoulders and unfastens his seat belt. "What were you expecting?"

"I don't know ..." I shrug. "Honestly, when you said you lived on your own, I just figured you lived in an apartment or something. This is way fancier than what I envisioned."

"If you think this is fancy, you should see the homes we grew up in," Hunter tells me, but his voice sounds a little off, almost like he's being strangled.

"No, she shouldn't." Zay shuts off the engine then shoves open the door. "No one should ever have to lay eyes on those goddamn fucking hellholes." With that, he climbs out and strides up the driveway and onto the front porch.

A beat of silence ticks by, and my mind wanders to what Harlow told me earlier. Well, vaguely told me about the families who run this town. It sounded very mobster-ish, and Jax said something that sounded mobster-like, too. If they do come from families that are kind of like mobs, I wonder what their childhood was like. By the way Zay just acted, probably awful.

Jax gets out of the car next with that wooden box in his hand, and Hunter follows. I scoot over and climb out, too. Jax is waiting for me then shuts the door.

We trail after Hunter and toward the front door that's now open and Zay is already inside.

"So, what's in the box?" I ask Jax, because it sounds like something inside it is jingling around.

"I made it in woodshop," he tells me as we walk up the stairs. "But it has a bunch of stuff inside that Hunter made in metal shop last year."

Hunter pauses in the doorway and glances at Jax. "Really?"

Jax nods as we walk into the house. "Mr. Johnson told me to take it and give it to you. Said he usually just tosses the stuff his old students make, but it felt wrong to toss stuff that's so well made." He hands Hunter the box. "He did make a joke that he should've sold some of it since you didn't seem that interested in keeping it."

As I enter the small foyer, I peer around, taking in the stairway in front of me, the hardwood floors, the living room to my left, and an office to my right. Black and white photos of scenery and buildings line the white walls that lead upstairs and a chandelier hangs above me.

How in the crap can three teenage guys afford *this*?

"I honestly don't even remember what I made," Hunter says as he heads down a hallway just to the left of the stairway. "I think it was a bunch of jewelry that I technically wasn't supposed to be making, but I was bored and Mr. Johnson liked me, so he didn't give a shit."

Jax starts after Hunter, and I just sort of lollygag in the foyer, wondering if I'm supposed to follow them. As stupid as this might make me sound, I have no idea how to act in this type of situation.

When Jax notices me just standing there, he gestures for me to follow him.

A bit of relief trickles through me as I hurry after him. He waits for me to catch up, and then we walk down the hallway and step into a kitchen that has a dining room adjacent to it. Zay is rummaging around in the fridge.

Hunter sets the box down on the granite countertop then rubs his hands together. "Let's open it up and see what my ever-so-awesome mind created a year ago." He lifts the lid and peers inside. "Huh? It's a little anti-climactic."

Jax walks by him and opens a set of doors that leads to a pantry. "What's in it?"

He gives a shrug. "Jewelry, like I said." He takes something out and examines it. "I guess this one isn't too bad."

I make my way across the kitchen to him to get a better look at what he's holding. My eyes nearly widen at the sight of a silver ring, the band engraved with roses that wrap around a black stone that has several tiny iridescent stones trimming it. "You made that?"

He presses back an amused smile. "What? Are you impressed or something?"

"Um, yeah. And I'm not ashamed to admit it." I look back at the ring. "It's pretty."

He considers something then reaches out and takes my hand. "Then it's yours." He slips it on my finger.

"Really?" I ask, staring down at the ring and watching it sparkle.

He nods then puts the lid back on the box. "One day, I'll make you a better one."

I don't really see how that's possible since this ring is gorgeous, but I get snagged on something else he said. One day, as in the future, like we're still going to be friends in the future.

Zay is still standing in front of the open fridge but glances over at us. He looks at Hunter then briefly glances at me, his expression unreadable. Then he looks away and grabs some stuff out of the fridge.

"I'm making grilled ham and cheese, and then we'll head over," he announces. "Hunter, go get the cameras together. Jax and Raven, help me make this shit." He pushes the door closed with his foot, cheese, meat, and butter in his hands. He cocks a brow at me. "Unless you can't cook."

"I can't cook fancy stuff." I round the counter toward him. "But grilled cheese is my specialty."

He doesn't appear too impressed, but I don't think Zay is the type of guy to get impressed very easily. He sets the food down on the counter then bends down to take a pan out of the cupboard. Hunter walks off down the hallway, and Jax exits the pantry with bread. He places that down on the counter then rolls up his sleeves and walks around me, offering me a small smile as he passes. Then he crosses the kitchen into the dining room and opens up the doors to an armoire. Inside is a stereo system, and he pushes a couple of buttons then returns back over to us, digging out his phone from his pocket.

He swipes his finger across the screen then hands his phone to me. "Do you want to pick the music?"

"Sure." I take the phone from him and start scrolling through his playlist, kind of excited to do so.

I honestly believe that you can learn a lot about a person from looking at their playlists. But when I see that Jax listens to a lot of the same music I do, I'm unsure what to make of it. Music is my security; it blocks out the noise and ugliness of the world and helps with my anxiety. I pick songs that speak to my soul, that sing about the dark stuff I can relate to. Is it the same for Jax? I don't know because I don't know much about him, but I find myself wanting to.

After scrolling through a handful of songs, I finally pick one. When I tap on it, music fills the room. I glance around and notice speakers are mounted on the walls.

Jax and Zay have already started on the grilled ham and cheese. Jax is spreading butter onto the bread, and Zay is tossing the bread onto the pan and adding slices of ham and cheese to it. As I head over to help, I notice how they seem to move in unison —all three of them do really. It's like they know what to do to get things done quickly, and it's just something they know, like they've done this hundreds of times before. They said they've been friends forever, but how much time have they spent together? A lot, I'm guessing.

As I step up behind them, Jax turns around to face me. "Nice song choice." He smiles then hands me the butter knife. "Here. Take my place. I'm going to heat up some mac and cheese to go with this."

I roll up my sleeves since I'm wearing Jax's hoodie still and the sleeves are long. Then I take the knife from him, step up beside Zay, and start buttering slices of bread while Jax digs out a box of frozen mac and cheese from the freezer.

For a few minutes, no one talks, and I'm okay with that. Music is playing in the background, and it's a good song, one I know the lyrics to. I quietly mouth them to myself. Normally, if I were alone, I'd belt them out, but like hell am I going to do that here.

"You're not buttering it all the way to the corners," Zay suddenly says in that bossy tone he uses a lot, I'm noticing.

"I'm doing it on purpose," I inform him. "It tastes better this way. The bread's less greasy."

He angles his head toward me. "Grilled cheese is supposed to be greasy."

"That might be your preference, but not mine." I pick up

another slice of bread. "If you want, I can slather butter all over yours."

"Do. I like mine greasy." He picks up the spatula to turn over the sandwiches he's cooking.

"Okay, one heart attack coming up." I slather a crap ton of butter all over the bread. He extends his hand to take it from me, but I move it out of his reach. "Hold on. I missed a corner." I butter a tiny spot that I missed, making sure to get it good.

Zay stares at me, unimpressed. "Do you always take things so literally?"

"No." I hand him the bread. "Do you always take things so seriously?"

Jax chokes on a laugh from behind us. Zay throws a look of warning at him, to which Jax just shrugs. Rolling his eyes, Zay returns to the grilled cheese while Jax trades a smile with me.

Still smiling, I turn back around and pick up another slice of bread to butter.

Zay moves the cooked sandwiches onto a plate to get ready to make another batch. "This thing with the cameras," he says, changing the subject, "we're all going to have to get into the house to install them. And while we do, we're going to need someone to keep an eye on the camera that's set up near the road to make sure no one shows up."

"And you want me to do that?" I ask.

He nods. "I know it's your house, but you don't know how to set up the cameras."

"It's fine." I pause. "You're not going to set up any in my room, right?" I mean, I know he already said that, but I want to be extra certain.

"I already told you I wouldn't."

"What about *near* my room?" You know, close enough that one of them could possibly hear what's happening during those nights my uncle sneaks in.

His gaze flits to me. "I'm not sure." He keeps his gaze on me as he takes the slice of buttered bread I'm holding. "What are you afraid of us overhearing?"

"Oh, you know, my off-pitch voice as I sing in the shower," I lie. "I suck at singing."

I don't think he's buying my bullshit, but that's okay. I won't crack. The wounds and scars on my side start to throb against his intense gaze.

"Having a stare down already, huh?" Hunter steps up behind me and reaches around to grab a sandwich off the plate, standing so close that his chest touches my back.

Zay returns to cooking, not bothering to remark on what Hunter said. "Did you get the equipment?" he asks.

"Yep." Hunter pries the butter knife out of my hand then laces his fingers through mine. "And now I'm going to go look at this beautiful girl's phone and see if I can figure out who the hell is sending her those texts while you finish cooking." He pulls me away from the counter and tows me with him as he heads back down the hallway. I grow nervous, knowing he's going to read those texts.

What the heck am I going to say to him if he does ask questions?

No answer comes to me, and by the time he pulls me into the living room, I'm sweating. When he lets go of my hand, I try to discreetly wipe off my damp palms as I take in the room. It has a fireplace, two sofas and a chair and, like the wall beside the stairway, framed photos hang everywhere. I get a better look at these ones, but one in particular snags my attention. It's of an old tree on top of a hill. The sky is shadowy, and the tree is shedding leaves that are floating around it. It's a haunting photo, but that's not why I'm staring at it. It's that I feel like I've seen the tree before.

"Where is this?" I wonder as I walk over to get a better look at the photo.

Hunter is standing beside me, digging through a box, and while I'm not fully looking at him, I can almost feel how tense he gets, as if it's so powerful it crackles through the air.

"It's on my father's land," he explains in an odd tone. "Zay, Jax, and I used to go there to escape the shit going on in our homes when we were too young to drive. It was a place of solitude until … someone we knew died. We used to spend time with her there. Now it's a place that reminds us of the worst day we ever had."

That was not what I expected him to say.

I look at him then, and his expression is crammed with anguish. This guy, who has been nothing but smiles and sunshine.

I want to ask him who died there, but I know how hard it can be to talk about stuff like that. So, instead I ask, "If this tree reminds you of so much pain, then why do you keep a photo of it on your wall?"

He collects an iPad from the box. "Because, while it's hard to look at, I don't want to forget about her either."

Her? Maybe it was a sister or one of the guy's sisters.

Again, I keep those questions to myself, not wanting to force him to talk about stuff that is clearly painful for him.

"Come sit down with me, and I'll see if I can figure out who's stalking you." He heads to the sofa, nodding at me to follow him.

I do, sitting down beside him. Then, with reluctance, I retrieve my phone from my pocket.

He extends his hand toward it, but I move it out of his reach. He cocks his head to the side, confused amusement written all over his expression.

"I'm going to need to see your phone, pretty Raven, or I can't do much of anything."

"I know." I clutch my phone. I know I'm going to have to tell the guys a little about my past eventually—I know this. And with that note I have balled up in my backpack, I'm well aware that people in the school probably already know. Add that to these texts, and it's inevitable. I don't want to, though. At all. But I think I'd rather them hear it from me. So, sucking in a deep breath, I say, "I need to tell you something before I do."

His puzzlement magnifies. "Okay, I'm listening."

"It's about me, and it's bad," I add, figuring I need to prepare him for this and prepare myself to get dumped by these guys who have been nicer to me than anyone else has for a long time— even cranky Zay. "And honestly, I don't really want to tell you, but these texts are going to make you have questions about it. Plus, I'm pretty sure someone at school has already found out about it, so it's only a matter of time before you guys do, too." I stare down at my lap while continuing because I can't look him in the eyes when I say this.

"When my parents were murdered, I was found with them

... with blood all over my hands and not a drop of memory of what happened ... I still don't remember. I became a suspect and was put in a psych ward for a bit before the police stopped investigating me. Then I was released and handed over to my aunt and uncle. But, even though I was released, there's no proof I didn't do it. There's just not enough proof that I did."

I squeeze my eyes shut as red fills my vision. Then I summon a deep inhale and open my eyes again, willing them to stay dry. I tell myself to look at him, because the silence is getting awkward. But I'm a coward. I never thought this would be an issue with me —I'm usually tougher than this—but I guess nice guys are my kryptonite.

Hunter fixes his finger underneath my chin and angles my head up so our gazes unite. Weirdly, not an ounce of disgust is in those pretty blue eyes of him.

"I already knew that," he tells me softly. "We already looked into your past, remember?"

My heart is thundering in my chest. "But you said you couldn't find much about my past, that I was off the grid or whatever."

"That's more of a recent thing. But there is info about what happened with your parents."

My lips form an O, my heart an erratic mess inside my chest as I wait for him to say what he thinks of this, for him to tell me that I'm a murderer like everyone else always does.

But all he says is, "No one's gonna judge you. We all have our dark pasts. And you're safe with us." With that, he lowers his finger from my chin.

Way, way into the future, when I look back at this moment,

I'll realize that I may have fallen in love with Hunter Hathingford just a tiny bit just then. Although, at the time, I wasn't aware of this, because I didn't know what love was.

He offers me the kindest smile ever. "Can I see your phone now?"

I nod unsteady, my heart still acting like a total lunatic, but for different reasons than being worried. When I hand him my phone, my fingers tremble like little shitheads, and he totally notices but doesn't remark, just giving my hand a gentle squeeze before taking the phone and plugging into the iPad.

I release a quiet exhale and pull myself together. "So, how do you even try to track down this person? Yesterday, you said the phone number was registered in a town in Wyoming, but how do you find out who it is?"

Amusement glitters in his eyes as he glances at me. "You wanna know how I hack shit?"

"Yeah, kind of."

Smiling, he scoots back in the sofa then pats the spot beside him, indicating for me to scoot closer. I inch closer to him, but apparently not enough since he gently grabs me by the thigh and drags me over until my leg is pressed up against his. Then he taps open my phone and opens the text thread from the unknown sender.

A beat of silence ticks by, and then he grips the phone. "This is what they sent you last night?" he asks, looking at me.

I nod, even though I'm sure it was a rhetorical question. "I have no idea how they got that photo of that pendant either, or why they think it's important, but I do know my uncle has it. He was actually trying to burn it before we moved, but I went out and picked it up. When he saw it on me, he freaked out and ripped it off me. Last night, while you were spying on him, he was actually sitting at the kitchen table, staring at it. But I have no clue why."

He nods, seeming distracted by the photo. "We'll look into that more," he mumbles. Then he blinks and looks at me. "But first, I want to deal with this little threat they sent you last night, because like hell am I gonna let this person threaten you."

"I'm not a fan of that either," I agree. "But how can we do anything when we don't even know who it is?"

"Oh, we're gonna find out who it is and deal with them." He lets out this eerie, almost manic laugh as he cracks his knuckles.

It might frighten me, but after spending months in the psych ward, only to be released into my uncle's cruel hands, it takes a lot more to scare me.

Zay enters the room then with a plate of sandwiches in his hand. "What's going on?"

Hunter taps a bunch of buttons on the iPad. "What's going on is that a stalker is gonna get their ass beat."

Zay slants against the doorway. "Sounds like fun, but you need to figure out who it is first."

"Oh, I will," Hunter assures him as my phone lets out a series of beeps.

Hunter sinks into silence then as he gets all intense, clicking buttons and muttering underneath his breath. Zay stares at me, something I'm starting to notice he does, and I'm not certain why. And he does it so openly, as if he doesn't give a crap if I'm aware he's doing it.

After a few seconds of simply looking at me, he pushes away

from the doorway and crosses the room, holding the plate out to Hunter. Without looking up from the screen, Hunter grabs a sandwich and takes a huge bite. Then, in a surprising move, Zay puts the plate out for me to take one.

I reach for one, but he moves the plate out of the way. "Not that one. Take the middle one." He puts the plate back in front of me.

"Why? Is that the one you poisoned?" I joke as I pick up the middle one.

He gives me a hardy har har look. "No, smartass, that's the one that didn't get butter all the way to the corners. You know, the less greasy one that you were raving about in the kitchen."

"Oh ... Thanks then." It was kind of nice of him to make sure I got that one.

At least, that's what I think until he shrugs and says, "No one else wants to eat it. We like greasy." He sinks down onto the coffee table that's in front of us.

"Well, you're all missing out, 'cause this way is the best." I take a big bite and lick up some cheese that drips onto the side of my hand.

Zay is watching me with an indecipherable, but I'm guessing it's more than likely due to my unladylike eating etiquette. But the whole term ladylike is stupid, in my opinion. Like, just because I have a vagina, I can't lick yummy cheese off my hand? Yeah, screw that.

Finally, Zay drags his gaze off me. "I heard a rumor today that one of the families might be sending trouble our way," he tells Hunter.

"Story of our damn lives," Hunter mutters, half-listening.

I freeze mid-bite. "Families?"

Zay leans back on one hand while taking a bite of his sandwich. "Yeah, families. Has no one explained this to you yet? I thought someone would've gossiped about it by now."

"No one's really talked to me except for you guys, and Harlow." I pick a chunk of sandwich off and pop it into my mouth. "And she mentioned it today but said she didn't want to talk about it while we were in school and someone could overhear us. She seemed kind of twitchy about it."

"She should be," Zay tells me. "The families aren't something anyone should be gossiping about in the hallways. Even Low."

"Why do you say it like that? Like she's ... I don't know ... exempt from certain rules or something."

Hunter, who up until this point has been pushing buttons like a mad man, freezes.

Zay looks at him then, and Hunter lifts his gaze to him. They exchange a look.

"We're going to have to tell her sometime," Zay says like they actually had a conversation. "She's with us now, which means she's at risk if she doesn't know."

Reluctance masks his expression. "I know but ... I like that she's unaware of the messed-up shit that we come from."

Zay's gaze turns cold. "You need to check yourself."

Hunter glares at him. "Fuck you."

I feel beyond uncomfortable and, to be honest, confused. Why is Hunter getting so mad at him? And what does he by, *he needs to check himself?*

"Zay's right; she needs to know." Jax enters the room with a sandwich in his hand and a plate of mac and cheese in the other. "She won't be safe if we don't tell her eventually." He looks at me then, and his expression softens. "I'm sorry if I'm scaring you."

"You're not," I tell him. "And I think we already established that I don't scare easily."

His lips remain in a thin line. "If something is going to scare you, this'll be it. And to be honest, I'd prefer if you could just stay out of it. But Zay's right; you do need to know. It's important if you're going to stay safe while you're here."

"You said this wasn't mobster stuff." I eye him over. "But again, with the way that you're acting, it sounds awful mobster-ish."

"That's because it is," Zay states. "Jax just likes to pretend it's not."

Jax scowls at him. "I don't like to pretend. No one's ever given anyone the official title of a mobster. Therefore, I prefer to see it in a different light."

"Yeah, the delusional one," Zay mumbles with an eye roll.

Jax shakes his head in annoyance then sets the plate of mac and cheese onto the table before sinking down onto the sofa beside me so that I'm not wedged between him and Hunter. I try to slide over to make more room for Jax, but Hunter is way too in La La Land to acknowledge what I'm trying to do, so instead, I just end up with my leg pressed against his along with my arm. I lean to the other side to give him some space, but that just makes it so I'm pressed up against Jax. I expect Jax to scoot over the other way, since there's room on that side, but he just reclines back in the sofa, keeping his leg resting against mine, along with his hip and shoulder—basically the entire left side of him. The scent of him floods my nostrils again, and I discreetly breathe it in. There's something about the way he smells that's familiar. I'm not sure why, but whatever it reminds me of, it makes me feel warm inside.

My thoughts fleetingly drift back to that memory of the butterfly …

"Well, whatever we want to call them," Zay says, drawing me back to reality. "Someone needs to explain it to her."

He looks at Hunter, who simply lowers his gaze back to the screen of the iPad. "I'm not doing it, so don't look at me."

"I'll do it," Jax offers then stuffs the last of his sandwich into his mouth.

Zay promptly shakes his head. "No way. You'll just mentally thesaurus all the scary words and use less scary ones."

Jax massages his temples with his fingertips. "You're giving me a headache."

Zay ignores him, focusing on me. "There are five families in this town who basically control everything. Us three are part of the Capperellie clan, which is probably the most powerful family in town. Although, other families will tell you otherwise."

Capperellie is Jax's last name, but not Hunter's. And I don't know Zay's last name. Katy had mentioned they were cousins, though.

"But how is Hunter part of this family if his last name is Hathingford?" I wonder. "And I don't know your last name, but I'm guessing it's Capperellie since you and Jax are cousins."

Zay's brow meticulously arches. "How do you know we're cousins?"

I shrug, a move that's awkward with how close Jax is sitting to me. "Katy told me."

"Right. Hunter's little fuck buddy." He tosses Hunter a look.

Hunter squirms. "She's not my fuck buddy. I just hooked up with her once."

"Whatever," Zay says. "My point is this is why you need to keep your dick in your pants. You get these groupies who like to run their mouths after you screw them over. And now we're going to have to add the jealousy factor into it, which is going to cause a lot more drama."

Hunter's gaze flicks up to Zay. "Jealousy factor?"

Zay glances from him to me.

It takes a second for it to click.

"Raven and I are just friends," Hunter stresses while scratching his wrist.

"So? She's a girl in our group, which means she'll be spending time with you, and all of those groupies, like Katy, are going to get jealous and do who knows what." Zay's hard expression sears into Hunter.

Hunter is way past annoyed, but also twitchy. I feel sorry for him, watching him get scolded by his friend.

Is this what all friendships are like?

"If you want, I can kick her ass for you," I offer. "That might keep her mouth shut."

Zay's gaze skates to me, shock briefly flickering in his eyes.

"Yeah, I think she's going to fit in just fine with our group," Jax mumbles, thrumming his fingers against the top of his knee.

Zay slants forward, resting his arms on his knees. "You seem perfectly okay with getting in a fight?"

"Does that really surprise you, considering the first time we met?" I quip then stuff another bite of sandwich into my mouth.

He observes me closely. "I guess not. It's probably a good thing, too, that you're a fighter, because this hellhole you now call home is going to test your fighting skills."

"Why?" I ask. "Why does it matter if I can fight just because mobsters or whatever reside in this town?"

"They don't reside in the town," Zay stresses. "They fucking *own* it. Everything that gets done here, they know about, and they get a say in it."

"They control everyone," Jax adds, his knee bouncing up and down again, like it did in first period. He has his elbow propped on the armrest and is chewing on his thumbnail. He's wearing a silver thumb ring that occasionally scrapes across his teeth. The noise is like nails on a chalkboard, so I reach over, place my hand on his, and move his hand away from his mouth. He blinks, brows furrowing.

I offer him a small smile. "Sorry, but the ring scraping against your teeth was making an awful noise. Plus, you shouldn't bite your fingernails."

Weirdly, my explanation seems to confuse him even more. He looks at me with almost desperation in his eyes as his gaze searches mine.

"But anyway." Zay's voice sears through the moment. "It's not just the power that makes the families dangerous. It's the rivalry. Every family hates each other and are always trying to dethrone each other. Since the Capperellies are the highest up, we're at risk most, but we're also the most powerful."

Yeah, this is definitely mobster stuff. Still ..."You guys are in high school," I say, feeling Jax shift beside me. He leans closer to me with his hands on his legs and his pinkie grazes mine. I doubt it's intentional, but I feel a soft shiver kiss across my skin anyway. "I mean ... does all of this affect you that much?"

Zay nods with zero hesitation. "We're always expected to honor our family's name, even when we've disconnected from our family, like me, Jax, and Hunter have ... You know Porter? Well, his family is constantly trying to dethrone the Capperellies, so it's not a good thing he was paying so much attention to you this morning."

"But I'm not a Capperellie," I stupidly state the obvious.

"But you're spending time with two of their sons. And Hunter, while his last name isn't Capperellie, his father is best friends with Jax's father, who is the boss."

"The boss seems like a very mobster term," I say.

Zay's gaze never wavers from mine. "That's because they are mobsters, despite what Jax tells you. And he's the scariest motherfucker you'll ever meet."

"She won't ever meet him," Jax bites out, straightening.

"You know that might be out of your control." Zay presses him with a look. "He's already shown an interest in her family."

"I don't give a shit," Jax snaps, rising to his feet. "She's not going to see him. I don't care what he wants. And if he tries to make her, I'll stop him myself." With that, he storms out of the room. Seconds later, I hear a door slam.

Silence ticks by, and my heart is beating deafeningly in my chest.

"He's right," Hunter says quietly. "We shouldn't let him see her. Or any of our fathers, for that matter." He swallows audibly. "Unless we want to risk history repeating itself."

Silence settles amongst them again, and Zay's gaze drifts to the painting of the tree. "Maybe," he utters, I think to himself. Then he glances back at me. "Maybe you shouldn't help us. I mean, now that you know all this, perhaps you should just change your mind."

Is he asking me or telling me? It's really difficult to tell.

"Even if she did, she'd still be at risk since they're already looking into her," Hunter reminds him as he sets the iPad down on the coffee table.

"So ... your parents are the ones looking into my family?" I ask, unsure how I feel about that.

Hunter pulls an *oh-shit* face, like he wasn't ever planning on telling me. "You technically weren't supposed to know that."

I restlessly ravel a strand of my hair around my finger. "I wouldn't tell anyone. I don't even have anyone to tell."

"I know you think that, but there are people here who have a way of getting the truth out of anyone," Hunter says with a remorseful look.

"Like Porter," Zay states. "So, you need to be careful if you're ever around him."

A chill slithers up my spine, but I remain calm on the outside.

"You'll be fine." Hunter levels his gaze with mine. "We'll keep an eye on you. You're not alone in this."

While I'm certain he means his words, I have a hard time accepting them—that I'm not alone in this. I've been alone in this —in life—for a very long time.

Zay's phone beeps suddenly, and when he glances at it, a frown forms on his face. "We should get going. We have about thirty more minutes before lunch is over." He gets to his feet without waiting for anyone to respond.

Hunter sighs then twists to face me, giving me back my phone. "We'll work more on this later, after Jax takes you to get you a new phone afterschool. I'm thinking that it might be easier to track the number from a device that's more compatible with the programs I use."

"Are you sure Jax will still want to take me?" I take the phone from him and pocket it before standing up.

"Of course." Hunter rises to his feet, too, and collects the box he took the iPad from.

"He seemed really upset."

He balances the box in one hand so he can brush a wisp of his blond hair out of his face. "That had nothing to do with you, baby. There's just certain topics that set him off sometimes, but he'll calm down in just a few minutes."

"Oh." I pause. "He doesn't like talking about his dad then?"

Hunter shakes his head. "No one does. And the same goes for our own fathers." He wavers. "Jax, Zay, and I worked really hard to get away from them. We saved up every ounce of money we made so we could get our own place. Unfortunately, while we remain in this town, we'll always be under their control, like when they force us to look into you and your family. After we graduate, though, we're out."

"I get that. I mean, wanting to take off after you graduate. I fully plan on, too." That is, if I can figure out a way to save up money. "Why don't you guys just leave now? I mean, you live on your own, so I'm assuming you're all either eighteen or have been emancipated."

"We're all eighteen. And while we'd like to leave, we made a vow to stick around until graduation, mostly to keep an eye on Low for as long as we can." He pauses, severe reluctance weighing in his expression. "And there are a few things tied to this town that not all of us are ready to say goodbye to." Again, his face turns solemn as he glances at the photo of the tree.

I find myself wanting to know what happened. Who did they lose that they used to spend time with at that tree? I won't ask. Not with how haunted Hunter's eyes look. So, I try to let it go as we leave the living room and walk out of the house. But even when we step outside into the chilly wind and clouds, surrounded by a neighborhood of picture-perfect houses, I can't stop thinking about that tree.

Like it's branded into my mind.

Chapter 8
Raven

Jax is upset, and I'm still a bit uncertain why. I'm also a little unsure why I decided to hold his hand. Maybe because he did the same thing for me earlier? I don't know ...

Whatever the reason, the gesture does seem to relax him, enough that he scoots closer to me and laces our fingers together. He doesn't say anything, just breathes softly while staring out the window as we drive toward my house. Hunter doesn't talk either, too busy setting up the gear. Zay's quiet, too, but I do see him glance at me in the rearview mirror a few times. Why? I'm not sure. What I am sure about is that these guys are really confusing.

The silence almost becomes maddening to the point where I'm kind of relieved when we park beside my house, something I never thought I'd ever feel. Zay parks in the trees where the car is out of view of anyone who pulls up into the driveway, but I can still spot the house through the cracks in the trees.

"Are we ready to go?" Zay asks Hunter as he turns off the car.

Hunter nods as he stuffs the last of the cameras and equipment into a backpack he brought with him. He keeps one of the iPads out and twists in the seat to look at me.

"However, this device goes to this pretty girl right here." He grins at me as I take the iPad from him.

I roll my eyes. "And there you go with your cheesy lines again."

"Aw, baby, I'm sorry," he says innocently. "I forgot I said I was gonna try to stop." He bats his eyelashes at me. "Please forgive me."

I roll my eyes again but can't help smiling. "I will, but only if you don't call me baby anymore."

"I'll try my best," he tells me with a mischievous smile.

"Great. That means you're gonna call me baby a lot, doesn't it?" I grimace.

He wets his lips with his tongue. "I think you're catching onto my quirks, aren't you, pretty Raven?"

"Quirks?" I question with my arms crossed. "Or obnoxious habits?"

He chuckles at that while Zay sighs and pushes open the door. "Make sure she knows how to use the app," he tells Hunter before climbing out.

Hunter gives him a salute, his gaze briefly flitting to Jax, who hasn't uttered a word and is still staring out the window. He momentarily frowns but erases it when he focuses back on me.

"All right, so all you need to do is keep this open." He leans over so he can tap the screen of the iPad, strands of his hair tickling my face as he gets close.

As he pushes the buttons, his gaze strays Jax and mine's interlocked fingers and freezes. He blinks, and I almost pull away but don't want to upset Jax. When Hunter's gaze skates back to me, he doesn't look upset or anything, just curious. He offers me a smile before tapping open an unlabeled app. When the screen goes black, I glance up at him in confusion.

"What am I looking at?"

"Nothing yet," he explains, rotating back around and pushing the door open. "We'll set up a camera in the driveway before we break in. Once I power it on, you'll be able to see the road and the driveway. If a car shows up at all, call my cell ASAP, okay?" He waits for me to nod then climbs out of the car and flips the seat forward so Jax can get out.

Jax doesn't get out right away. Hesitancy consumes his face as his eyes slide from me to Hunter. "Maybe I should stay with her, so she won't have to be alone."

Hunter's expression crams with sympathy. "You know we need your help setting up the cameras. Raven will be fine. If I thought she wouldn't be, I wouldn't leave her out here by herself."

When Jax continues to remain hesitant, I try to reassure him. "I'll be fine. I know how to throw a punch if I need to." Of course, I don't know why I'd need to punch anyone in this situation, but Jax seems worried.

His gaze meets mine, and I want to retract my initial statement.

Jax doesn't *seem* worried. Jax *is* extremely worried.

"I just ... I don't like the idea of you being in the car alone when we're doing this sort of stuff," he offers an explanation. "And the car's parked in the woods."

"I'll be fine," I continue to try to alleviate his worry, but I'm a bit perplexed over what specifically he's worried about. "I promise." I smile, hoping that'll help, but it only causes him to start bouncing his knee up and down like crazy.

Hunter sighs. "If you want, you can keep her on the phone with you," he tells Jax. "That way, you'll know exactly what's going on."

Jax wavers for a heartbeat before nodding. "Okay, yeah, let's do that." He turns to me. "I'm going to call you, okay? And then keep you on the line with me. That way, if anything goes wrong at all, I'll know ASAP."

To lighten the mood, I give him a salute, but I have to wonder what he's so worried about, what he thinks might happen. The guys said this town was sketchy, that their fathers are, too, and the idea of me even meeting Jax's father is what I think caused him to take off out of the living room. But I doubt that could be a risk of happening while I'm hanging out in the woods, playing spy ... right?

Hunter smiles at my salute, and even a trace of one touches Jax's lips. But it swiftly fades as he slowly gets out of the car.

Hunter lowers his head and looks at me. "Are you good?" he double-checks.

I nod. "Yep, let's do this."

He smiles again, but this time it doesn't quite reach his eyes. He's worried, too, but is hiding it better than Jax. Again, why? Why are they so worried?

He stares at me for a beat before closing the door. A second later, my phone rings, and Jax's name flashes across the screen. I answer, "So, what're we supposed to talk about? Or do we need to just be quiet and listen to each other's heavy breathing?"

A soft chuckle drifts through the phone. "Talking should be fine since no one's around."

"Cool." I recline in the seat. "So, what do you want to talk about?"

"Hmm ... How about why on earth there's a collection of creepy-ass gnomes lined up in the backyard?" he replies with hilarity in his tone.

I snort a laugh. "That's my aunt's collection. And she's super weird about them. Like, she once caught me moving one of them out of my way so I could water some of her flowers, which FYI, she asked me to do. But anyway, when she saw me move it, she freaked out. Said some crazy crap about how they all had their proper positions in the yard and I had messed it up."

"Seriously?" Jax says. He sounds as if he's feeling a bit better, and I'm glad. "What a weirdo."

"She really is," I agree, my thoughts drifting to something I've often pondered.

Does she know what my uncle does to me? Sometimes, I think she does and doesn't care. If she does, then she's just as bad as him, in my opinion.

"Maybe she thinks they're alive," Hunter calls out.

"I've wondered that, too," I reply then ask, "Am I on speakerphone?"

"Yeah," Jax says. "Wait. Hold on."

I hear a muffled conversation, and then Jax gets back on the line and asks, "Can you see the video feed on the iPad now?"

I glance at the iPad and, sure enough ... "Yep."

"Awesome," he tells me then says to either Hunter or Zay, "She's good."

The line goes quiet again, but I hear one of them say something every so often.

Finally, I can't take the quietness anymore.

"Are you guys in my house yet?" I wonder.

"Yeah," Jax answers. "Zay's setting up a camera in the kitchen, Hunter almost has one up in the living room, and I just put one up in the upstairs hallway."

Crap. There's one in the upstairs hallway? That could be close enough to my room where they might overhear something. But I know if I say anything about it, he'll question why.

"Which one's your room?" he asks.

I chew on my bottom lip. "Um ... Why?"

"I was just curious what it looked like," he tells me. "It's okay if you don't want me to go in there."

I relax a smidgeon. "No, it's fine if you want to go in there ... It's the second door on the right."

Jax doesn't say anything right away and, for some dumbass reason, that makes me nervous.

"There's not a lot of stuff in here," he finally says.

"I know ... My aunt and uncle made me get rid of a lot of stuff when I moved in with them. And I haven't really gotten a lot of new stuff, so ..." I shrug, even though he can't see me.

"You should have more stuff," he mutters, but I'm unsure if he's talking to me or himself.

"It's fine ... I mean, I wish I had some of my old stuff, like my dad's old record collection, but that's long g—"

"Where did you get this photo?" he suddenly cuts me off, his tone trembling.

I'm beyond confused, not just by his question, but by his reaction. "What photo?"

"This one with the man and woman and a little girl in a purple dress?" His tone is equally, if not more, shaky now.

"That's a photo of my parents and me, when I was little, obviously. It's the only photo I have left of them. My aunt threw away the rest, said I didn't need to dwell on the past or some shit like that." Tears burn my eyes as I remember how angry I was when I watched her toss all the boxes of my family photos in the trash. She said it was making me too emotional whenever I looked at them. "She didn't know I kept that one. I hid it in my shoe. If she did, she'd probably freak out." I give a short pause as something dawns on me. "Jax, you don't think she made me toss them because I'm off the grid or whatever, do you?"

"I don't know." His voice is barely a whisper now, and I'm not positive why, what's making him so upset.

"Jax, are you okay ...?" I trail off as the driver's side door opens.

At first, I assume it's one of the guys since I didn't see a car pull up to the house, but when the person ducks their head into the car, I know I'm in deep shit.

Because they're wearing a ski mask.

I immediately scoot over to the other side of the car to high-tail it out the passenger side, but that door opens up, too, and that person is also donning a ski mask. Panic soars through me as I put the phone back to my ear.

"Jax," I hiss but get no response, so I open my mouth and shout, "Jax—"

The person on the driver's side dives over the seat and smacks my face hard enough that my ears pop and I drop the phone onto the floor. I'm fuming with rage as I hurriedly fumble to pick up the phone, but the people have already flipped the seats up and are grabbing at me from both sides. I put up a fight, kicking and screaming, throwing punches. I manage to clock one of them in the face, and they curse, leaning back for a moment. I try to shove around them, but the person behind me wraps their fingers around my throat while pinning me against them.

Before this point, I wasn't quite certain what was going on, but now I get it. Whoever these people are, they are trying to kill me. I scramble to get free, but the person I punched has recovered and climbs on top of me. I attempt to kick them, to no avail.

In the back of my mind, I question why Jax didn't answer me when I screamed into the phone, and while I don't want to think it, I wonder if perhaps they're behind this. I mean, they are the ones who had me sit out in the car. I didn't see anyone pull up to the house and the car is hidden in the forest, so how did these people know I was here? Unless this was a setup.

"Shh ... ," the person who's holding my neck whispers. "No one's gonna hurt you as long Jaxon, Hunter, and Zayden give me what I want."

Okay, maybe the guys didn't have anything to do with this—

Suddenly, the person basically sitting on top of me shoves a pill into my mouth. I start to spit it out, but they hold my mouth shut. I wiggle and thrash around, trying to get the fucker off me while keeping the pill in my mouth. It dissolves, and then I start to feel a little dizzy.

Panic whirls through me as my arms start to go limp and slump to my sides. As they do, I feel my fingers brush against my phone that I dropped on the floor. With every ounce of strength I have in me, I pick it up and discreetly put it in the pocket of the hoodie I'm wearing. Hopefully, they won't search my pockets so that maybe I can try to call someone when I get a chance ... unless they're just going to kill me.

Maybe the drug is going to do just that, is the last thought I have before dizziness overtakes me.

Then I pass out.

Chapter 9
Raven

I'm in a large room with a massive, domed ceiling and a huge light decorated with crystals hanging from it. I feel in awe as I take everything in—the paintings on the walls, the fireplace, the way the air smells like cinnamon.

"This place is so big," I tell my dad as I turn in a circle, taking everything in.

He nods, seemingly distracted as he glances at his phone. "Yeah, I know it is, Ravenlee."

He's called me Ravenlee three times since we arrived at this strange house in the middle of nowhere and hasn't given me an explanation as to why we're here. The large guys who greeted us at the entryway led us into this room before wandering off after telling us not to go anywhere.

I haven't seen the scarred boy that one of the men called "Kid" since he wandered into the house. Honestly, I haven't seen anyone besides my dad since the men left us here. I haven't heard anything either.

This place is spookily quiet.

I chew on my thumbnail. "How long do we have to stay here?"

"I'm not sure." *His frown deepens as he reads something on the screen, worry written all over his face.*

"Daddy?" *I ask, starting to get really worried.* "What's wrong?"

He glances up at me, his face really pale. "Ravenlee, I'm so sorry that this ..." *He trails off as a tall man with dark hair enters the room. Then he swallows hard.*

Something's very wrong.

"I'm glad to see you made it," *the man says to my dad then glances at me in a way that makes my skin crawl.*

"Did I really have a choice?" *Dad mutters in an annoyed tone.*

"No, but some men in your position might do something stupid, like try to run," *the man replies.* "Glad to see you aren't one of those men. I didn't particularly feel like chasing anyone down today." *He glances at me again with a curious look on his face.*

Wanting him to stop looking at me, I inch behind my dad.

A trace of a smile touches the man's lips, as if my move amuses him. "She's afraid of me," *he muses.* "Smart girl."

As a cold chill rolls through my body, I grab my dad's hand. "Daddy?" *I whisper.* "Why does he want me to be afraid of him?"

He grips my hand tightly in a reassuring squeeze. "Don't worry about it." *He sounds the complete opposite of his words.*

The air grows quiet as the man sinks into silence, staring at me like I'm a complex puzzle he desperately wants to solve.

"We should get this done," he finally says, looking at my dad. "Leave the girl here and come join me in my office for a drink. I'll have Kid brought in."

I have no idea what's going on, but I grasp my dad's hand desperately. "Don't leave me," I beg.

He glances down at me with remorse in his eyes. "I'm sorry, Ravenlee." Then he pries my hand out of his. "Stay here," he orders in a cold tone I've never heard him use before.

Tears burn my eyes as he starts to walk away.

When he notices I'm about to cry, he sighs, walks back to me, and crouches down so his gaze is level with mine. "Suck it up, Ravenlee," he says in a quiet but firm tone. "Crying makes us weak. Do you want to be weak, or do you want to be strong like your mom and me?"

I shake my head and sniffle, trying to suck back the tears. "Strong."

He offers me a small but sad smile. "Good girl." Then he stands up and walks away without a glance back.

I watch him leave with my fingers curled into fists and my stomach winding into knots, but my eyes are dry.

Once the man and my dad leave the room, I move to sit down on the sofa, not sure what I'm supposed to do. But before I can sit completely down, the door is opened and a woman with long, red hair walks in. She's wearing a black dress, a lot of sparkly jewelry, and her hair is done up like she's going someplace fancy. She's also not alone.

The sad boy with the scar trails in behind her, the boy everyone keeps referring to as Kid. He looks even sadder than before, which doesn't even seem possible.

As the woman with the red hair walks toward me, she assesses me with a curious look on her face, like I'm some weird creature she's never seen before.

"So, you're the little girl everyone's been fussing over?" She stops in front of me and tilts her head. "Honestly, I don't see what the big deal is. You don't even look like her. Makes me wonder if you're really hers or if he was just bullshitting everyone. He does have a reputation for being a liar."

"So do you, Diane," the boy says with a shake of his head.

Her lips twitch in annoyance. "You little shit ..." She trails off, putting on a sugary sweet smile. "You know what? Say whatever you want about me. At least I'm not a monster."

The kid smashes his lips together, his gaze shifting to me, and I swear I see remorse in his eyes.

"What's going on?" I speak. "Who are you guys? And where's my dad?"

The woman's attention returns to me, the smile still on her face. "What's going on is that you're about to pay your whore of a mother's debt."

Anger burns under my skin as I curl my hand into a fist. "Don't call my mother that!"

The woman smirks at the sight of my balled-up fist. "Are you seriously thinking about hitting me? You're just a kid—"

I step forward and punch her in the stomach.

She grunts, her face contorting in pain. "You little brat," she seethes then starts to storm toward me.

"Diane," Kid calls out. "If you touch her, the bosses are gonna be pissed off."

She slams to a halt, breathing furiously as she glares at me then at Kid. "*Fuck off,*" she spats but doesn't move toward me again.

Bosses? *What does that mean?*

I'm about to ask when the woman suddenly relaxes, the tension leaving her body.

"You know what? I don't need to listen to this shit. I was told to bring you here and nothing more." She turns, her heels clicking against the marble floor as she starts to leave. "You know what to do," she says as she passes Kid, and he visibly tenses.

Smirking, she strolls out of the room and shuts the door behind her.

Silence stretches between us as Kid just stands there with his hands balled into fists and his gaze fastened on the floor.

Finally, I can't take the silence anymore. "Your name's Kid, right?" I ask.

Shaking his head, he looks up at me. "No."

"Oh." I'm so confused. "But everyone keeps calling you that?"

"I know," he says flatly.

"Why do they call you that if it's not your name?"

He shrugs, not saying a word, just staring at me.

The silence is making me uncomfortable, so I try to think of something to say to him.

"Well, my name's Ravenlee," I tell him. "But almost everyone calls me Raven."

He studies me for a moment. "I have a pet raven."

"Really?" I ask, stepping toward him. "How the heck did you get one of those for a pet?"

He lifts a shoulder. "I caught it."

"That's really cool. Is it here? Maybe you can show it to me."

He shakes his head. "It's at my house."

"This isn't your house?" I ask, and he shakes his head. "Whose is it?"

He frowns. "The boss's."

"Who the heck is that?"

He seems to grow nervous, scratching the back of his neck. "No one you want to know."

"Oh." I pause. "Do you know why I'm here?"

He swallows hard, not answering me. It grows quiet again, and that sad look returns to his face.

Honestly, the only time he didn't look sad was when he was talking about his pet raven.

"Um ... What's your raven's name?" I ask, hoping he'll relax again and maybe tell me why the heck I'm at this house.

He lifts a shoulder. "I haven't named it."

"Well, you should," I say. "Every pet needs a name."

"Giving names to things make us weak," he mutters automatically.

"No way," I disagree, stepping toward him. "Naming things is really fun, especially pets, because you can name them just about anything. Like this one time I named this stray cat Cat. Although, he wasn't really my pet. He just wandered into my backyard sometimes."

"You named a cat Cat?" he questions.

I shrug, smiling a bit. "I thought it was funny."

"And you like to be funny?" He seems confused by this.

I shrug again. "I like to be a lot of things, but yeah, I like being funny sometimes ... Why do you seem so confused about that?"

He lifts a shoulder, staring at me like he's completely mystified. "It's just that you ... I don't know ... You seem ... happy?"

"And that's confusing?"

He shrugs again.

The boy really likes to shrug.

"Well, I am happy sometimes," I inform him. "Just like I'm sad sometimes. And angry. And scared. That's totally normal."

A crinkle forms between his brows. "Not in my world." Then he sighs loudly. "Look, I can't name my raven anything or else my dad will get mad at me."

"Really?" I ask, and he nods. "Your dad's really strict then."

"Yeah, he is," he agrees in a hollow tone.

I get the feeling his dad is a really mean guy. No wonder he looks so sad all the time.

I find myself wanting to make him happy, like I am sometimes.

An idea comes to me then. A pretty awesome one, too.

"Well, maybe you can give it a name without him knowing," I suggest. "Like how I named my cat Cat."

He gives me a funny look. "You think I should name my raven Raven?" he questions. "Like, after you?"

I give an innocent shrug, pretending like that just occurred to me. "Well, you really don't have to name it after me. It could just be a weird coincidence that we have the same name."

He sinks into silence again, giving me a suspicious look. But then the look fades. "I'll think about it."

I nod, smiling to myself. For a crazy second, he looks as if he's smiling, too. But the look swiftly erases and fills with panic as an intercom inside the room clicks on.

"Kid, stop fucking around and do what you're supposed to," a male's voice floats from the speaker.

Kid swallows hard. "I'm sorry," he whispers then steps toward me.

My heart rate quickens, and I'm not sure why. Then he touches my arm, and I hear the flap of wings—

My eyelids snap open as I'm tugged from the memory. At first, I can't figure out what jolted me from it, my mind clogged with disorientation. Then I feel a gust of cold air hit my cheeks, and I'm suddenly wide awake. Although, I kind of wish I wasn't.

"Please, please let me be dreaming," I mumble as I gape down at the thin, metal beam I'm standing on that extends across a river. "What the hell?" I glance around and stiffen.

I'm on a bridge.

And someone is standing behind me, holding my hands behind my back.

Shit. Shit. Shit.

"Let me go." I jerk my hands, but the person only tightens their grip.

"You're feisty, aren't you? I'm not surprised," a guy whispers in my ear.

It's the same guy who shoved the pill down my throat, and I think he's about to shove me off the bridge. And maybe that wouldn't be so awful, since the water looks deep enough for me to handle the fall without hitting the bottom. The only problem is … "I can't swim," I sputter, my legs beginning to tremble. And I hate it. Hate that I look weak. Hate that I have a weakness at all.

"Hurry up!" someone shouts. "It's freezing out here!"

"I think I saw a car coming!" a girl shouts. "Hurry up before we get caught!"

Great, not only is this guy trying to kill me, but I have an audience.

The guy holding me hesitates. "She says she can't swim!" he shouts at them.

"She's lying!" the girl yells back. "Who doesn't know how to swim by the time they're seventeen years old?"

"She's the one who's lying," I whisper, a shiver rolling through me as the cold air seeps into my skin. "Please don't do this. If I go into that water ... I won't be able to get out. Please don't do this—"

He clutches onto my neck so tightly I can't breathe. "Shut the hell up. You don't get a say in this. You're just a pawn."

I freak the hell out and start to wiggle around in an attempt to escape, but he only tightens his grip. Well, for a split-second. And then he lets go ... and shoves me forward.

I fall. And fall. And fall.

I hear shouting, something about hurry and getting the hell out of here, that someone is running up the road. But then the words get stifled as I crash into the river, my body instantly locking up as I sink.

Holy shit, the coldness takes my breath away. It also feels like a thousand needles are piercing my flesh. That pain is the easiest to handle, though. It's kind of like the pain that comes when those words are carved into my flesh.

Freak.

Loser.

Murderer.

Freak.

Loser.

Murderer.

Freak.

Loser.

Murderer.

The girl who killed her parents.

And now I'm going to be the girl who killed her parents and paid for it when she sank to the bottom of a river and froze to death.

This is going to be my tomb.

But as soon as my feet touch the bottom, my instincts kick in, and I try to swim to the surface.

"Just kick your feet, Raven," my dad tries to encourage as he stands in the pool with me, helping keep me afloat as he tries to teach me how to swim. "You can do this, sweetie. You can do anything if you put your mind to it. You've got to learn how to swim. If you don't, you'll be at risk."

As the chill of the water burns my muscles, winding them into knots and making them useless, I start to sink again, darkness taking over. And I start to let it ...

Blood on my hands.

"Hide, Raven," my mom begs. "Hide and don't come out. Do you understand?"

I frantically shake my head. "No. I can't leave you."

She grabs my shoulders and looks me in the eyes. "You have to. And you have to promise to forget what's about to happen. Promise me."

I shake my head again, tears burning my eyes. "No, I'm not going to. I'm staying with you. I'm not going to hurt—"

Arms wrap around me, and then I'm being pulled upward, toward the sky. I'm dead, and I'm going upward. But that can't be right.

No, when I die, and if there is a heaven and a hell, I definitely won't be going up.

You've got it wrong.

You're going the wrong way.

I need to go back down—

I gasp as I break the surface of the water then cough as the air burns my lungs.

"I got you," Jax breathes out as he holds me in his arms, swimming us over to the shore, the water rushing around us.

I want to answer him, want to ask him how he found me, but I'm chattering too hard to form any coherent words.

My eyelids start to lower as water drips down my face.

"Don't go to sleep," he says as he drags me onto the shore. "Whatever you do, keep your eyes open."

My clothes are soaking wet. Everything feels heavy, even breathing.

"Willow, please just stay with me," Jax begs as he swims us out of the water.

I give a feeble nod. Or, I think I do. My head feels so heavy.

Moments later, I'm being laid down. I peel my eyelids open and try to move, but my arms are useless lumps of frozen flesh. So, I just slump into the dirt.

Jax is muttering incoherently under his breath, panic taking over him as he stares down at me, water dripping from his face.

"What do I do?" he mutters as his gaze sweeps across mine.

Snowflakes start to drift from the cloudy sky.

"You were right ... It did snow today," I whisper, totally out of it as I reach up and brush my fingers along Jax's lips.

Hunter's gorgeous face appears in my vision, right beside Jax's, his skin as pale as the snow. In fact, he looks sick.

"Holy shit," he whispers. "We need to ..." He chokes up as he crouches down beside me. "We need to get her somewhere warm."

Jax just stares at me, seeming frozen in some sort of horror-induced trance.

"Jax!" Hunter snaps while picking me up. "We need to get her into the car before hypothermia kicks in. And you need to warm up, too." Hunter stands up, holding me to him. A drop of warmth starts to seep into me as his body heat engulfs me, but the cold hastily takes over again.

Numb.

I feel numb.

I feel nothing.

Weightless.

And it's kind of blissful.

Jax snaps out of his trance and stands up, too. Then they hurry ... somewhere. I'm not sure where since everything is becoming blurry. And I'd ask, but my lips are too frozen.

"I'd call an ambulance, but with how slow they are, it'll take probably half an hour before they get here," Hunter says. "We can get her out of here quicker."

"Why?" I whisper, my voice hoarse.

"Why what?" Hunter asks, glancing down in confusion.

"Why ...? Why did Jax save me?" The question might sound simple, but deep down, I know it's much more complicated than he probably realizes. That while I may be confused about why and how Jax was here to save me, I'm also a tiny bit disappointed that he did.

For a moment, I was ready for this hell of a life to be over.

Pity fills Hunter's eyes as he stares down at me, as if he can see through the cracks in my mind, see the secrets hidden inside them.

He doesn't answer. Instead, he quickens his pace.

I turn my head toward his chest and close my eyes.

He feels so warm ...

I could drift away in it ...

Drift away back to that peace I felt for a split-second as I sank ...

"Raven, look at me," Hunter says, yanking me out of my daze.

My eyes roll in my head as I try to do what he said.

Dizzy. Everything is spinning. But I'm starting to not feel cold anymore.

"Dammit, open your eyes," he orders with a trace of anger in his tone. "I need you to open your eyes now."

My eyes roll into the back of my head as I try to open them, to no avail.

"Dammit," he curses, quickening his pace.

I continue fading in and out of consciousness until Hunter sets me down. That startles me enough that I force my eyelids open to see where I am ... Lying on the back seat of Zay's car, soaking wet and shivering.

"Are there any blankets in the trunk?" Jax's voice floats from somewhere.

"Yeah," Hunter says. "I'll get them. You get in the car. You need to warm up, too, or you're going to get hypothermia."

A beat of silence skips by, and my eyelids slip close again.

"So, we're gonna just what? Wrap her in blankets?" Zay asks. "Will that even work?"

A beat of silence ticks by.

"We ... we have to take her clothes off first," Jax finally says quietly and with a heavy amount of discomfort in his tone.

Again, it grows quiet, and panic manages to rise inside me, lacing with the cold.

Wait ... They're going to take my clothes off?

No, that can't happen.

I try to flip over so I can crawl off the seat and out of the car. The door is open and the seat is shoved forward, so all I need to do is get that far. Then I can tumble out and ... Well, I don't really know where I'll go from there. All I know is I've got to get out of here.

By some miracle, I get my body turned over. But as I'm dragging myself toward the edge of the seat, Zay steps up in front of the open door.

His hoodie is off and his short, brown hair is covered in snowflakes. His eyes widen when he sees me. I start to slide back on the seat to try to climb out the other side of the car. The movement seems to draw him out of his shock, and he moves, climbing into the back seat with me. Then he shuts the door and peels off his wet shirt.

I attempt to move, panic soaring through me. Holy hell,

being frozen makes it really freakin' complicated to move, so I barely get anywhere before Zay grabs the sleeve of my plaid shirt.

"I'm just going to help you," he mutters as he sits me up and pulls me toward him with me putting up a fuss. He sighs, like I'm being a nuisance. "Raven, if we don't get you undressed, you might freeze to death."

I guess I kind of get what he's saying, but if I take my clothes off, they'll see ...

All of my sins and secrets.

I try to push him away, but my limbs are so heavy I barely tap him.

He holds his hands in front of him then stares at me undecidedly. "You're gonna have to chill while I do this. Don't fight, or it's going to complicate things."

"N-no," I chatter.

He sighs then slowly reaches for me. "I'm just trying to help." He pauses then slowly starts taking off my plaid shirt. I lift my hand and push against his chest, but he merely removes my hand and yanks the soaked fabric off me, tossing it into the back. Then he reaches for the hem of my shirt and hoodie.

I try to fight back, but I can't even get my eyes open. I feel him hesitate, his fingers lingering on the hems. In my mind, I fight back, but my body isn't cooperating with my thoughts, and with shaky fingers, Zay tugs my shirt and hoodie over my head.

Oh my God, this is really going to happen ... He's going to see it.

I force my eyelids open and look up at Zay, silently pleading with him to stop. But he's not looking at me. His gaze is locked on my side. I know what he's looking at, and I hate it. Hate that he can see all the ugliness all over me. Hate that he can see me at all.

Blinking then shaking his head, he leans down and tugs off my boots. I slump back against the seat, my eyelids lowering as I veer toward passing out.

Zay works on peeling my tights off, then moves toward my shorts. That's when I really begin to freak the hell out. His fingers are going to be right by my side, right where those words are carved.

"Stop ... Stop ... Stop ..." I tip to the side, digging my fingernails into the edge of the seat, trying to pull myself away from him and toward the door.

"Goddammit," Zay growls. "You've got to let me finish. It's getting so bad you can barely keep your damn eyes open!"

I shake my head as I grab the door handle to the driver's side door, but the door swings open on its own. Hunter appears on the other side with an armful of blankets, snowflakes falling around him. When he catches sight of me, he frowns, his gaze straying to Zay.

"Why don't you have her clothes off already?" he asks. "You need to move more quickly, Zay. I mean, I know you have issues with this shit, but get over it."

"I'm trying to take off her clothes," Zay grumbles. "But she's trying to get away from me. I don't know what she's thinking, but she clearly doesn't realize the severity of the fucking situation."

Hunter shakes his head then returns his gaze to me, his expression softening. "I know this is terrifying, but you've got to let us get your clothes off and warm you up before you get hypothermia." He must see it, too, because he leans down, levels his gaze with mine, and cups my face between his hands. "No one's going to hurt you, I promise."

I want to argue more, but that's when I just sort of give up. The cold is too much, And to be honest, I just want to go to sleep. So, I manage a nod.

Relaxing a smidgeon, he asks, "Can you get your shorts off on your own?"

I try to move my fingers toward the button, but I can even feel my fingertips. Grimacing, I shake my head.

Reluctantly, Hunter climbs into the car beside me and rolls me over, putting my head onto his lap. "I'm going to take them off, okay?"

He waits for me to nod then reaches to the hem of my shorts and undoes the button, carrying my gaze the entire time. I can barely feel the movement as Zay tugs my shorts down my legs.

Once those are off, Hunter reaches up and strokes my cheek. "This is going to be the hard part, okay? In order for you to get warm, you're going to have to share body heat with me and Jax while Zay drives us back to the house."

I shake my head and manage a, "Can't …"

His gaze never wavers from mine. "I know it's scary and uncomfortable, but it's the best way to keep you from freezing to death."

I don't want to do it at all and part of me considers the idea of just letting myself freeze to death. But then my survival instincts kick in, and I nod. "O … kay."

He exhales in relief then looks over my shoulder at I'm assuming Zay.

"Let me get my clothes off," Jax says from behind me. "Here are some more blankets."

Apparently, while I was in and out of consciousness Zay and Jax switched places.

Hunter takes the blankets from him then strips off his shirt while I lean slumped against the back seat, barely able to keep my eyes open. Once Hunter removes his shirt, he unfolds a blanket.

"I'm going to lean you against me," he explains, carrying my gaze. "And then Jax is going to lean against you. Then I'll wrap us up in blankets."

Even the little scraps of clothing I have left give me no sense of security. Even worse, Zay has climbed into the driver's seat, so all three of them are in the car now.

This is so damn uncomfortable.

Zay cranks up the heat, flips on the windshield wipers, then casts a glance back at us. "Is everyone good for me to drive?"

"Yeah," Hunter answers, reaching down to pick up the blankets.

Zay locks eyes with me briefly, and I swear I detect the slightest bit of worry. Then he looks away and drives forward.

Hunter reaches for me then, carefully wraps his arms around me, and pulls me forward until my chest is flush with his. I might manage to be embarrassed over the situation, but then his body heat seeps into my skin.

Warmth.

I thought I'd never feel it again.

Never thought I'd be this close to anyone ever again.

I've been so cold for the last handful of years ...

"Wrap the blankets around us," Jax whispers as he slips his arms around my waist and presses his bare chest against my back.

Unlike Hunter, he's cold.

I shiver against him.

"Sorry," he whispers, his lips brushing my ear. "For everything."

His words don't make much sense, but I can't form any words to ask him what he means. I can feel his heart beating. *Soaring.* So, so fast. He's either got a lot of adrenaline rushing through him or he's freaking the hell out.

What would scare him, though?

Fabric touches my back and more warmth spills across me.

My eyelids lower as I breathe the feeling in, wanting to go to sleep.

"Just keep ahold of her until we get to the house," Zay says. "Although, if her condition doesn't improve, we may have to take her to a hospital."

"She seems like she's getting warmer already." Hunter brushes his hands up and down my side. "Jax, are you doing okay?"

Jax presses closer against me and rests his head against my back. "Yeah," he whispers. "Did you see who did this to her?"

"No," Zay replies, annoyance ringing in his tone. "I tried to chase them down but couldn't catch the fuckers before they jumped into their vehicle. They were all wearing masks, so I didn't see any faces and the vehicle didn't have a plate. All I know is that they drove a black SUV that looked like maybe it was a Cadillac, but I didn't get close enough to be positive."

"So, basically, all we know is that they drive a black SUV and that they're from one of the families," Hunter states in irritation. "Great, that narrows it down to basically anyone who's a part of a family."

"My money is on Porter," Zay replies. "He saw us with Raven this morning and made those subtle threats."

"I agree, but we can't retaliate until we know for sure," Hunter reminds him. "Even though we're technically not part of the family, we still have to follow the rules, or we'll be in deep shit."

"I'm aware of how the rules work," Zay snaps. "I don't need a reminder."

"Don't snap at me, man," Hunter tells him. "I'm not the one pissing you off right now."

"I know that," Zay grumbles. "I'm just pissed off ... I don't like it when people get the upper hand over me."

"None of us do." Jax's voice is weighed with exhaustion. "But we're not the one who suffered. She did." He hugs me closer against him and buries his face in my neck.

Time and time again, everyone has said how scary Jax is, but all I've seen is this sweet, soft side, so I don't really get it.

"I know," Zay chokes on the word and quickly clears his throat, his tone dropping to an eerie, dark tone. "We're going to find out who did this, and then the fuckers are going to pay. They want to play a game, then let's show them how to play. We may all hate are families, and everyone may know that, but they forgot that, while we may have detached ourselves from them, for a very long time we were raised by the scariest motherfuckers this town has ever known. We know things, and I think whoever did this to her stupidly forgot that."

"I completely agree, but I also want to point out that you sound very protective right now," Hunter remarks with a hint of a taunt in his tone.

"Oh, shut the hell up," Zay snaps. "I'm just pissed off, and I ..." He trails off.

As they grow silent, that tiredness I've been fighting off finally wins.

Chapter 10
Raven

Warm blood covers my hands as I stare down at my parents. Blood is all over them, covering their clothes, their hair.

Why is there so much blood? And why is it all over my hands?

"Mom," I whisper as I collapse to my knees.

I can't remember how I got here. Can't remember where the blood came from. All I can remember is the screaming. So much screaming.

"Raven! No!" my mom shouts a plea. "Run!"

"I'm sorry," I whisper.

She screams—

My eyelids flutter open and gasp for air. I hate it when I have memories like that, ones I feel like I barely experienced. I usually only have one or two every few months, but today, I've had three total. But the last one might be because of what happened to me.

Drugged. I was drugged.

Then I fell from a bridge and Zay, Jax, and Hunter saved me.

What happened after that, though?

Where am I?

My stomach twists with nausea as I peer around at ... well, I'm not really sure where I am. From what I can tell, I'm in a large bed with lots of pillows and blankets around me.

The bedroom the bed is in has dark blue walls with photos hanging on them, making me wonder if I'm in Hunter's room. But how did I get here?

As I slowly sit up, I realize I'm wearing someone else's shirt, and my body feels like it was run over by a truck. Or like it slammed into a freezing cold river ...

As memories of what happened gradually surface, I throw the blankets off me. Then I frown. My legs aren't covered up by anything.

"Crap," I breathe out, recalling how Hunter held me while Jax tugged down my shorts.

At first I'd panicked, but then I realized they were just trying to help me not die from hypothermia. Still, I'm a little unsettled at the idea that they saw me without my clothes on.

They probably saw my scars.

Swallow shakily, I start to scoot toward the edge of the bed so I can figure out what happened and where I am. But the door to the bedroom opens up before I can even get my feet to the floor.

A slamming instant of a heartbeat later, Hunter walks in. He blinks in surprise when he notices me then relief washes over his features.

"Thank God, you're really awake," he says, the tension in his muscles unraveling.

"Really awake?" I say confusedly. "Was I fake awake before?"

He wavers, raking his fingers through his hair. "You've been coming in and out of consciousness for a while."

"Oh." I tuck a strand of my hair behind my ear. "Where am I exactly?"

He enters the room. "In our house. This is my bedroom."

I chew on my bottom lip, fiddling with the hem of the shirt I'm wearing that covers up the scars on my side, so many question marks flooding my thoughts. "How did I... I mean, how did I get this shirt on?"

Hunter tracks the movement. "I put it on you. I promise I was careful, though, and didn't look or let my hands wander..." He trails off with uncertainty. "But I did see something while we were taking your clothes off in the car. And I don't want to make you feel uncomfortable, but what I—Jax and I saw has us concerned."

My cheeks warm as I feel so exposed. "It's not really a big deal." *Please, please don't ask me how I got them.*

Pity floods his eyes. "No, pretty Raven, it is a big deal. A big, huge fucking deal." Sucking in a breath, he sits down beside me. "I'm going to show you something. It's something no one else knows about other than Zay and Jax."

He opens and flexes his free hand and takes an uneven breath.

He's nervous.

Why's he nervous?

When he lifts up the hem of his shirt, I have my answer.

Long, thin, but deep scars cover his sides, chest, and waist.

"Holy shit, what happened?" I ask, glancing up to meet his gaze.

He lowers his shirt, then a breath trembles from his lips. "My stepmom ..." He crosses his arms, tucking his hands underneath his armpits. "She's a bitch who gets off on using her power on people who are weaker than her. And when I was younger, I was a lot weaker than her ... And, well, she used to do things to me a lot ... And she would scratch me a lot while she did those things to me."

He doesn't specify what the *things* are, but with the way he's trembling, I get a pretty good idea. And it makes me feel sick. And angry. Not at him, but at his stepmom and at the fact that we have to live in a world where adults can hurt children likes this.

But I'm not really certain what to say to him. I've never had anyone confide in me with something so personal. It makes me feel out of my element, enough that I kind of want to leave. But he's also sitting here, shivering from probably fear of the memories connected to those scars, and the sight of it tugs at a memory of me trembling in a bed while my uncle leaned over me, and carved the word *disappointment* into my side. It was the first time he did it, and I was terrified. But I learned quickly to numb myself.

"I'm sorry," I say, deciding to start there. "That that happened to you."

He promptly shakes his head. "It's not your fault. And I just wanted to show you so that maybe you'd trust me enough to tell me where you got those scars on your side." He uncrosses his arms, his eyes searching mine. "They looked like words."

I smash my lips together. "They're... They're just..." I can't get a good lie to leave my lips.

This isn't my typical MO, but it's been a pretty damn traumatic day.

A day I may not have survived if it hadn't been for Hunter, Zay, and Jax.

"You don't have to tell me if you don't want to," he tells me softly. "I just want to make sure you're okay. But if you want to talk about it, I want you to know that you can trust me."

Trust? When's the last time I've trusted someone? I can't even remember. But he trusts me enough to show me his scars. And he saved me. Him, Zay, and Jax didn't have to do what they did. And sadly, a lot of people would have been perfectly content to ignore the situation. Trust me, I've been bullied enough to know that people like to look in the other direction when that sort of stuff is going on.

So, with trembling fingers, and before I can back out, I reach for the hem of my own shirt and lift it up, putting all my scars and the fresh wounds on display for him. The blanket is still covering my legs so all I reveal is my side.

As soon as the air hits my skin, a shiver courses through my body.

"Jesus," he whispers, reaching out and tentatively touching my skin. He starts at the top, tracing each letter marking my flesh with his fingertips, slowly working his way to the bottom. When he reaches the fresh wound, he pauses, his gaze traveling up to mine. "Who did this to you?" he asks, his gaze searing into mine.

"I..." *Just say his name, Raven. Just say the truth for once in your damn life. Stop being so scared of him.* "It was my uncle." Holy shit, I can't believe I said that aloud.

He doesn't look completely surprised. "Your uncle did this to you—the sheriff did this to you."

I give a shaky nod. "Unfortunately, yeah."

He looks down at my scars. "Did he put all of these on you?" He doesn't remove his hand, keeping it on my scars just underneath my shirt.

I nod again, trying not to shiver as he touches my scars, this time the urge not stemming completely from fear but by the unfamiliarity of his touch. "He started doing it years ago. He does it when I do something that really pisses him off. Although, he's been doing it more frequently the older I get. But that might be because I get in more trouble now than I used to." I sink my teeth into my bottom lip, wavering. "I don't know. He kinda seems to ... get off on it, so maybe he just likes doing it."

His brows furrow. "What do you mean by that exactly?"

"That he seems to like doing it to me." I shrug, feeling a bit mortified talking about this. "The last time he did it, I think he went and had sex with my aunt. At least that's what she implied the next morning... so ... yeah ..." I shrug again, my cheeks on fire.

He remains silent for a beat before biting out, "He sounds as fucked up in the head as my stepmom." He looks at me with a crease between his brow. "What about your aunt? Does she know?"

I laugh hollowly. "If she does, she wouldn't care. Trust me, she hates me."

"I'm so sorry." He tucks a strand of my hair behind my ear. "For everything."

"Why are you apologizing?" I wonder. "None of this is your fault."

Remorse reflects in his eyes. "Actually, it was. At least the reason why you were thrown off the bridge."

My brows start to furrow in confusion until a faint memory tickles at my mind. The person who forced the pills down my throat had said something about Zay, Jax, and Hunter.

"I actually think I remember them saying something about you guys and wanting something from you... That that's why they pushed me off the bridge," I say. "But they never said why."

"We're still trying to figure it out, but we think it might be this game that some of the families kids have started where they basically go to war against each other. But we still need to look into it more." Guilt reflects in his eyes as he reaches up and cups my face between his hands. "I'm so fucking sorry we brought you into this mess, but I swear to God we won't let anything happened to you again. We're going to protect you. Not just from whoever did this but from your uncle... We... Jax, Zay, and I talked about it and we want you to move in with us for a while."

My eyes widen. "What? No... I can't do that."

He frowns. "Why not?"

"Because... I don't want to be a burden to you," I say quietly. "Plus, I doubt my aunt and uncle will let me." Although, I'm not totally positive about that part.

"We'll figure out a way to convince them... Jax, Zay, and I can be very persuasive when we want to be." He says it in this dark, ominous tone that makes me question if they're going to like hurt my uncle or something.

Not that I really care. What that says about me, I'm not sure.

"And you wouldn't be a burden. You're our friend and we want—need to protect you from a mess we brought you into." He skims his thumb along my cheekbone, looking straight into my eyes. "Please let us do that."

I want to say yes. How could I freaking not want that, however...

"Maybe I could pay rent or something," I say. "And be like a roommate, so that I'm not just living here for free."

The corners of his lips quirk. "If that's what I want."

Relief washes over me. "It's what I want."

Silence takes over as he searches my eyes for something; what I'm not sure, though.

Then he drags the pad of his thumb along my bottom lip, this intensity consuming his expression. "I... I just..." He sucks in a shaky breath then starts to lean in, "I want to fucking kiss you. I can't stop thinking about it."

My heart is pounding in my chest to the point that I can barely breathe.

He wants to fucking kiss me? *Hunter? Gorgeous Hunter?*

He hesitates suddenly. "I'm sorry. I didn't mean to scare you. I just..." He blows out a quiet breath.

"You didn't scare me," I say quietly. "I just... I don't know what I'm doing." As soon as the words leave my lips, I want to smack myself across the face.

Did I seriously just say that aloud?

He wets his lips with his tongue. "You've never kissed anyone before?"

I shake my head. It's not a total lie. The one and only other kiss I had was completely unwanted on my part, so I don't count it.

He nibbles on his bottom lip. "Can I kiss you? You can totally say no, but I..." He suddenly seems nervous. "I really want to fucking kiss you. I have since the first time I laid eyes on you."

I should say no... right? It seems like it'd complicate things, but part of me want to kiss him. Maybe it's because I really am crazy or perhaps I'm too tired to rationalize. Whatever the reason, I find myself nodding.

"Are you sure?" he double checks.

I nod again and then he's leaning in slowly, so slowly that all I can feel is my heart pounding in my throat. It's loud and unnerving and—

His lips brush mine and suddenly everything inside me seems quiet.

His lips are so soft.

He remains that way for a while and I think that he's going to leave it at that when his tongue suddenly parts my lips. And just like that, he's kissing me. And I mean, really kissing me, his tongue tangling with mine as his hands find my back. He moans and so do I and all I can think is this—this moment—is something I didn't think existed.

Perfection.

He kisses me deeper, groaning as his hands travel down my waist, his fingers delving into my flesh.

Oh my god, I want this.

"Oh my god, I want you," Hunter groans, apparently thinking the same thing as me.

Then someone knocks on the door and the perfection stops as he pulls back.

Then someone knocks on the door and the perfection stops as he pulls back.

He stares at me for a moment, his eyes searching mine. "Are you okay?"

I nod. "Yeah... I'm great." And I sound stupidly breathless.

The corners of his lips quirk and his mouth opens probably to tease me, but something knocks on the door again.

He sighs. "That's probably Jax wanting to see if you're all right." He sweeps his thumb along my bottom lip before lowering his hand. "Just a warning, he might freak out a little bit... What happened to you... With you being in that water like that... He's kind of experienced something like that before." I'm about to ask him what happened, when he calls out, "You can come in, man."

The door opens up and Jax walks in. His eyes instantly find mine and so many emotions flash across his face at once that it's kind of overwhelming. To be honest, seeing him is stirring emotions inside me.

He saved me. Jumped into that water and didn't let me drown. I thought no one would care if I died. But he did.

"Are you okay," he says as he steps into the room, his intense gaze searing into mine.

I nod then stand up, tugging down the hem of the shirt I'm wearing. "I am thanks to you."

He takes another step toward me. "Don't thank me. It's our fault you were ever in that situation."

"Don't blame yourself," I say, wanting to alleviate some of the anguish in his tone. *I wonder what he's been through to cause that kind of sorrow.* "Honestly, if I'd known how to swim, the situation probably wouldn't have ended up that bad. But I hate water so learning how to swim has never really worked for me."

For some reason, his breathing quickens. I start to worry that something I said might have triggered some sort of panic inside him when he steps all the way to me, his gaze never wavering from mine."

"Can I hug you?" he asks softly.

That's not what I was expecting him to say and I'm not used to being hugged, but he looks like he's desperate for me to say yes, so I do.

"Y-yeah." I don't know why I stammer.

"Are you sure?" he double checks.

I nod, telling myself to chill out. That it's just a hug. But the moment his arms wrap around me, I become aware that it's more than that. It's comfort and intensity and weirdly, familiar.

Are all hugs like this?

And why do I keep getting the feeling that I know these guys?

"I'm never going to let anyone hurt you again," Jax whispers in my ear as he holds me tightly against him.

Breathing in, I wrap my arms around him and hug him back. I thought it would be awkward, to hug someone, but it's not. At least, this hug isn't.

"Thanks for saving me, Jaxon," I whisper with my head resting against his chest where his heart is racing.

He pulls me tighter against him and his body starts to shake. I think he might be crying. I think about what Hunter said, how he experienced something similar to what happened to me. It must've been awful for him. And I hate that he feels this, this pain. I want to take it away from him but I don't know how. So I do the only thing I can think of. I let him hold onto me, and hold onto him right back, letting him cry.

Letting him cry out his pain.

"You okay, brother," I hear Hunter say from close behind me.

Jax gives a nod then sucks in an inhale and then steps back. He hurries and wipes his eyes with the sleeve of his shirt before looking at me.

"I'm sorry about that," he tells me apologetically.

"You're fine," I try to reassure him.

Then I reach out and hitch my pinkie with his.

I don't know why I do it, but the move causes his brows to knit. Then he trades a look with Hunter.

"Is everything okay?" I wonder.

He nods, returning his gaze to me, a small smile touching his fine.

Hunter moves up beside me and drapes his arm around. "How about we let you shower then we'll come up with a plan to get you out of that house?"

I nod, a drop of panic stirring inside me as I wonder if Hunter will tell Jax what my uncle did to me. But then I think about how Jax just cried on my shoulder and I decide that I don't think he'll judge me for anything.

"Okay, yeah, a shower sounds nice." What I want to say, but I don't, is that all of this sounds nice.

I just hope it stays.

Chapter 11
Hunter

I can't stop thinking about that kiss. It replays over and over in my mind. I've kissed a lot of women, but that kiss with Raven, it was different. It had meaning behind it. Feeling. Emotion. Connection. God, I can barely breathe even thinking about it.

But despite the fact that I just had the most amazing fucking kiss of my life, I need to address a huge problem.

"Are you okay?" I say to Jax after we leave Raven in the bathroom so she can take a shower.

He nods, releasing a shaky breath while stuffing his hands into his pocket. "Yeah, I think so." He gives a short pause, his gaze straying to the shut bathroom door where Raven is. "Hunter, I really do think it's her... She seems so familiar. And the way she hitched her pinkie with mine... Willow used to do that."

"I know," I agree, my heart quickening at the realization.

"We need to get her out of that house, but from the way she acted and some of the stuff she told me, I think her uncle is going to make it a pain in the ass."

He straightens. "Did something happen to her?"

I'm not sure if Raven wants me to tell Jax everything, but I think he needs to know that... "He's hurting her, Jax. I think similar to like how we were hurt."

Anger flashes in his eyes, his fingers curling into fists. "Then that motherfucker is going to pay."

While Jax is usually a calm person, he does have his moments when he loses his cool. And this time, I'm right there with him.

"Oh, I know he is," I agree. "And we're going to protect her from everything like I promised her we would. We just need to come up with a plan."

Zay appears at the end of the hallway then with his arms crossed. "I'm sure I can think of one."

"Really?" I question. "Because I thought you were against her moving in with us?"

He just shrugs. "You know I'm always up for destroying someone's life that deserves it."

He's such a liar. I know he has a soft spot for Raven. So do Jax and me, which could get really complicated, especially after the fact that I just fucking kissed her.

"So we all agree on that," I ask. "That we're going to help her?"

Jax nods and then with a bit of hesitation, Zay does too.

Then to seal the deal, I stick out my hand. Zay rolls his eyes, but places his hand on mine and Jax puts his on top of Zay's. We haven't done this in a while, since Willow actually. I just hope this vow between us goes better than the last one.

But I'll do whatever it takes to make sure it does.

No matter what, I'll protect Raven.

No one will hurt her ever again.

Chapter 12
Raven

Broken, broken girl. My aunt used to tell me that all the time. She was trying to break me. I got that. I refused to let her, though. At least, that's what I thought. Now, thinking about what it felt like to sink in that water—that brief flicker of relief I felt—maybe I was wrong. Perhaps my aunt did break me. It was just a slow break; tiny cracks in my skin that I barely noticed until I almost shattered from crashing into the water. It was like I was made of glass. But Jax saved me. Then he and Hunter picked up the pieces and put me back together again.

Can someone else actually put you back together right, though? Can someone else know which of the pieces go where? Do I even know?

"Shit, it's so late," Hunter mutters from the driver's seat as he pulls up to my house.

Despite me agreeing to move in with him and his friends, I'm still being forced to sleep at my aunt and uncle's house. Why am I doing that? Well, because my aunt is a bitch.

When I called her to see if I could at least spend the night at the guys' house, I had my apprehensions that she'd say no. Although part of me had convinced myself that she'd agree to let me just to get me out of the house. I mean, it makes sense. She hates me, so why not let me stay the night at someone else's home? I had actually told her I was staying at Harlow's. She had almost let me, but then she abruptly said no, and that was that. Begging her wouldn't do any good—I know this.

Jax and Hunter had freaked out, but we ultimately agreed that, for now, it was best for me to sleep at my aunt and uncle's until the guys could get some blackmail material to hold over their heads.

"I hate this," Hunter adds as he parks the car.

It's dark, the night sky cloudy, but the soft glow of the porch light offers just enough light that I can see the worry consuming Hunter's features.

"I'll be fine," I try to reassure him. "I'm always fine."

He shakes his head, wisps of his blond hair falling into his eyes as he looks at me. "Baby, you're not always fine." He reaches out and lightly brushes a strand of hair out of my eyes, the touch causing my heart to flutter. "You just think you are."

I smash my lips together, mainly to catch my breath before I speak. "Dude, what's up with you calling me baby? I thought we were friends." Right? He said we were, like, a dozen times, but he kissed me before leaving his house. Pressed his lip to mine and gave me my first real kiss. We haven't said anything about it, and I'm starting to wonder if perhaps he regrets it.

While Hunter is usually all calm and collected, I detect the faintest sound of a gulp. "We are."

"Okay." I force a smile. I'm not sure why I'm forcing it or why I feel the slightest bit of disappointment. I've always wanted friends, and here he is, offering me that, and what do I do? I feel disappointed.

Yeah, one of my pieces is being super ungrateful.

"Thanks for everything." I lean over to hug him. It's a strange instinct for me, seeing as how it's been years since I was hugged. Well, minus the hug Jax gave me earlier.

When my arm goes around him, he goes stiff. I start to pull away, thinking I've done something wrong, but then he's hugging me back. Tightly. And it feels ... well, new and unfamiliar, but I kind of like it. Like, a lot.

"You smell like my shampoo," Hunter mutters as he smells my hair.

Before I had left the guys' I had taken a shower, and ... "There were like five bottles in the shower. Yours smelled the best," I inform him. "It kind of reminded me of a rainstorm, though I'm not a huge fan of rainstorms." In fact, they freak me out a ton. I'm not even sure why other than the sound of snapping thunder scares the living crap out of me.

As if the sky heard my words, lightning illuminates the night, followed by thunder suddenly booming..

I crinkle my nose as I peer up at it through the windshield. "Well, that's ominous."

"Honeyton gets a lot of storms," Hunter informs me with his hand still on my waist. My arm is still around him, and the console is digging into my abdomen, but I'm not about to lean back, not when it's thundering and lightning and he's bringing me comfort. "Is there a reason you're afraid of them? Storms, I mean?" he asks, his breath dusting across my cheeks.

"I'm honestly not sure. It could be just a weird phobia, or maybe the answer is locked inside my mind with everything else I've forgotten."

As another zap of lightning lights up the sky, I decide that, even though I wish I could stay in this car with him forever, I should get my butt inside.

"I should get going"—sighing quietly, I lean back—"before it starts raining." I turn away from him and move to reach for the door handle, but he captures a hold of my hand. Confused, I twist back toward him. "What's wrong?"

He chews on his bottom lip, glancing from the house to me. "I was thinking—and you can totally say you're not cool with it if you're not—but I was thinking that maybe I could, like, sleep on your floor, or in your closet, or something. That way, I'll know you're safe."

My eyes widen. "You wanna sleep in my closet so that you can make sure I'm okay?"

He nods without zero hesitation. "It's not like I'm going to get any sleep, anyway, because I'll probably be watching the security footage on your house all night just to make sure you're okay."

Guilt rises inside me. "I'm sorry for putting this shit on you guys. It's—"

He places his finger against my lips. "Don't you dare blame yourself for this. First of all, I'm choosing to be a part of this. And second, it's your fucking uncle's fault that any of this is happening, not yours."

My heart rate quickens, and not because I'm scared. I feel … I don't know, kind of breathless, I think it's overhearing him say words I always wished someone would say. Sure, I had thought them myself, but it's hard to believe your thoughts when everyone around you is always telling you that you're wrong.

It's your fault.

All of this.

You did it.

You made me do it.

You are a murderer, Ravenlee.

"Thanks for saying that," I tell him quietly, my lips brushing against his finger as I speak.

"I'm just saying the truth." He lowers his finger and brushes his knuckles across my cheekbone. It's something he's done a few times, and I'll admit I like it. It's just a little weird, not only being touched but being touched by a guy … a gorgeous guy. "Please let me stay."

The way he says it has me nodding without thinking, and it's in that moment that … "You know, I can see how you make girls like Katie obsessed with you. It's hard to say no to you when you have that look on your face and use that voice."

"What look and what voice?" he asks innocently, but he's trying not to smile.

I roll my eyes. "I think you know exactly what look and voice I'm talking about."

He gives an exaggerated shake of his head. "I have no idea what you're talking about."

"Whatever." I can't help smiling. Then my smile fizzles when I notice my aunt peering out of the living room window. Why? What's she looking for?

"If you're staying the night, how will you get up to my room without being caught?"

He rubs his jawline as he considers this. "Does your aunt and uncle leave the back door unlocked?"

"Until they go to bed, yeah. I can make sure to unlock it once they do," I tell him. "But, how will you get in without getting caught?"

"Well, I do have access to security cameras all over the house," he reminds me with a cheeky grin. "I can look at the footage from my phone and should be able to sneak up to your room."

My stomach flutters at the idea of him in my room while I sleep.

Jesus, you're a freak, Raven. It's not like that for him. He's told you multiple times that he just wants to be friends.

"What about your car?" I wonder.

"I'll park it in the trees like Jax did the other night," he replies simply.

"Okay." I reach for the door handle, but he stops me again.

"Be safe," he whispers with a hint of worry in his eyes.

I nod then push open the door and hurry inside with the snap of thunder and lightning chasing at my heels.

Chapter 13
Raven

My aunt is waiting for me when I walk in, which is a little odd. Sure, she sometimes gets eager to confront me when I've done something that's gotten myself in trouble, but I haven't really done anything. At least, not that I can think of.

Of course, as I'm shutting the front door, it dawns on me that I cut school today, so maybe that's why.

"You're late," she tells me like I have a curfew.

"How can that be possible," I say as I turn toward her, "when I don't even have a specific time that I'm supposed to be home? And I thought you liked it when I wasn't here?" Which again leaves me wondering why in the heck she didn't let me spend the night. Why not take a break from my smart-mouth comments that seem to crawl under her skin?

She's wearing a nightgown, and her hair is done up in curlers. She's clearly ready for bed. Again, odd, since it's only nine o'clock.

"Oh, I do, but I also know you were lying to me about spending the night at someone's house since I know there's no way you have any friends."

The muscle in my jaw ticks. "I do, too—"

"Liar," she cuts me off with her arms crossed. "I know you were probably doing something that I'm sure will get you in trouble. And, while I don't care if you ruin your own life, I'm not about to let you ruin our family's reputation." She steps toward me. "You're going to behave while you live here, or else there will be severe consequences ... worse than anything you've ever suffered." With that, she turns and heads toward the stairs, leaving me standing alone in the foyer.

I release a shaky breath. What the hell is her deal tonight? And, why does she give a crap if I get home at a specific time?

Who the hell knows? Still, she's definitely acting sketchy.

I want to find out why. I think it might be time to start looking into this family more and find out what secrets they're keeping from me. It's the perfect timing, too, since the guys are also looking into them.

Game on, Auntie, game on.

Chapter 14
Hunter

I'm completely screwed. I know this. And yet, I still did it, anyway. I kissed Raven when I knew Jax liked her. I messed up, and the shitty part is that it's not even a surprise. It's what I do all the damn time. I hate that I am this way.

But this time ... this way ... with Raven ... it feels different. I don't want to just hook up with her. I want to kiss her. I want to touch her skin. I want to feel every inch of her with my lips until she's all I can think and feel.

"Shit," I mumble as I grip the wheel and lower my head.

I parked in the trees as it's beginning to rain, droplets splattering against the windshield. I can barely see anything due to the trees surrounding me and the cloudy sky above. But that's a good thing. My car needs to be hidden. Just like I need to stay hidden.

Sneaking inside Raven's house isn't going to be too complicated if I wait until everyone is in bed. I'll admit, though, that

I'm freaking out. Not about sneaking inside. No, I'm kind of freaking out about spending the night in her room.

I'm not entirely sure what's going on with me. I mean, I've known her for a few days. Well, unless she's Willow. Even then, I don't really know Raven. And yet, I felt this connection to her the moment I laid eyes on her. It's like she was the thing that I didn't even know I'd been searching for. Again, the massive issue is Jax. He likes her a lot. I can see it in his eyes and the way he worries about her.

"What the hell am I going to do?" I mumble, part of me just wanting to leave. I can't do that, though. I can't leave her in this house of horrors. Just thinking about those scars on her side makes me want to strangle her uncle. I'm not usually a violent person, but with this ... with Raven ...

Why does she affect me so much?

Too much?

I feel like I'm crawling out of my skin.

I can't fucking deal with this.

Closing my eyes, I take a deep breath, but it doesn't help, so I reach into the glovebox and take out the bag filled with powder as white as the moonlight. I hate that I'm this way, that I have to resort to this shit, but the feeling is exhausting.

It's agonizing.

Sucking in a deep breath, I cut a line right there on the console then snort it up. A few moments later, after the drip comes, I feel calmer.

I feel *nothing*. And it's *everything*.

As I sit and wait around for the lights to go out in the house, I decide to check the video footage inside Raven's house. It's driving me crazy that I can't text her because she dropped her phone in the river. Apparently, it's driving Jax crazy, too, since he messaged me three times about it already.

Jax: Is she okay?

Jax: I'm worried about having her stay at that house.

Jax: Dude, why aren't you messaging me back?

Jax has always been the worrier out of the three of us. While I think it's okay to worry about stuff ... to an extent, Jax deals with his intense worry in unhealthy ways—by cutting. He's been good for a while, but I'm worried he's going to revert back with all this extra stress.

I chew on my bottom lip, trying to decide how to reply to him in a way that won't make him panic more.

Me: She's fine. I'm actually going to stay at her place tonight and sleep in the closet. I'm just waiting to sneak inside. It's going to be uncomfortable as hell sleeping on the floor, but at least we'll know she's safe.

His reply is almost instantaneous.

Jax: That's probably a good idea. I just wish I was there, too.

Me: It'd be harder to sneak both of us in. Plus, there'd be even less room on the closet floor.

Jax: True. Keep me updated and let me know if anything goes wrong.

Me: Okay.

I blow out an exhale as I end the conversation and open the

security footage app. I know he's probably going to stay up all night and not sleep at all.

I decide to send Zay a text, telling him to keep an eye on Jax. He doesn't respond right away, but that's just Zay. Then I go to the live footage of Raven's house. It looks like it's pretty quiet, and I can see past footage of her aunt going into her room. The same goes for Dixie May. Her uncle, though, I don't think he's home yet. I could wait until he arrives before I sneak in, but I'm eager to get in and make sure Raven's okay. Plus, I'm sure she's nervous, and that means the back door should be unlocked.

Before getting out of the car, I grab a hoodie from the back seat and pull the hood over my head. Then I hop out, lock the door, and shut it before rushing through the rain and toward the back of Raven's house. I make sure to stay in the shadows and keep near the trees for as long as possible to avoid getting caught. When I reach the door, however, I realize I have a huge fucking problem.

My boots are covered in mud. If I try to walk into the house with them on, I'm going to leave a trail of dirt across the floor. So, I slip them and my socks off then wrap my finger around the doorknob and turn it, hoping it's unlocked.

Sure enough, the door opens.

I check inside to make sure the kitchen, where the door leads, is empty. It is, and the lights are off. I take out my phone with my free hand and recheck the cameras to make sure I'm still good to go. I can't see anyone wandering around outside the bedrooms, so I quietly step inside and shut the door behind me. Then I tiptoe across the kitchen and toward the stairway. The house is quiet as I start up the stairs, moving as silently as possible. I manage to make it to the top without any hiccups, but the second I start down the hallway, I hear a door open.

"No, I totally don't get it, either." The sound of a high-pitched female voice floats down the hallway as light creeps into the darkness.

Dixie May.

She steps out of her room, and I freeze, peering around in a panic.

"She's such a freak," she continues to yammer on with the phone pressed to her ear.

I panic and duck into a room that I know is some sort of office because Jax, Zay, and I snooped around when we set up the cameras.

Once I'm inside, I softly shut the door and hold my breath, hoping to God she didn't see me.

"Are you sure it was her?" Dixie May asks, and it sounds like her voice is right outside of the door. "I mean, why would they save her?"

That statement captures my full attention. I press my ear to the door and listen.

"Whatever. Even if they did, tomorrow is going to be awesome when that footage gets sent to the entire school." She laughs in a high-pitched tone that makes my skin crawl. "Okay, yeah, see you tomorrow, baby." She hangs up then, and I hear the soft steps of her heading off.

Moments later, a door clicks shut, and I'm left standing in the dark room, wondering what exactly I overheard. Was she talking about Raven? If so, what exactly was she talking about? She said something about saving someone. Could she mean the bridge incident? If so, does that mean someone took a video of what happened? That thought makes my skin crawl even more.

I decide to text Zay so he can look into it, because Jax is too on edge right now, and this might send him right over. I give him a quick recap of what I heard, and he responds within a minute.

Zay: Wait. Why are you in Raven's house? I thought you were just dropping her off.

Me: Jax didn't tell you?

Zay: I'm working out right now, so I haven't seen him.

Me: Oh, well, I'm staying the night at her house to make sure she's safe.

Zay: You think that's a good idea?

Me: I'm sleeping on the closet floor.

Zay. Whatever. Do what you need to do, I guess.

I roll my eyes.

Me: Glad I have your permission. But anyway, this is all beside the point. What're we gonna do if they do have a video of her falling off the bridge? Do you know how traumatizing that'll be for her to see?

Zay: I'll look into it. Give me a few hours, and I'll let you know what I find out.

I put my phone away, not sure if I feel any better. The truth is that I'm not sure if Zay can find out much since we don't even know who pushed her off the bridge. Dixie May, however, may know something ...

Hmm ... Just how brave do I want to be?

Chewing on my bottom lip, I pull my phone back out and

check the cameras. No one appears to be wandering out in the hallway, and after viewing the footage from a few minutes ago, I see she headed into her room. I'm going to give it a while, and then I think I'll try to sneak in there and get a hold of her phone. Because if I can pull that off without getting caught, I'll be able to find out who she was talking to. And they could have the answers to who tossed Raven off that bridge.

Of course, if I get caught, I could end up arrested.

Chapter 15
Raven

O nce I got up to my room, I changed into a pair of comfy sleeping shorts and a black tank top, turned my lamp on, and then shut off the overhead light so it appears as if I went to bed. Then I wait around for Hunter to come up. After a while goes by, I peer outside to see if I can see his car anywhere or him creeping around, but I can't. I wish I had a phone so I could text him. Instead, I'm left stuck in my room, waiting while rain showers down outside and thunder and lightning boom and spark. The longer this goes on, the more I start to wonder if perhaps he changed his mind and went home. It's not like I can be upset with him if he did. He doesn't owe me anything.

I'm just about to give up and climb into bed when my bedroom door starts to open. I instinctively tense since, whenever my door usually opens at night, my uncle is the one to walk through. But a second later, Hunter pokes his head in, sweeping his gaze over the area then landing on me. A smile curves at his lips in a way that makes my heart rate quicken.

"Hey," he says as he slips into my room and shuts the door softly behind him. "Should I lock the door?"

I nod, scooting to the edge of the bed. "Yeah. That way, no one will walk in."

His expression slightly falters as he turns the lock. "How often do people come into your room at night?"

By people, I think he means my uncle.

"Not all the time," I tell him, hugging my knees to my chest. "But there's always a chance."

He smashes his lips together and remains silent for a beat while opening and flexing his hands. "Well, no one's coming in here tonight. I'm going to make sure of that."

I slightly smile. I'm not sure I've ever smiled while I've been in the same house as my aunt before. "Thanks, Hunter, for doing this."

His expression softens. "You don't need to thank me, baby. You shouldn't even have to stay here."

My heart flutters, but I manage an even tone. "*Baby?* I thought we talked about this?"

Amusement tickles at his lips. "We did. And I thought we both agreed it was the perfect nickname for you."

I narrow my eyes at him, but it's a playful move. "That's not how it went at all, and you know it."

He steps toward me. "Maybe you're right." He pauses when he gets right in front of me, and I have to tip my head up to meet his gaze. When our gazes collide, he chews on his bottom lip, contemplating something. I'm about to ask him what it is when he says, "But I thought maybe after I kissed you that you'd be okay with me calling you baby. I probably should have asked you, though, right?" He measures my reaction, but I'm not quite sure what reaction he wants. What does happen, though, is I blush like a dumbass.

"Yeah, you should've," I manage to get out.

He continues to study me, his lips threatening to turn upward. "You're blushing."

"I am not," I lie. When he grins, I roll my eyes and sigh. "Fine, you know what? I am blushing. But you're standing there, looking at me like that and talking about how you kissed me, so ..." I shrug, unsure what else to say.

His gaze continues to dissect me. "Look at you like what?"

I lift a shoulder. "I don't know. Like you mean to look at me."

A strange look flickers on his face. "Can I sit down?" He nods at the bed.

Um ... That so was not what I thought he was going to ask me.

"Yeah, of course," I say without much thought of my answer.

Of course, once he sits down on the bed beside me, I become hyperaware that he's sitting down on the *bed* beside me. In fact, we're sitting close enough that our legs and hips touch.

He doesn't say anything for a moment as he stares at the floor with a pucker at his brow. Then, letting an exhale ease from his lips, he turns toward me. "About the kiss ..." he starts, "you said it was your first kiss?"

Nervousness webs through my stomach. "Yeah." At least from what I can remember, but I choose to keep that thought to myself.

He reaches out and tucks a strand of hair behind my ear. "Are you okay with what happened? I kind of feel like maybe it was a horrible moment to kiss you. You had just fallen off a bridge, for hell's sake." He sighs, his shoulders slumped as his hand falls to his lap. "I generally mess a lot of stuff up, and I think I may have messed up your first kiss."

Again, that *so* was not what I expected to leave his lips. "You didn't mess it up at all ... I liked it ... Like, a lot."

He presses his lips together, wariness flooding his expression, and all of my insecurities rise.

Did he not like the kiss?

Oh my God, he didn't like the kiss!

I am the biggest dumbass.

I start to get up so I can go hide in the bathroom and never come out again, but he captures my arm.

"Raven, wait," he says, rising to his feet with me.

I slip my arm from his hold then cross my arms. "No, it's okay. Really. If you didn't like the kiss, that's totally cool. I just need to use the bathroom." I move to step around him, but he sidesteps, blocking me.

Pissed-off Raven is biting at the surface, claws coming out, ready to peel back any open wounds. Not necessarily because I'm pissed off. No, she's coming out because I'm totally mortified, and she's trying to protect me.

She's a feisty one, that motherfucker.

Then he says, "I liked the kiss," and slowly, pissed-off Raven's claws begin to retract. "I loved the kiss," he mumbles, and it feels like a thousand cracked-out butterflies have taken residency in my stomach. "I just ..." He swallows hard then steps back, raking his fingers through his hair. The strands go askew, sticking up in all sorts of directions, and I have the strangest urge to touch them. "I shouldn't have kissed you." He drops his hand to his side.

"Oh." I'm not sure what to make of what he said. I'm definitely in unchartered territory here, seeing that I'm not an expert at all when it comes to kissing, or dating, or anything related to them. "Okay, cool." Not sure if that's the right thing to say, it's all I can think of.

"*Okay, cool*?" he questions with an arch of his brow. "That's all you have to say?"

I gape at him. "What else do you want me to say after you just said you didn't want to kiss me?"

"I didn't say I *didn't* want to," he corrects. "I said I *shouldn't have*."

"Okay." I'm getting defensive—I know this—but I don't know what else to do. I feel out of my element, which I hate. Usually, I would get stoned, but he's right here, and I don't want to announce right in front of him that he's making me feel so uncomfortable that I need to self-medicate.

Self-numb.

Self-destroy.

He knits his brows. "That's really all you have to say?"

What the heck does he want me to say? Because it clearly feels like he wants me to say something.

Screw that. Just because we kissed doesn't mean I'm going to stand around and try to read his damn mind.

"Yep. And now I'm going to bed." I point toward the closet door. "The closet's over there. There's a couple of folded-up blankets in there already." I grab one of my two pillows and toss it at him, probably too roughly, but what-the-fuck-ever. "And here's a pillow."

He catches the pillow with a confused and somewhat astounded look on his face.

I ignore him, climbing into the bed with my back to him. I hear him quietly sigh, and then his soft footsteps lead toward the closet. The house grows quiet except for the rustling of blankets as he gets situated and the thunder booming outside. My stomach churns every time that happens, and I cross my fingers that the storm will end quickly, but it only seems to pick up intensity the deeper into the night it gets.

Through the limited breaks of thunder, I can hear Hunter tossing and turning on the closet floor. The longer that goes on, the more I start to feel like a terrible person. He didn't even do anything wrong except say he shouldn't have kissed me. And that might not even be bad. He was just being honest. I'm the one who acted all butt hurt, and after he offered to come stay with me so I would feel safe.

Now my stomach is churning for different reasons.

Guilt.

I feel awful.

Stupid.

Broken. Broken. Broken.

Disappointment.

Sucking in a breath, I whisper, "Hunter?"

Painful silence skips by.

"Yeah?" he finally says, sounding as if he's wide awake.

"I'm sorry for being a jerk."

He doesn't respond, and I assume he's upset with me, but then soft footsteps creep through the breaks in thunder grumbling from outside.

I turn and find him walking toward my bed. When he reaches it, he crouches down so he's eye level with me, and I turn all the way over so I'm facing him.

He's not wearing a shirt, which surprises me since he says he never lets anyone see his scars. I guess he already let me see them, though, so maybe he's more comfortable around me now.

I can't help glancing at his chest and abs. Not at the scars, but how defined his muscles are. I mean, he's not huge or anything, but he's definitely in shape.

"You don't need to apologize for getting upset with me." He tucks a strand of hair behind my ear, drawing my attention to his face. He's always doing that, and I'm really starting to get attached to it. And that might be scarier than the thunder. "I was trying to get you to specifically ask me something instead of just saying it aloud. And that isn't right."

"Oh." I knit my brows. "What were you trying to get me to say?"

He skims his fingers down my cheek, his gaze briefly tracking the moment before returning to my eyes. "I was trying to get you to ask me *why* I shouldn't have kissed you, but I should've just said that."

"That's a lot of should'ves," I try to joke because this conversation and the way he's looking at me feels intense.

A lopsided smile touches his lips, and it's so gorgeous. He's so gorgeous. I can admit that to myself. Just myself, and no one else.

"Yeah, it is." He gives a short pause. "I said I shouldn't have kissed you not because I didn't want to kiss you, but because ... well, for starters, it could complicate things with you working and moving in with us."

"How so?"

"In a lot of ways," he replies evasively. "Some of which I can't tell you because it's not really for me to tell."

I have no idea what he's referring to, but I'm not about to force him to tell me more.

"And also because I'm me," he adds with an apologetic smile, but I don't get what he's apologizing for.

"Okay." Confusion laces my tone. "What do you mean by that exactly? Because, when I think of you, I think of the guy who's offered to be my friend, given me rides to school, fed me, saved me from nearly dying, and"—my fingers unconsciously drift to my side, and my chest tightens—"you saw my scars and didn't judge me." That part comes out softer.

He pauses with his fingers against my cheek. "Baby, that's nothing anyone should ever judge you for. As for the rest of the stuff you said"—he swallows hard—"you don't know me very well, but you know of my reputation. You've heard the rumors about me. You ... you saw Katie chase me through the parking lot." His voice drops to a whisper. "That's who I am. I hook up with people then bail the next day."

"So, you just want to hook up with me?" Again, these are words that leave my lips without any forethought. I really need to stop doing that, because I'm starting to sound like a clueless dumbass. "I didn't mean to ask that," I hurriedly say.

Dude, I'm such a dork when it comes to guys.

He looks like he's choosing his next words cautiously. "It's fine that you asked. And the answer is no."

"Oh." Again, I don't know how to feel, because this is unchartered territory for me. Honestly, what I want to do is roll over, pull the blankets over my head, and stop talking.

"I don't want to hook up with you," he repeats then adds, "because I feel different about you. I just ..." He sighs. "If I could, I think I'd probably try to date you. That is ... if you'd even want to. But I worry that I'd fuck it up. Plus, the whole thing with you working for us and living with us, and—"

He bites down on his tongue.

"And what?" I ask.

"It's just part of that thing that's not mine to tell," he replies with a sigh.

I nod like I understand, but I don't. I hate that I don't. I hate unchartered territory and not being able to know what to do in this situation.

I start to shut down. I can feel it, like a light turning off inside me.

"I should probably get to sleep," I tell him.

His lips tug downward, but he nods then moves to stand up. I snag a hold of his hand.

"You can sleep in the bed with me if you want," I tell him, letting go of his hand.

Wariness floods his features. "I don't know if that's such a good idea."

"You'd rather sleep on the floor?" I question with an arch of my brow. "Dude, quit being weird and just get in my bed with me."

He bites back a smile, and I realize what I said.

"I didn't mean it like that," I clarify, my cheeks warming.

His smile breaks through. "You're blushing."

I roll my eyes and slide over. "Come on; I need to get some sleep."

Apprehension crosses his face, but he ultimately climbs into the bed beside me. I'll admit that it's kind of weird. Ever since I met him, everything between us has been odd, from the way that I feel like I know him to how quickly I trusted him. Perhaps those two may coincide.

I watch as he gets situated, moving around a bit before rolling on his side and facing me.

"You good?" I ask, and he nods.

I remain looking at him for a second, scanning his face, searching for the answer as to why he sometimes feels familiar. However, it's like this wall is pushing back against my mind, like a dam that wants to crack under the pressure but won't.

"Everything okay?" he asks, his forehead creasing.

I could just ask him, but I chicken out, which is definitely a first for me. "Yeah ... I'm just nervous because of the stupid lightning."

I roll over so my back is to him, mostly so I'll stop staring at him.

Silence stretches between us, and I try to will myself to go to sleep. But between the storm and having him lying in bed next to me, I can't get my mind to turn off.

"Raven?" he suddenly asks, startling me.

"Yeah?"

"Can I turn the light off? I can't sleep very well unless it's dark."

Shit. I can't sleep well when it is dark. But he's staying here for me, so I probably need to tough it out.

"Yeah, that's fine," I tell him.

He turns and the light clicks off. Darkness smothers my room except for when a brief flicker of lightning zaps across the sky outside. This goes on for about ten minutes, and then Hunter scoots closer to me.

"Are you okay?" he whispers, his lips close to my ear.

I bob my head up and down. "Yeah. Why?"

"Because you're trembling," he says.

I become aware that I am. "It's because of the storm ... and the dark. I have issues." Understatement of the year.

"Fuck, you should've said something. Let me turn the light on." He moves to do just that.

I quickly roll over and stop him. "It's fine. I promise I'll relax in a bit."

"Raven—"

I place my hand over his mouth. "You're my guest. Keep the light off and let's get some sleep." I wait for him to nod, and then I lower my hand and turn over, trying to get comfortable again.

He lies down, too, and he must be facing me because I can feel his breath touching the back of my neck. It's strange, but I find comfort in it.

As discreetly as I can, I inch just the slightest bit closer to him. Everything stills for an instant, and then he scoots closer to me until we're almost spooning. My heart is beating so deafeningly inside my chest that it's almost as loud as the thunder.

"Is this okay?" he whispers in my ear.

I nod. "It's actually helping with the storm."

Another pause, and then he slides his arm around my waist and pulls me closer. "You still good?"

I close my eyes and nod. I am more than good. Minus the hug from Jax, I don't even know how long it's been since I've been this close to someone. I don't think it's just because of that, though. It's his warmth, his scent, the way he actually knew what I needed.

I curl in closer to him, and I feel his breath falter against my ear. He pulls me even closer until he's basically wrapped around me.

I almost instantly start to doze off, and right before I do, I swear I feel him softly kiss my cheek. But perhaps it was just a dream.

If it was, then the dream shifts straight into a nightmare as I tumble back into a memory where blood stains my hands and my parents' lifeless bodies are right in front of me.

Chapter 16
Hunter

I t's been a couple of hours since Raven dozed off. I don't want to let her go, but I need to get Dixie May's phone. I'm worried that if I so much as budge, she'll wake up. I hate the idea of doing that—of just leaving her here by herself when she's clearly afraid of the dark and of lightning storms—but I have to if I ever want to figure out who the hell pushed Raven off the bridge.

Sucking in a deep breath, I remove my arm from around her and carefully roll off the bed. Once I'm standing, I wait for a beat to make sure she's not going to wake up. She's breathing softly while she lays on her side, quietly sleeping.

I turn and pad over to the door, grateful that the storm is still going wild outside. The noise will help hide my movements.

I slowly open the door and step into the hallway. Then I make my way toward Dixie May's room. The only reason I know it's hers is because of when we installed cameras. I remember thinking that I knew it was hers and not Raven's due to the abundance of pink and frilly things covering the room.

Before I walk in, I press my ear to the door, listening to figure out if she's awake or not. It's late enough that she shouldn't be awake, but I'll admit I'm extremely nervous as I crack open the door. No lights are on, which is a good sign. Holding my breath, I push open the door, resisting the urge to sigh in relief when I spot Dixie May fast asleep on her bed. She's lying on her side with her back to the nightstand where I'm hoping she put her phone. Normally, that's where people leave it at night, but I once knew a girl who left hers under her pillow.

Crossing my fingers that's not the case, I make my way over to the nightstand. Sure enough, her phone is there and plugged in. Giving one last glance at Dixie May, I pick it up and swipe my finger across the screen. When the password entry pops up, I dig out my phone and open the app that decodes passwords. It's a rare app that I only have access to because Zay's brother created it. It usually works fairly well, although it gets a bit testy when trying to crack through fingerprint passcodes. Luckily, Dixie May only has a four-digit passcode, and the app deciphers it rather quickly.

Once I'm in, I open her recent calls. She received three within the timeframe of when I snuck into the house, so it's going to be a tiny bit more complicated to figure out who she was talking to. Not impossible, though.

I type down the phone numbers into the note section on my phone then set the phone down. Then I hurriedly sneak out of her room, quietly shutting the door behind me. Everything is going perfectly until I hear someone coming up the stairs.

Shit.

It has to be her uncle. He hasn't gotten home yet, and I haven't heard anyone else get up.

I try to hurry into Raven's room, but when I spot the outline of someone on the stairs, I panic and duck into the office again. Worried he'll hear the door shut, I leave it cracked open. Then I hold my breath as I hear someone getting closer. I wait for the footsteps to pass by because, if it is her uncle, he should be heading to his bedroom. But no one ever does. Finally, after about a minute goes by, I dare a peek through the crack in the door. What I see makes me want to strangle someone.

Raven's uncle is standing in her doorway, staring into her room. I know it's her uncle because I can make out the gun holster on his belt. He isn't doing anything, just watching her sleep, but that's enough to make me want to kill him. How dare he even look at her, the perverted piece of shit?

If I wasn't convinced before, I sure as hell am now that this fucker has some sort of sick, twisted fetish for her. And if he so much as takes a step into that room, I'm going to go after him. I don't care if I get arrested.

Part of me wishes he would just so I could beat his ass. But I also don't want to scare the living hell out of Raven. Plus, if I got arrested, she'd be in this alone, and I don't want to do that to her.

Thankfully, he closes the door and walks away without doing anything but gawking. The moment he goes into his bedroom, I tiptoe out of the office and into Raven's bedroom, shutting the door behind me and locking it. I pocket my phone before carefully climbing into bed with her. I've managed to get in without waking her up, but then the loudest boom of thunder that I've ever heard reverberates across the sky and makes the house shake.

Raven jolts, her eye snapping open as she quickly rolls over so she's facing me. She latches on to the bottom of my shirt, her fingers grazing my abdominal muscles as she blinks up at me, a little disoriented.

As I stare down at her, my heart quickens.

She's so beautiful. I want to take a photo of her. Capture the look of her forever.

"Hey," I say, skimming a finger across her jawline. "It's okay."

She blinks a few more times. "I was having a nightmare ... and then I thought I heard this loud bang ..."

I tuck a strand of hair behind her ear. I've done this a ton of times, but with how her head is resting in the crook of my arm and with the way she's clutching me, it feels more intimate.

"It was the thunder," I assure her.

"Oh." She stares up at me, trying to catch her breath. Or, well, that's what I think is happening at first. But instead of her breathing calming down, it quickens. Every time she breathes in and out, her chest rises and crashes, brushing against mine and driving my body mad. So many feelings are stirring inside me that I'm struggling to deal with them.

I can deal with being the jokester, putting on fake smiles, pretending everything is okay. I can pretend I don't care. I can pretend a lot of things. But this ... this fierce pounding in my heart is definitely new to me. It makes me want to get up and leave, do a line, and just stop thinking altogether.

But I don't—can't—leave her.

"You're breathing heavily," I whisper, swallowing hard.

She smashes her lips together for a beat. "Oh. Sorry. I didn't even realize I was doing it."

"It's fine, baby. I'm just wondering why ... if everything is okay."

"It's just the storm. I always sleep like crap during them ... They seem to sort of just"—she wavers—"trigger fear in me, I guess would be the best way to describe how I feel."

I can hear the fear in her voice, and it makes me want to help her.

Help Raven ...

Help Willow ...

I tear myself from that thought.

You don't know if she's her yet.

I hesitantly reach out and tuck a strand of hair behind her ear again. "Is there anything I can do to help?"

She shakes her head. "You being here is enough."

A frown tugs at my lips. "But you're still freaked out."

"I know." She sighs. "I'm sorry."

I let my fingers linger on her cheek. I can't seem to stop touching her. I'm not even sure why. I just feel this connection to her. And not just because I believe she's the girl from my past, but because I've felt this pull toward her ever since I ran into her in the office and she smarted off to me. She's so gorgeous, and feisty, and funny, and broken. I want to help her, but I'm so messed up myself that I'm not even sure I can.

I want to, though. Desperately.

Shit. I've got it bad.

"You don't need to be sorry for being afraid of something," I promise her.

She carries my gaze, her eyes searching mine. I want to know what she's thinking. I want to know everything going on inside her head.

"Why are you always so nice to me? It ... It doesn't make any sense," she whispers in a tone that nearly rips my heart in two.

"Why doesn't it make any sense?" I question. "You're beautiful, sweet, smart, and sassy when you need to be." I cup her cheek. "Everyone in your life should be nice to you."

But I know that hasn't been the case for her. I have seen it with my own eyes.

"You've been nicer to me than anyone has in a long time." She is still gripping my shirt, her knuckles grazing my abs again. It sends heat through my body. And desire. Want. Need.

"I haven't even been that nice," I whisper shakily. Her touch is driving me crazy in the most unfamiliar way possible.

Sure, I've had a lot of sex, but I always keep most of my clothes on so no one sees my scars. Raven has seen my scars, though, and now she's touching them.

"Are you okay?" She knits her brows. "You seem tense all of a sudden."

"I'm fine." I suck in a deep breath then release it. "I just ... You're touching some of my scars, and I'm not used to that."

She pauses, and then her gaze drops to where she's fisting my shirt. She quickly pulls away. "I'm so sorry. I didn't even realize I was doing that. I won't ever touch you again like that—"

"No, don't say that," I quickly cut her off, skimming my

fingers down her cheekbone. "I don't *not* want you touching me. I'm just not used to my scars being touched."

She wets her lips with her tongue, hesitancy written all over her face.

"What's wrong, baby?" I ask.

"Other than the fact that you keep calling me baby?"

Have I been?

A smile curves at my lips. A real one, too, something that rarely happens but seems to frequently around her. "What? Is that not what BFFs call each other?"

"You know they don't," she says flatly. "And I know you know that because we've already talked about this."

"Did we?" I bring my free hand up toward my mouth so I can tap my finger against my lip. "Man, Jax and Zay must really be confused then, since I'm always calling them baby. I thought I was just being a good friend, but they probably think I want more. No wonder Jax sent me flowers last Valentine's Day."

She giggles, and I grin. Then, as lightning flashes from outside, her smile quickly fizzles.

As I detect that her attention is drifting toward the storm again, I decide I need to keep distracting her since it seems to keep her relaxed.

"Tell me what that look was on your face early," I say, drawing her attention back to me.

She meets my gaze, confusion briefly flickering on her face, but then it's quickly replaced by recognition and, ultimately ... embarrassment.

Wait ... "Are you blushing?" I ask as lightning briefly illuminates the room just enough to give me a glimpse of her pink cheeks.

"No," she lies, looking away.

"Raven," I say, so damn curious as to what in the hell is going on in that head of hers. "Come on. Tell me. I want to know."

She promptly shakes her head. "No way."

I hook a finger under her chin, forcing her to look at me. "Come on." I pout. "I want to know."

She makes a big show of rolling her eyes then sighs. "Fine. Earlier, when we were talking about your scars, I was just wondering"—she avoids eye contact with me—"how no one has seen or touched them, because ... you've had ... sex, and that seems like it should happen during ... sex."

Every time she says *sex*, she trips over the word. And it's literally the most adorable thing I've ever seen.

"During what?" I pretend like I can't hear her just so I can hear her trip over the word again.

"During sex," she mutters, pulling the blanket tighter against her, as if she can hide underneath it.

"What?"

"Oh my God, sex," she gripes, bobbing her head back. "But I get the feeling you heard me just fine."

When I let a grin spread across my lips, she narrows her eyes at me.

"I did hear you," I divulge, and her face turns into a full-on glare. "I just like hearing you say sex."

She narrows her eyes, and I become aware that I'm flirting with her again.

I seriously have no self-control.

I'm about to make myself stop when she scoffs. "I don't say it any differently than anyone else. See? Sex. Sex. Sex. Sex. Sex—"

I kiss her, just a light brush of my lips against hers. I'm not even sure why. Or, well, maybe I do and just can't admit it to myself yet.

When I pull back, neither one of us say anything. We just breathe softly, our breaths dusting against each other's faces.

"That's the second time you've kissed me," she whispers, shattering the silence.

"I know." I sound breathless—a mess. Like the Hunter I am, who needs a drink or a one-night stand, it's why I do what I do—sex ... drinking ... It calms me the fuck down, usually when thoughts of my past are haunting me. They're not really haunting me right now. I'm just ... kissing her because I want to.

Well, that's new.

Deep down inside me, I'll admit that I want to taste it again. Want that just because of want and not because I'm trying to bury painful feelings inside me.

I splay my fingers across her cheek then skim my finger along her cheekbone, my pulse soaring inside my chest.

"Are you ...?" She swallows audibly. "Are you going to kiss me again?"

I wet my lips with my tongue. "I was ... I was thinking about it." I briefly pause. "Are you okay with that?"

Part of me worries her answer will be no, while the other part worries it'll be yes.

She sinks her teeth into her bottom lip then gives an unsteady nod.

A faltering exhale leaves my lips, and then I'm leaning in.

The move is deliberate, and I know that in doing so—kissing her —it'll change a lot for me. But I'm not about to stop. I don't want to stop.

"Hunter," she murmurs as my lips brush hers. Her hands find my sides, her palms touching my scars again, and her chest presses against mine. I can feel so much of her, and she can feel so much of me.

My body starts to tremble, but I don't tell her to move her hands. No, instead, I kiss her again softly, slowly. I'm taking it slow on purpose for so many damn reasons, one being that I don't want to pressure her into doing anything. I also don't want to take things fast like I always do. Not with this. Not with her. And, in the back of my mind, I know there's another reason.

Jax.

Jax likes Raven. I know he does. And I don't know what to do about that.

I should pull away from her. Be a good guy for once.

I pull back, struggling to breathe evenly.

"Are you okay?" she whispers, still clutching me, her chest brushing against mine with each breath she takes and driving my body mad.

I nod with my eyes shut and rest my forehead against hers. "I just don't want to move too quickly with this. For once, I want to take things slow." I put part of the truth out there.

"This?" she asks confusedly.

I realize I'm not even sure what I mean by the word. What is Raven to me? A potential long-lost friend? My new friend? The girl who I feel such a connection to that I'm letting her keep her hands on my scars right now?

I don't have an answer for her, and thankfully, a loud boom of thunder seems to distract her from the conversation. She latches on to me, inching closer to the point where her head is resting right above where my heart is racing.

"How long do you think the storm will last?" she asks with her fingers splayed across my back.

"I'm not sure." I wrap my arms around her, pulling her closer to me. "You should try to get some sleep. I'm here. Nothing's going to happen. I promise."

I honestly don't expect her to believe me. I expect her to stay awake and stress over the storm, but she surprises me when she nods. Then, a few minutes later, I can hear the soft sound of her breathing as she drifts into dreamland.

I'm so glad she fell asleep, but now I'm wide awake. Not because of the storm, but because I have her pressed up so closely against me. I've never been a cuddler, but this is so much more than that. Everything about her, from the way she feels to the sound of her soft breathing rings with familiarity. And I have this desperate need to protect her. It's like this long-buried need that's clawing its way out of the grave.

I want to protect her.

I want to feel her skin.

I want to taste her lips again.

Shit. I am so damn screwed.

Chapter 17
Raven

I'm running through a forest. Blood is on my hands. I can hear screaming from somewhere. It sounds like my mother. Birds scatter through the air, and fog laces from my breath. And the air? It tastes like fucking death, and I don't even know how I know that. I just do.

"Run, Raven!" someone shouts from the trees. "Run quickly!"

Tears burn in my eyes as I recognize the voice. "Mommy?"

But my mom is dead. I saw her back at the house, lying on the floor with blood surrounding her. I just don't know how she got there. All I know is that I have blood on my hands—

"Raven!"

"Raven, wake up."

My eyelids flutter open, and I suck in a huge breath at the sight of someone leaning over me. For a panicking moment, I think it's my uncle. Then Hunter's beautiful blue eyes come into focus, and I relax.

Concern is creased between his brow as he stares down at me. "You were whimpering in your sleep." He tucks a strand of hair behind my ear. "You did that a lot ... Do you have nightmares?"

I release a shaky breath and nod. "Yeah ... It's not a big deal. Honestly, at this point in my life, it's just part of my sleeping pattern."

A frown forms on his pretty, pierced lips. The pretty, pierced lips that have kissed me. Twice.

"That shouldn't be something you just get used to," he says in concern.

"You've never had nightmares before?" I question, no longer wanting to talk about this. While I appreciate his concern, it's making me think about the nightmare, and I want to erase it from my mind.

He wavers. "Yeah ..."

"So, it's not a big deal, then."

"I guess not." His frown remains as he stares down at me. He's propped up on one arm, shirtless, and wisps of his blond hair are hanging in his eyes. He's so gorgeous. And I've kissed him. But I'm not sure what that means, especially since he seemed a bit uneasy last night afterward.

"We should get ready for school," he suddenly murmurs. Then his gaze briefly drops to my mouth.

Is he going to kiss me again?

Do I want him to?

I probably would except for the fact that I have some extreme morning breath going on, so I turn my head and pretend to yawn and stretch.

He slants back, appearing slightly confused, like he knows exactly what I just did.

"Do you have to go home and change before school?" I ask in an attempt to distract him from my spazziness.

He nods, sitting up and raking his fingers through his hair. "I do." He glances at the time on his phone. "I'm probably going to be late." He sighs heavily then looks at me. "I hate to say this, but I don't think I can drive you to school unless you want to be late."

I try my best not to frown. "As much as I like being a rebel, I think, after missing the last half of school yesterday, I should probably make sure I go today." I act as casual as I can, but deep down, I loathe the idea of getting on the bus.

"You sure?" he double-checks. "Because I can get you a tardy pass."

The thing is, while he's saying words that would make me believe he wants me to be late for school, I get the vibe that he doesn't want to drive me.

"I'm good," I assure him. "It's not going to hurt me if I have to ride the bus for a day."

A crease forms between his brows. "I'm not going to make you ride the bus."

"Oh." Now I'm the confused one. "Who's going to drive me, then?"

"I was going to have Low do it."

Low is his sister. She seems super nice, but I have to check.

"You think she'd be okay with that?"

He nods with zero hesitation. "She'd probably be happy to. She ... Well, she doesn't have a lot of friends."

"That's something I can totally relate to," I tell him. "Or, well, not now, I guess since you're my friend, but ..." Jesus, did I seriously just call him my friend like I'm twelve. I clear my throat. "Anyway, yeah, if she doesn't mind driving my ass to school, I'd totally love a ride."

He smiles with those lips that I've kissed. Twice. And yet, I have no idea what any of that means.

Clueless Raven. Apparently, this is becoming my permanent title.

"Sounds good, bestie," he says in a teasing tone. "Let me text her really quick." He begins texting away while I scoot to the edge of the bed and stretch my arms above my head, arching my back. When I lower my hands, I peer over my shoulder to find him looking at me with his teeth sunk into his bottom lip.

"Is everything okay?" I ask, wondering if maybe Low said no.

He nods, sweeping his gaze across my face. "Yeah, every-thing's good. Low's completely fine with driving you. In fact, I think she's excited about it." He erases the intense look on his face and rises to his feet. "She'll be here in, like, thirty minutes. Is that enough time for you to get ready?"

I nod, standing. He seems a bit off, like he's being formal with me, and I'm not sure why.

"I can get ready pretty quickly," I assure him. "But, how are you going to get out of the house without being caught?"

He grins as he rounds the foot of the bed. "It's easy to sneak out of a girl's house when you've got cameras all over the place."

"True." I wonder how many houses he's snuck out of. Hunter seems like the sort of guy who has probably snuck out of quite a bit. "Still ... be careful. My uncle is a cop, and if he busts you, he's going to be a douche about it," I stress, combing my fingers through my tangled hair.

A flash of what looks like anger flickers across his face but is quickly erased.

"Don't worry about me. I got this, baby." He starts to reach for me—I think to brush his fingers along my cheek, something he's done a couple of times—but halfway, he suddenly pulls back and stuffs his hands into his pockets. "See you at school," he says, giving me what looks like a forced smile. Then he pulls out his phone, checks the video footage, and slips out of the room without uttering another word.

And I'm left feeling utterly confused.

Last night, he kissed me—twice. And now he's acting as if we're barely friends. It's weird, and I feel like I did something wrong, which pisses me off.

I'm not going to do this—sit here and overanalyze some guy.

Blowing out a breath, I march over to my dresser and grab an outfit for the day. I decide on a pair of torn, black jeans and a grey, fitted shirt. I top that off with my boots and leather jacket. Like always, I keep my makeup simple with just a dab of lip gloss, a glide of kohl eyeliner, and a swipe of mascara. I leave my long, wavy brown hair down, using my fingers to comb through it.

By the time I'm good to go, it dawns on me that I don't have a phone, which means I don't have any way to keep in contact with anyone. Not even Low. I guess I'm going to just have to watch out the window for her.

While I do, I decide to take a few hits, even though it's weird to be smoking from a joint that I know my uncle knows I have. I still don't get why he left all the drugs on my bed, but while it may be sketchy, I'm not going to not smoke it.

I open the window, lean out, and suck in a few inhales. As the smoke slides through my lungs, I feel slightly calmer, my worries of Hunter acting weird and me not having a phone drifting away. By the time I spot a sleek, black car with tinted windows rolling up the driveway, I'm feeling pretty damn good. Although, it is kind of confusing because the car looks way too luxurious for a teenager to be driving. And to add to my confusion, Harlow hops out of the back of the car.

She has her blonde hair down and is wearing jeans and a purple shirt, along with a pair of clunky heeled boots. She pulls down her sunglasses slightly and looks at the house as if she's wary of approaching it.

I don't blame her. My uncle's patrol car is parked out front. And seriously, who wants to deal with a cop? And a perverted one at that. Not that she knows that.

Jesus, Raven, stop being stoned and focus.

"Hey!" I shout down at her.

She jolts, darting her gaze up to my bedroom. "Oh, hey, bestie!" She slides her sunglasses back on. "You want me to knock, or do you wanna just come down?"

"I'll just come down. Give me a second." I put the joint out on the side of the house, aware that she saw me and wondering if she's cool with it. My bet is yes, but you never know sometimes.

Once the joint is out, I tuck it in my pocket because my bag and stuff are still in my locker. Then I shut the window and head out of my room, crossing my fingers that I won't run into anyone. But luck is not on my side. It never is.

"Oh, look, it's loser bridge girl," Dixie May sneers as we just so happen to exit our rooms at the same time.

"Wait ... What?" My heart rate increases.

Did I hear her right? Does she know about the bridge?

Her overly lipstick'ed lips spread into a grin. "You don't know? Oh God, that's even better."

I hate to ask it, but I need to know. "Know what?"

She taps her finger against her lip. "I could tell you, I guess, but I think I'll wait and let you figure it out on your own." She turns to leave, but I reach out and grab her arm.

She's in a pair of pink stilettos that match her dress, so she stumbles when I jerk her back.

"What the hell?" she whines, trying to yank her arm from me. "Let go of me, you freak!"

I hold on to her arm tightly. "Not until you tell me what you're talking about." I know I've only got moments to spare before my aunt shows up and goes crazy on me.

She glares at me. "No. You deserve to show up at school blind about this."

I tighten my grip on her. "Tell me or else."

"Or else what?" She smirks at me. "You tell your friends to beat me up? Who the hell cares? I have my own protection, thank you very much." Again, she jerks her arm away, and this time I let it go, mostly because her words have thrown me off.

She has protection? Who's protecting her?

"You're lying," I say, but I'm losing some of my confidence.

The way she said it, her words seem to carry some truth. But who could offer her protection against Hunter, Jax, and Zay? From what I understand, everyone at school is afraid of them. Then again, someone had the balls to push me off that bridge.

Wait ...

"What did you do?" I inch close to her, trembling with rage. "Were you there yesterday?"

She doesn't answer, but she does look a bit worried when she notices my balled-up fists. Of course, at that precise moment, my aunt materializes from out of her room.

"Mom, Raven's being a bitch," Dixie May immediately complains.

My aunt glides her gaze to me and parts her lips, but I walk off before she can utter a word.

"Ravenlee!" she calls out. "You come back here right now so we can talk about your behavior."

I just flip her off from over my shoulder and quicken my pace, barreling down the stairs so swiftly that I nearly trip over my own feet. I manage to keep my balance and hurry out of the house, breathing in relief at the feel of the crisp morning air against my skin. Then I powerwalk toward the car, anger buzzing underneath my skin.

"Hey," Low greets me as I approach the side of the car where she's waiting. "I'm so glad Hunter asked me to pick you up. I've been wanting to hang out with you, but he's being a friend hog ..." She trails off. "What's wrong?"

"It's nothing." I'm unsure how much I'm supposed to tell her about what's going on. Then again, if what Dixie May said is true, then she's going to find out about it, anyway.

She shakes her head. "It's definitely not nothing."

I sigh heavily. "Yeah, it's definitely not. But, can I tell you on the way to school? I don't want to make us late." I don't want to walk into class late, either, or I'm going to have to deal with staring again.

Concern laces her voice as she turns and opens the car door. "Sure." She climbs in back, a reminder that she didn't drive here. I was too distracted when I walked to her car to pay attention to who was driving. Maybe I won't tell her what happened if someone we go to school with is driving the car. When I slide into the back seat, however, I see an older man with grey hair sitting behind the wheel.

"This is Larry, my driver," Harlow explains when she notices where I'm looking.

Right. Harlow is from a wealthy family, so it makes sense that she has a driver.

Okay, that's a lie. That doesn't make any sense to me because she doesn't seem like the kind of person who would want a driver. Although, I don't know her well.

"My dad likes to keep tabs on me," she explains, as if reading my thoughts. "And this is one of the ways that he does." She gestures at Larry, who hasn't said a word. I'll admit, it's kind of creepy

"Oh," is all I can think of to say as I reach for my seat belt.

"I wish I had my own car," she continues, buckling her own seat belt as Larry starts to back out of the driveway, "but my father thinks it's too dangerous."

I think of what happened to me yesterday and wonder if perhaps her father is right. Then again, Hunter has told me enough about his father that I get he's probably a scary man.

"So"—she twists to face me—"what's going on that's got you worried? And worried enough that you had to get stoned this morning?"

So, she did see me get stoned. I could tell her that I do that all the time but decide not to for now.

"Some kids were bullying me yesterday," I give her the partial truth. "And my stupid cousin knows about it and basically told me that school is going to be hell today."

Her lips sink into a frown. "God, I fucking hate this town." She blows out a frustrated exhale. "What did they do to you?"

I shrug. "Just your typical bullying." I feel bad for being vague, but again, I don't want to tell her about this weird game the families are playing. Not when Hunter asked me not to tell her.

She shakes her head and mutters some stuff under her breath. "Well, they're going to regret it. You're friends with my brother and his friends, and they'll make them pay. You just got to tell them."

"They already know," I inform her, wishing I had a phone so I could ask Hunter if it's okay to tell Low what happened. Or at least tell him what happened with Dixie May. With how strange he was acting when he left my house this morning, maybe it's better if I handle this myself.

"That's good." She pulls out her phone. "I'm going to text him and make sure he's handling it."

"No, you don't need to do that," I say quickly. "Everything is good. In fact, we already have a plan." It's a total lie, but I don't want to be that girl—the girl who always needs saving. They already saved me last night from the river. That's enough saving for now. I just wish there weren't those few moments, like the ones that happened between Hunter and me, the soft touches and brushes of lips. Those confuse me the most and make me want to text him, talk to him, seek comfort in him. Then I remember how offish he was this morning.

"You sure?" she asks, her finger hovering over the screen of her phone.

"I'm positive," I assure her as we drive out onto the road.

She momentarily hesitates before pocketing her phone. "Well, if you change your mind, let me know." She reclines back in the seat. "So, want a little distraction for a bit?"

I nod, grateful. "Yes, please."

"Okay." She brings her leg up onto the seat between us. "So, about this club I want you to go to with me."

Right, the club. In the midst of the drama, I'd almost forgotten about that.

"First off, my brother and his friends can't know which one we're going to or they're gonna freak."

"That's fine." I give a short pause. "Can I ask why they'd freak, though?"

"Because it's a club my father owns," she explains. "And while my father sucks, this club is the shit. It's like super exclusive, and there's this band that's going to be there that's awesome. They're not super huge or anything, but they really should be ... They're called Alyric Bliss."

"You know what? I think I've heard of them."

"Really?"

"Yeah, I love music."

"Dope. Then you're down to go, I'm guessing."

"Sure." I tuck a strand of hair behind my ear. It sounds fun and everything, but going to Hunter's father's club sounds sketchy at best.

"You sure you're sure?" she wonders, noting my expression.

"Yeah," I assure her with a flick of my wrist. "My mind's just a bit wandering today."

"You're worried about what's going to happen at school." It's not a question.

"Kind of. But honestly, I can handle it." Because, while I may be scared shitless, it's nothing I haven't had to handle before. I may be clueless when it comes to guys, but I'm an expert when it comes to dealing with bullies.

Sometimes, I wish I wasn't. That I was never the kind of person to get bullied. That I wasn't a murderer.

"So ... do you have a thing for my brother or Jax?" Low asks so abruptly that I nearly get whiplash from the subject change.

"What?" I blink at her.

She shrugs. "Sorry for the abrupt subject change. I figured you could use it. And I'm also super curious to hear the answer to my question because, the day before yesterday, when you, my brother, and I went to lunch, you seemed to be vibing. But then, yesterday, you were with Jax."

"He was just walking me to the car," I explain, "where Hunter and Zay were."

"Maybe that is true, but I've known Jax for a super long time and, trust me, that guy is not the sort of guy to walk a girl to a car," she informs me. "Not that he's an asshole, although he can be. Jax is just"—she wavers—"the quietest and more mysterious of The Raven Three."

"The Raven Three?"

"That's what people sometimes refer to them as."

"Oh." Weird, considering my name's in it. "Why?"

She lifts a shoulder then turns forward in her seat as we near the school. "Honestly, I'm not sure." She leans over and picks up her backpack from the floor. "They've had the name for a while ... since they were kids."

I nod, absorbing this all in. I know it's just a name, but it has my name in it. And I wouldn't think much of it except for the fact that, every now and again, I get this feeling that I know the guys. I swear I've even seen memories of them of when we were younger.

She starts digging around in her bag, seeming sort of distracted as the car rolls up to the curb in front of the school entrance. People are wandering around the campus yard, and I more than notice a few glances in our direction. It has to be because of Low, right? Because no one would know I was in here.

"Ah-ha," she whispers as she retrieves a pack of cigarettes from her backpack. "I didn't forget to put them in there." She stuffs them back into the bag then unfastens her seat belt and slings the handle of the bag over her shoulder. "You wanna come smoke with me?" she asks.

"Um ..." I peek at Larry, who hasn't said a word, but is clearly an adult and Low is underage.

"Don't worry about him," she assures me then throws Larry a

cheeky grin. "Larry's cool, right?"

Larry nods but doesn't so much as glance at us.

A Cheshire cat smile spreads across her lips. "See?"

I smile back, but to be honest, Larry's sort of creepy. Still, I can smoke with her. I usually don't smoke cigarettes, but I do occasionally. And I get high at school all the time. Plus, it's kind of fun to have a friend to go with.

"Sweet." She shoves the door open and hops out of the car, her boots scuffing against the asphalt.

I climb out, too, and the instant I do, I want to shrink back in the car. Almost everyone starts staring at me. And it's worse than it was yesterday when I was with the guys and me being with them was drawing attention.

Swallowing hard, I try to put on my best brave face, but I'm nowhere near high enough. Still, I manage to hold my head high enough as I walk by Low, following her as she heads toward the back of the school. She doesn't say anything to anyone, but I get the feeling she wants to.

The staring is almost maddening, and by the time we duck behind the school and out of sight of everyone, I feel like I'm crawling out of my skin.

We head back by the dumpsters and tuck ourselves between them and the wall of the school where Low tells me no one ever goes, so we should be safe. The moment we're settled, she reels toward me.

"Dude, what the hell? That was bad. Like worse than when I ..." She shifts her weight. "Anyway, I was going to tell people to fuck off, but I wasn't sure if you wanted me to draw more attention or not."

"I honestly don't know." I chew on my bottom lip. "I mean, I've never been one to totally cower down—you can ask Zay that —but at the same time, I hate drawing attention to myself." I wrap my arms around myself as the wind kicks up. "I usually enter school with earbuds in so I don't even have to hear what people are saying."

She swings her bag off her shoulder, drops it to the ground, and digs her pack of cigarettes out of the front pocket. "You say that like you've spent a lot of time having to deal with people talking shit about you."

"I have," I admit. "My cousin is a bitch and gets off on getting her followers to torment me. If I wasn't so outnumbered and didn't have to live with her, I'd kick her ass. But I could end up homeless if I did." Not that I completely care about that. To be honest, I've thought about getting kicked out and how living on the streets might be better than living under a roof that belongs to a sadistic asshole.

"That's gotta suck living with people like that," she says as she pops a cigarette into her mouth.

I can tell she wants to ask more, like maybe why I'm living with them. But thankfully, she doesn't and instead offers me a cigarette. I take one and put it into my mouth. She lights up then hands me the lighter, and I light up, too.

We take the first drag in complete silence, smoke circling the air.

"I feel like I need to do something," she finally mumbles. "It's not fair that this school is doing this to you. You're new and that's hard enough."

While I appreciate what she's saying, I still feel the need to say, "More than likely, if you try to stop it, you're going to end up getting bullied, too."

Although I'm not even positive what it is, what's going on exactly, I have a guess, and that has to do with what happened on the bridge yesterday. Someone probably spread a rumor. That's how it always starts, right?

"So?" She sucks another drag of her cigarette. "I can't let you go through this alone. It's too much to deal with on, like, your third day of school."

"Well, to be fair, I'm not totally coherent."

"True." She eyes me over curiously. "You got any more on you?"

I pat my pocket. "Yeah. Why?"

She waggles her eyebrows at me. "Wanna share?"

"Seriously?" I ask, surprised.

She lifts a shoulder. "Sure. If you don't mind."

"I totally don't." I dig the joint out of my pocket and hand it to her.

She immediately lights up and takes a hit, holding it in before letting it out. Then she hands the joint to me, and I do the same.

"I've never actually gotten high with anyone before," I divulge as smoke snakes from my lips.

"Me, neither," she admits. "And, while I'm being totally honest, you're like the first friend I've had since middle school."

"Really?" I ask, and she nods.

"I used to have friends." She lifts the end of the joint toward her lips, frowning. "But then they stabbed me in the back with a big fat knife."

I want to tell her I feel her pain—at least when it comes to being friendless—but she receives a text that distracts her.

She fishes her phone out of her pocket then frowns. "Someone sent a message to everyone at school. Or, well, a video." She taps the screen to watch it. I think I already know what's on it.

Sure enough, I hear a voice.

"You're feisty, aren't you? I'm not surprised."

It's the same voice that whispered in my ear while I was standing on the bridge.

And it's the exact same words.

Which means everyone is about to see my humiliation times ten.

I could run away, but instead I just take another hit, letting myself become more numb.

Low watches the video, her eyes widening. "Holy shit."

"Holy shit is right." My voice sounds so hollow.

She looks up at me. "This is what happened to you yesterday?"

I bob my head up and down.

"And my brother and his friends know?" she asks, her tone shaking with anger.

"Yeah ... they actually saved me when I fell into the water. Does the video not show that?"

"No ... it cuts off before then."

A thought occurs to me. "Does it show who pushed me?"

She shakes her head. "No. The person was wearing a mask." She hesitates. "You don't know who did it?"

I sigh as I ash the cigarette, the joint still burning in my other hand. "No. They drugged me before they took me."

"*Took you?*" she gapes at me. "Okay, so I don't want to force you to talk about this, but if you feel comfortable enough, could you tell me what happened?"

Hunter told me not to tell her, but she already knows enough about what happened—everyone at school does—so I take a deep breath and proceed to tell her, leaving out the part about the game because that was the part Hunter didn't really want me spilling the beans about. By the time I'm finished, both our eyes are wide ... and bloodshot.

"Dude, I can't believe someone took you like that." She grows quiet, wavering her head from side to side as she ashes her cigarette. "You know what? I actually can. Honeyton is so messed up."

"I'm kind of starting to realize that." I take one more drag off the joint then gently put out the tip and stuff it back into my pocket, which will probably stink by the end of the day.

She inhales off the cigarette then exhales a cloud of smoke. "So, what do you think the point of it was? Do you think, if it was your cousin, she was just being a bitch? Or do you think there was an ulterior motive?"

"I have no idea." I hate lying to her and really want to just divulge about this game. Although, I'm not even positive what the game is exactly. And I'm not going to betray Hunter like that, either. Sure, Low is nice, and I want to be her friend, but Hunter is ... well, he's been so damn nice to me. Even this morning when he was a little distant, he made sure I had a ride to school. And

Jax? Jax freakin' saved me from drowning. And Zay ... he's still an asshole, but not as bad.

"You really need to learn how to swim." She drops her finished cigarette onto the ground and puts it out. "Like as soon as possible."

"I know," I agree. "I've tried to learn quite a few times, but my fear of water makes it nearly impossible."

"You should ask the guys to help you." She takes out a perfume bottle and sprays a few spritzes onto herself before handing it to me. "They're all pretty good swimmers. I think Zay's the best, though."

I spray the perfume onto me, trying to visualize what it'd be like for Zay to teach me how to swim.

She laughs softly at my expression. "I'm guessing, from that look on your face, that you're not a huge fan of Zay."

I hand her back the bottle of perfume. "He's just really intense, and I don't know ... I'm kind of a smartass, so it's not a good combination."

"He's definitely intense." She puts the perfume back into her bag, zips it up, and slides her backpack on. "Still, I think asking him, or even Jax or Hunter, to teach you is a good idea. I'd teach you myself, but I'm not that great."

The bell rings then, announcing that we have to leave the safety of the dumpsters. And yes, I know how crazy that sounds, but being near a dumpster sounds way better than going into school. Hell, I'd take being in one over having to go in.

"You ready for this?" she asks.

I nod and force a smile onto my face. "Yeah."

It's a total fucking lie. I'm not ready for it. Not even close. But I square my shoulders and follow her out from our spot, walking beside her as we round the school and enter the building. The hallway has cleared out a little, but enough people are lingering around that I have to endure the gawking and whispering.

I pretend not to notice, but when I reach my locker, any ability to pretend goes *peace out*. Because painted across the front, in what looks like blood but is probably just red paint, is the word: *murderer*.

Chapter 18
Hunter

Part of me hates that I'm not driving to school while part of me is relieved.

I kissed her. I fucking kissed her and slept beside her for an entire night. I may have had a lot of sex, but I've never spent the night with a woman before. And that kiss ... damn, I think I could've probably spent the entire night doing that. But deep down, I know I can't. Not just because I'm screwed up and scared shitless of intimacy, which I am—I can admit that. It's not just that, though.

Jax likes Raven. I could tell from the moment she climbed into the car with us after busting me for snooping around in her house. He was defensive of her, spoke to her. And that's not Jax's typical MO. He clearly likes her. He fucking saved her, for God's sake. And here I am, kissing her.

But God, she tasted so damn good.

"You got the list of phone numbers from the calls she

received and made last night, right?" Zay asks, drawing me from my thoughts of the most beautiful girl I've ever seen with the saddest eyes.

I nod, sweeping strands of hair out of my eyes before lowering my hand back onto the steering wheel. "Of course I did, bro. I'm not an amateur."

I'm speeding, not necessarily anxious to get to school, but to get back to Raven. I hated sending her to school on her own today, but I needed a few minutes to talk to Jax and Zay about what happened at her house without her overhearing. It's not that I want to keep it a secret from her; I just want to make sure it's what I'm thinking it is before I have to tell Raven.

Tell her that I'm sure her bitch of a cousin helped aid what went down on the bridge yesterday.

"You aren't, huh?" Zay challenges from the passenger seat with his brow raised.

I flick a glance at him. "What the fuck are you implying?"

"That you shouldn't have left her to go to school by herself," Jax mumbles from the back seat. He has his arms crossed and is staring out the window with his jaw set tight. "She doesn't even have a phone on her."

"She's with Low," I stress, but guilt is creeping up inside me. I hate to admit it, but a teeny, tiny part of me needed to take a breather from Raven. "She'll be fine."

"She better be," Jax says, throwing me a dirty look.

My brows rise toward my hairline. Shit, this thing he has for her is way worse than I thought. What I don't get, though, is why Zay's acting so weird about it, too.

"You shouldn't have let her go on her own." He pulls the hood of his hoodie over his head as we near the school. "If the game is really starting, she's clearly meant to be on our team. And if something happens to her this morning, that's going to make us look even weaker than we already do."

He acts as if his worries are solely selfish—and they could be—but I have to wonder: if Raven is Willow, does Zay have an ulterior motive behind his concern over this? You never know with him. He's an unreadable sort of guy, and that's coming from me, one of his best friends.

I nervously suck on my lip ring as I pull into the parking lot and find a spot near the back.

I get out of my car when my phone rings. I dig it out of my pocket while Zay lights up a cigarette. He's never been one for giving a shit if he gets busted. When I see that Low is calling, my stomach twists with nerves.

"Hey," I answer, trying to sound upbeat.

"Hey," Low replies in a tone that makes that twisting sensation increase. "Something happened this morning ... something bad."

Blood roars in my eardrums. "What?"

Zay watches me from over the roof of the car with the cigarette dangling from his lips. Jax has just climbed out of the seat and is reaching back to grab his binder, but he pauses to look at me.

"Well ... have you guys gotten a text from someone today, with a video attached to it?" Low asks with worry in her voice.

Dread prickles at my skin. "No. Why?"

"Huh? Whoever sent it must've kept you, Zay, and Jax off the text list on purpose, probably so you'd be blindsided. That's just my guess." She's rambling. She does that sometimes.

"Low," I say, avoiding Jax's and Zay's dissecting gaze. "What was on the video?"

She releases a quiet sigh. "It was of what happened to Raven on the bridge yesterday. And then, to top it off, when we went into the school, the word ... *murderer* was painted on her locker in what I'm guessing is paint, but honestly, it could be, like, blood or something."

That roar in my eardrums turns into a full-on raging scream. "Where is she right now?"

"We're in the bathroom," she answers. "I'm with her, but she's sitting in the stall and won't come out. I don't want to leave her alone."

I lock my door and shut it. Zay's talking to me, but I ignore him, heading for the entrance to the school. "Okay, we just got to school. I'm heading in right now, so stay with her until I get there." I wait for her to agree before hanging up.

"Hunter, tell me what the hell is going on," Zay demands as he jogs after me, tossing his cigarette to the ground before we reach the curb.

"Something happened," I mumble as I powerwalk to the school.

"No fucking shit," Zay snaps at me. "But I want to know what."

Jax rushes up beside me, the chain in his belt loop jingling. "Is Raven okay?"

As we near the doors, I take a breath then give them a quick recap of what Low told me. By the time I'm done, we're by the bathrooms, Zay looks livid, and Jax even appears to be annoyed. And me? I feel sick.

I had convinced myself that having her drive to school with Low was so I could talk to the guys about the phone numbers. Really, I was being selfish. But I should've put those feelings aside. I should've known better than to let her go to school without our protection.

I failed her.

"You don't need to look at me like that," I mumble, yanking my fingers through my hair. "I already feel bad enough."

"You should," Jax mutters, glaring at me before moving to head into the women's restroom.

I grab the sleeve of his black shirt, stopping him. "Let me go talk to her first," I say, lowering my hand from his arm. "I'm the one that screwed this up."

The tick in his jaw lets me know that's the last thing he wants to do, but when I give him a pleading look, he complies.

Sucking in a breath, I head inside, rounding the corner and stepping into the stall area.

Low is standing near the sinks and relief washes over her face when she spots me. "I'm so glad you're here."

"Where is she?" I ask.

Low points to the last stall. "In there."

Nodding nervously, I make my way over to the stall. I lift my hand to knock on it then pause and glance at Low. "Can you give us a second, please?" I want to apologize without an audience.

Curiosity flashes across her face, but she collects her bag. "Sure. I should get to class, anyway. Stepmother Dearest has been trying to play the mom role lately, for some reason, and has been on my ass about my tardiness." She waves at me then exits the bathroom.

The mention of our stepmom makes my scars twitch, but I shove that sensation aside and focus on Raven.

"Pretty Raven," I say, "you doing okay in there?"

I hear her quietly sigh. "I'm fine."

I press my lips together, pausing for a beat. "Baby, you can be honest with me. I know ... I know this has to be hard for you." I lower my head against the stall door as guilt pushes down on my shoulders. "I'm so sorry. I know that doesn't make this better, but I need to say it."

She doesn't respond right away, and I worry that she's not going to forgive me. Then I hear the soft *click* of the door being unlatched and lift my head as the door opens.

Raven is standing on the other side. She's wearing a pair of black jeans, a grey shirt, and her leather jackets and boots. Her wild hair is swept to the side and, fuck, if it's possible, I swear she's even more gorgeous than she was when we parted ways this morning. My fingers crave to photograph her, but at the rate I'm screwing up, she will never let me.

"Hey," she says with a sort of miserable look on her face, but at least she's talking to me.

"Hey." I offer her a small smile, hoping it'll help her feel more at ease. "Are you okay?"

She nods but folds her arms across her chest, as if trying to curl within herself.

"I know that's not true—there's no way it can be." I eye her over, how red her eyes are. "You've been crying?" God, my heart hurts.

She shakes her head, meeting my gaze. "No ... I'm stoned as hell, which is probably a good thing, or else I might be crying." She winces at the words. "Please forget I just said that."

"No way. I'm glad you told me the truth." This morning, I kept my distance because I had been a selfish asshole and was thinking about my own feelings. Well, and Jax's. But not once had I thought about hers. And after what happened yesterday, she deserves better. I'm going to try to give it to her now, if she'll let me.

I step toward her. Then, breathing in quietly, mostly to steady myself, I reach out, place a hand against her cheek, and carry her gaze. "I want to say that I'm sorry."

A crinkle forms at her brow. "For what?"

"For bailing on you this morning." I'm known around school for being a joking, rarely serious sort of guy, but right now, I'm probably acting more serious than I ever have. "I shouldn't have done that. Not with everything going on."

She chews on her bottom lip. "It's okay. None of this is your fault. And you don't need to apologize for not driving me to school."

"Yeah, I sort of do. I also need to apologize for being distant this morning."

Her expression reveals that she picked up on my distant behavior this morning. Not that I'm surprised. Raven seems to be an observant person.

"You don't owe me anything. I swear you don't." She gives a

short pause. "But, why did you act that way? Was I, like, being weird last night or something? I know I got a little bitchy this morning."

I promptly shake my head. "You did nothing. I just have issues. That's all."

She drags her teeth along her bottom lip, deliberating. "Is it anything you want to talk about? I mean, I don't really know the rules of being a BFF, but it seems like talking about shit is a thing?" She gives a shrug.

At that moment, she's so goddamn adorable that I almost can't take it.

A smile slips through, causing the crease between her brows to deepen.

"What?" she wonders confusedly.

"It's nothing." But my broadening smile contradicts my words. So, I decide *fuck it* and just be honest with her because that's what she deserves. "It's just that you're so fucking adorable."

She pulls a face. "I am not."

"Oh, you are," I disagree, lowering my hand and dragging my finger across her bottom lip. It's like they're magnetized there, and I can see the problem forming, the draw I feel to her and how I'm not sure if I can navigate around it. I need to, though, for everyone's sake, which is why I decide to be honest so she'll understand. "Is it okay if I'm honest with you right now?"

"Of course," she replies without missing a beat.

I lower my hand from her lips, internally sighing that I'm no longer touching her. But it's for the best, which is why I stuff my hands into my pockets. "I can't kiss you again."

Her expression fleetingly falls, but she quickly puts on a neutral face. "Okay."

"It's not because I don't want to," I continue, trying to read her, but it's complicated as hell when not a drop of emotion is on her face. "I do. Like, really, really badly." Just stop. This isn't helping. "But I can't. There's just ... stuff that makes it complicated if I do."

"I already said it was cool." She scratches her arm, drifting her gaze to the mirror over my shoulder. "I'm so screwed." She changes the subject. "I look high as a kite. And on top of that, that stupid video is going around. And someone painted *murderer* on my locker." She lowers her head and pinches the brim of her nose. "I sometimes fucking hate my life. And I don't even think I'd be saying this in front of you, but I'm stoned and not thinking clearly."

My heart feels heavy in my chest as I fix my finger under her chin and elevate her gaze to me. "The video and the paint aren't going to be a problem. Jax, Zay, and I are going to handle that, I swear. As for being high, I've got eyedrops in my car that'll fix the redness."

"What if I get called on by the teacher?" she wonders. "And, how are you guys even going to handle the video? Sure, the paint is nothing—it can be washed off. Although, now everyone knows I'm a murderer. And the video ... everyone at school saw it."

"No one knows you're a murderer. It's just a word. That's all. And they may have seen the video, but by the end of the day, something more dramatic will take up everyone's minds." I haven't quite come up with a full game plan yet, but I'm going to find out who did this, dig up everything I can on them, and let the whole school know about it.

"How are you going to do that?" she questions with an arch of her brow.

I let a slow smile spread across my face. "Because everyone has secrets, and digging them up just happens to be my specialty."

Chapter 19
Raven

I wanted to be tough about what happened, but I'm struggling. I've been bullied before. Humiliated. But this has reached an entirely new level. And now I'm just supposed to what? Go to class and pretend like nothing happened?

Even when Hunter tells me his plan, I'm still skeptical. Plans take time and will not be erased by the time I walk into first period. Late and high, I might add.

Still, I'm grateful he's at least trying to help me. I've never had that before.

"Thanks." I try to smile, which feels weird, like my lips don't want to stretch.

"You don't need to thank me. This is my fault. And Jax's and Zay's. We brought you into our group, and we should have protected you better." He sweeps a strand of hair out of my face. "The bridge thing never should've happened."

"Actually," I say, "I think Dixie May might have had something to do with that."

His expression drops. "How do you know that?"

I shrug. "She said something to me this morning that kind of implied it. From what she said, I should've known that video being sent to everyone was going to happen. And the paint on my locker ... that reeks of Dixie May. Well, she probably got someone to do it, because she was too worried about getting paint on her clothes ... if it even is paint. It kind of looked like blood." God, what if it is? The thought makes me want to vomit.

"We're going to get that cleaned off." He gives my hand a squeeze.

He keeps touching me, and yet he said he shouldn't have kissed me. It's confusing, but I'm not an expert on friends, especially having a guy for a friend, so maybe this is normal. It doesn't seem like it, though ...

I really need to talk to Low about this.

I really wish I hadn't gotten so stoned.

I heave a sigh unintentionally. "Thanks, Hunter. Not just for trying to take care of this, but for checking in on me."

"You don't need to thank me. It's my fault," he says. When I open my mouth to argue, he places a finger against my lips. "Shh ... No arguing. I'm right about this." When I narrow my eyes, he grins, going back to his joking self. "It's cute when you pretend to be mad at me."

I roll my eyes, but a smile plays on my lips. He smiles, too, as he lowers his finger from my lips.

"I guess I should get to class." I grimace as I start toward the bathroom door. "I'm just dreading walking in late."

He turns, rubbing his lips together, contemplating. "I know this morning you said you were worried about being late because you missed part of the day yesterday, but I'm going to throw this offer out there just in case you want it ... You and I, we can ditch, go get you a new phone, and maybe go driving. That way, you won't have to be here while Jax and Zay fix everything."

Hunter has done a lot of stuff for me. He became my friend. He brought me into his group. He showed me his scars when I was freaking out about him seeing mine. He gave me my first kiss. Spent the night at my house because I was freaking out about a storm. But this? It might be the nicest thing he's ever done for me, because I've had to deal with a lot of bullying all by myself, and I've never had another option other than to just endure it. And, while I'm not a huge fan of missing school again, I'd way rather ditch and deal with those consequences than to have to spend the day getting stared at.

"You wouldn't mind doing that?" I ask, not wanting to seem too eager so he won't feel pressured to do so.

His smile is so damn warm. "Of course I wouldn't mind. I'd way rather spend the day with you than in this hellhole."

"You won't get in trouble for ditching?"

He laughs. "Baby, did you see me in the office the other morning? I never get in trouble for being late or ditching. In fact, I can usually get a pass."

He keeps calling me baby, and while I'll never admit it aloud, it's really starting to grow on me.

"And I may even be able to get you one," he adds enticingly.

What he's saying ... I want it. Part of me is afraid to take it, though, mostly because it never works out when I want something. But the alternative—going to class—isn't any better than taking the risk, so ... "Okay, yeah, let's ditch."

"Yeah?" He seems happy about it ... and kind of nervous. Not sure what the nervousness is about, other than maybe he's worried he'll get caught ditching? That seems a bit odd.

He nods his head toward the door. "Let's go, then. Jax and Zay are waiting outside, so I can fill them in on the plan."

I give him a salute, and a genuine smile graces his lips.

"What's that look for?" I ask as I follow him toward the exit.

He gives a half-shrug. "It's nothing. I just thought your little salute was cute. That and you seem a bit more relaxed than you were before."

I tug at my jacket. "That's probably because we're leaving. Although, I'm kind of worried that maybe I'm taking the coward's way out." I crinkle my nose at that.

We are at the exit when he pauses, extends his hand toward my face, and traces the brim of my nose with his fingertip. "You're not a coward at all. In fact, you might be the bravest person I know." His voice rings with genuineness.

I want to believe him. Desperately. But the truth is ... "I haven't done anything to be brave," I point out, shifting my weight uncomfortably.

"Yeah, you have." He appears so confident in his answer, like he knows something about me that I don't. But that doesn't make any sense, since he's only known me for a few days ...

Unless that's one big fucking lie.

I attempt to convince myself that I'm just being paranoid as we walk out of the bathroom, that Hunter doesn't know me, that these surfacing memories that almost seem as if him, Jax, and

Zay are in it, are just me being crazy. But that's difficult when those memories are the most vivid ones I've had in a long time.

If they keep up, I may have to look into it. Secretly. That might seem weird, but this feeling in my gut tells me I need to.

The moment we're out of the bathroom, my thoughts become distracted by other things. Those things being Zay and Jax, who are hanging out in the hallway just outside. Zay is leaning against a locker, reading something on his phone with the hoodie of his jacket pulled over his head, which seems to be his trademark look, and Jax is sitting on the linoleum floor, staring at his shoes, wisps of his dark hair hanging in his eyes. He looks stressed out, but when he looks up at me, relief cascades over his face.

Jax. Jax. Jax. The guy who saved me from drowning. I haven't seen him since I left his house last night, but seeing him sends a drop of comfort through me as I remember him saving me.

"Hey." He rises to his feet while Zay flits a glance in my direction. Then he steps forward as if to hug me yet hesitates. "Are you okay?"

I nod, even though the answer to that is up for debate. "Yeah, I'm good," I try to reassure him.

He walks toward me with his hands stuffed in his pockets. "Are you sure? If there's anything I can do to make it better, just tell me and it's yours."

"Easy there, Romeo," Hunter says. "We already have a plan."

Jax fiddles with his brow piercing. "So, what is it?"

Hunter gives Zay and Jax a quick recap of what we

discussed in the bathroom. By the time he's finished, tension is rolling through Jax's body.

"We have to retaliate," he mumbles with his arms crossed. "We can't just let whoever is doing this to her get away with it."

"Of course we're going to retaliate." Zay slips his phone into the back pocket of his dark jeans. "We just need to figure out who's doing it. We look like weak fuckers right now." He cracks his knuckles. "Scare tactics are definitely the way to go. And I think I know who to start with."

Jax glances at him. "Who?"

Zay lifts a broad shoulder. "Porter."

"You think that guy from yesterday had something to do with this?" Rage pierces through my veins. "Like with me getting thrown off the bridge?"

"We've speculated that he has." Zay stuffs his hands into his pockets. "But that's about it so far."

My rage swells. That stupid piece of crap that I met yesterday might have been the one to toss me off the bridge?

Hunter must feel the tension radiating off me because he says, "We're going to retaliate. I swear we are. We have to, anyway, because of the game."

Right. The weird game that keeps getting mentioned.

My mind is getting flooded with all sorts of thoughts when a person wanders down the hallway. She's probably a senior, and while I've never seen her before, she's for sure eyeing me. Or it could be in my head. Doubtful. She's probably seen the video.

Still, I'm grateful when Hunter gives her a dirty look that causes her to lower her gaze to the floor and haul ass.

"We should go," Hunter mumbles, glancing at me.

"I can go with her," Jax offers.

"I can take her." Hunter scratches his arm. "You have that test in third period, anyway."

Jax stares at him hard. "So? I can miss a test."

"That's math? You know you're struggling in it." He offers Jax an apologetic look. "I'll take her this morning, and you can see her at lunch."

Zay's gaze strays between the two guys. So do mine. I get the sense that something is happening, something I don't quite understand.

"Whatever." Jax practically glares at Hunter, but his expression softens when he looks at me. "I'll see you at lunch?"

I smile at him, hoping that'll make him feel better. "Yeah."

He returns my smile, but it doesn't quite reach his eyes. Then he walks off down the hallway without so much as a glance back.

Zay arches a brow at Hunter. "Is that gonna be a problem?"

Hunter stiffly shrugs. "I don't know."

"Well, you better handle it or things will end up getting out of control." He aims a firm look at Hunter then eyes me warily before striding down the hallway. "Keep in touch today," he calls from over his shoulder.

Hunter gives him a salute then sighs and shakes his head.

I fiddle with the zipper on my jacket. "Everything okay?"

He nods, an easy smile spreading across his lips. That doesn't mean I believe him. I'm learning Hunter is good at pretending when he needs to.

"Yeah. We should get going before we get busted for not being in class."

I nod in agreement, and then we rush down the hallway. At first, our steps are normal, but then we sort of increase our pace together without discussing it. We continue to do so until we're jogging down the hallway, in a kind of racing.

A laugh slips from my lips as we near the exit doors, and he laughs, too.

"Last one out owes the other a favor," he announces then takes off running.

"Hey! No fair!" I run after him, laughing, something I didn't think I'd do this morning. "I never agreed to that. Plus, you're a freakin' athlete; of course you're going to win."

He's ahead of me and, to show off, he turns around and runs backward. "Come on; I thought you were a daredevil, pretty Raven."

I increase my pace. "Says who?"

He elevates a brow. "So, you're saying you're not?"

I stare at him for a moment before taking off in a mad sprint. He busts up laughing, spins around, and runs out the damn doors about a second sooner than I do.

I grimace as I burst outside into the cool breeze and underneath the cloudy sky. Despite the crappy morning and the crappy weather heading our way, I feel light at the moment, like I can finally breathe through a haze that's been filling my lungs.

Or maybe that's just the weed talking.

Hunter is laughing, his eyes crinkling around the corners. "That was fun, right?"

I narrow my eyes at him playfully. "It was until you made that little wager."

A smug smirk spreads across his face. "A wager that I won."

I cross my arms. "Because you cheated."

His lips part in shock, and then he presses his hand against his chest. "How the hell did I cheat?"

I quirk a brow. "Because you didn't even wait for me to agree to the wager. Plus, you're faster by default."

"Says who?" he challenges, stepping toward me, the breeze blowing through his blond locks. "You have killer long, lean legs. For all I know, you could be some kind of superstar."

I roll my eyes. "Dude, I just smoked, like, half a joint, so even if my legs were killer, which they're not, my lungs are like power-walk champions at best."

He chuckles.

So do I.

Then his laughter fades, and a soft expression consumes his features. "You have a pretty laugh."

"Laughs can be pretty?" I question.

"Absolutely. And yours is definitely the prettiest I've ever heard." He smiles, and I return it. Then his gaze darts over my shoulder, and his expression falters. "Shit, we need to go." He grabs a hold of my arm and yanks me with him as he spins around and rushes across the grass toward the parking lot.

While I hurry with him, I peer over my shoulder, half-expecting to find a hall monitor or something. Nope. It's a group of people exiting the school. They're all wearing red and grey, which is super weird. They look intense, too.

"Who are they?" I whisper to Hunter as we reach the edge of the parking lot.

"That'd be the Melford family," he replies in a low tone with his eyes fixed on his Camaro parked near the back. "If the game has started, the last thing I want is to be around them by ourselves without backup."

"You mean without Zay and Jax?"

"And Zay's brothers. They're older and don't go here, but they'll have our backs in this. And we're going to need it."

By "in this," I'm assuming he means the game. What's really frightening, though, is how worried he seems. Then again, I did get pushed off a bridge yesterday because of this game.

"So, if this game has started again, what's the endpoint?" We reach the car, and he unlocks the passenger door and opens it for me.

He holds up a finger and signals for me to get in. I do, climbing onto the leather seats. He shuts the door then quickly rounds the front of the car, unlocks, and opens the driver's side door. He pauses before he climbs in, though, and I'm guessing he's looking at the group of people who seem to make him uneasy.

When I turn and look out the window, I notice the group are definitely paying attention to us. They're not necessarily walking toward us, but they've taken up residence near a massive, lifted truck with tinted windows. A few of them have lit up and are eyeing Hunter and me.

"Hunter?" I hiss because I have a bad feeling and really just want him to get into the car.

He ducks his head and slides into the seat, shutting the door. His eyes immediately wander to the group as he revs the engine and reaches for the shifter.

"Are you sure everything's okay?" I ask worriedly.

"Yeah ..." He sounds the exact opposite, worry leaking out of his voice.

He rests his hand on the shifter, not driving forward, just letting the engine idle as he stares at the people.

One guy in particular stares back. His hair is as dark as his eyes, and he's tall. I can tell that even from in the car. He has an arrogance about him in the way he watches us while perched on the tailgate, people surrounding him.

I reach for my seat belt. "Who is he?"

Hunter rubs his lips together, staring at the guy for a beat longer before tearing his gaze off him. "That would be my ex-stepbrother."

My seat belt clicks into place. "You have an ex-stepbrother?"

He bobs his head up and down, finally tearing his gaze off the guy and pulling out of the parking lot. "His mother was briefly married to my father, but it was a while ago. Then she had an affair with the Melford boss, and my father divorced her."

"So, your ex-stepbrother is your rival?"

"Yeah ... And he's a sadist. Seriously, the shit he used to say when we were younger ..." He winces then hastily erases the look. "You know what? Let's not focus on this right now. You've already had to deal with enough stress for the day."

He may not realize it, but that's like the nicest thing anyone has ever said to me.

"Thanks, Hunter, for being so nice to me." I may be being a little more honest because I'm stoned, but I don't really care at the moment.

He turns his head and looks at me, scanning my face. "Aw ... Baby, I'm not being that nice."

"To me, you are," I say quietly. "You're like the nicest guy I've ever met."

He sucks on his lip ring. "I think you might be a bit stoned, because I don't think the feisty Raven who threw a pillow at me last night would be admitting these things."

"I know I am, but I'm still telling the truth."

A contemplative look flashes across his face. Then, keeping one hand on the steering wheel, he reaches over with his other hand and tucks a strand of hair out of my face. "I promise that, no matter what, I will always be nice to you," he assures me with sincerity.

"That doesn't seem like a viable promise." Although, I do like the sound of it.

"It is if I say it is."

"You're going to get mad at me at some point. It's inevitable."

"So? Being mad at someone doesn't mean you should be mean to them. You can be upset with someone but still not be an asshole."

I crack the smallest of smiles. "You're wise."

"Ha! Now I know you're stoned." He flicks me a grin, to which I giggle in response. A funny look crosses his face. "You have the most beautiful laugh I've ever heard."

I rub my lips together, trying not to get all squirmy, but I usually get that way whenever someone gives me a compliment.

"Sorry if I'm making you uncomfortable." He lowers his hand from my face and returns it to the steering wheel. "But it is true." He grows silent then as he flips on his blinker to turn into a parking lot of an electronic store.

I study him out of the corner of my eye, the way he focuses

so intently on parking the car, the way wisps of his hair hang into his eyes. He's so gorgeous. He really is. And he's so damn nice. Like, really, really nice. And I think I might be in some real damn trouble. Because I think I might be starting to like Hunter Hathingford as more than a friend. And that's not even stoner Raven talking.

However, he's already told me that he doesn't want to kiss me again. Plus, guys like Hunter don't fall for girls like me.

They just don't.

Chapter 20
Raven

"You're being really quiet," Hunter says.

We're in the electronic store, waiting for the cashier to bring out my new phone. The phone is way nicer than the one I wanted, but Hunter insisted I needed a good one. He wanted to purchase the most expensive one for me, but I protested, so we settled on a medium price range one.

I'll admit, I have been fairly silent, stuck in my own head of how I'm starting to get a crush on Hunter.

This is bad. Really, really bad. I know this. I cannot have a crush

"Sorry." I rest my hands on the display case and peer at the phone cases inside, not necessarily interested in them, but it's better than having to look at Hunter. Not that he's bad to look at. I just feel like if he stares at me for long enough, he'll be able to read what I'm thinking or something, which yeah, realistically, I get that that's probably not possible.

"You don't need to be sorry." He shifts closer to me so he's facing my side. "I just wish you'd tell me what's up."

Yeah, that's not going to happen.

Still, I need to tell him something.

"I think I just smoked too much this morning." I elevate my gaze to him. "Plus, I'm just stressed out about what's going on at school."

"You sure that's it?" He searches my eyes as he waits for a response.

I nod, a big fat fucking lie. Still, it's better than telling the truth. That I like him.

He looks disbelieving, like he can read through my bullshit. He doesn't press, though, his attention straying to the door as someone enters.

The second he spots who it is, so much tension floods his body that I can actually feel it. I turn to see a woman walk in. She looks only a handful of years older than us, at least in her face. The way she's dressed, in what I'm guessing is a designer dress and heels, gives her a more mature look. When she spots Hunter, a grin spreads across her face.

"Well, well, look who's been caught ditching school," she says to Hunter. She doesn't appear to be upset by the fact that he's ditching. No, she seems positively delighted. She saunters over to him, raveling her necklace around her finger. Then her smile falters slightly when she notices me. "Who's this?"

"Who are you?" I throw back at her because I can tell Hunter despises her.

Her lip twitches, clearly annoyed with me. "I'm Hunter's stepmom."

His stepmom? The woman who put those scars on his flesh?

Tension rolls off Hunter. "Leave us alone," he says curtly to her. Then he turns his back to her and stares at the counter.

She stares at him, and I can tell she's calculating something to say. Probably something mean and cruel.

I stare at her for long enough that her gaze shifts to me.

"What are you looking at?" she asks in a cold tone.

"Nothing." I keep staring at her, wanting to say more, to say everything, to let her know I know about his scars, the secrets staining her hands, the dirty things she's probably trying to hide underneath all those flashy designer clothes.

Her lips twitch again. "Hunter, please tell your little friend to stop staring at me."

In a way, she reminds me of my aunt, only maybe a bit more confident.

"His little friend can speak for herself," I tell her then mouth, "*I know what you did to him.*"

Her face turns bright red as she glares at me. She stares at me hard, and I stare right back, daring her to say something. Maybe she would have if the cashier didn't walk out from the back room with my phone.

When I first saw the guy, he looked like a pothead with his bloodshot eyes. He looks even more high than he did when I first saw him, so my bet is he took a little smoke break while my phone was being set up.

"Here you go." He sets the phone down on the counter.

Hunter quickly takes it and hands the guy a credit card. "Can you make it quick, please?"

"Don't you want me to go through the features?" the guy asks in confusion as he takes the card.

"Dude, Del, you know I know more about electronics than you do," Hunter replies as he picks up the phone and the box.

"True." The guy swipes the card through the machine, and I cringe at the price on the display screen.

Hunter doesn't even bat an eye as he punches in his pin.

"Why are you even getting a new phone?" his stepmom suddenly asks. "Better yet, why are you buying a phone for some girl you barely know?"

How does she know we barely know each other? Does she know who I am?

I glance at her, ready to throw down, because she's seriously getting on my nerves, but Hunter beats me to the punch.

"That's none of your fucking business," he says as he stuffs his credit card back into his wallet. Then he pockets the wallet and turns to me. "You ready to go?"

I nod. "Yep."

He nods, too, then moves for the door until his stepmom actually sidesteps right in front of him.

"Are you going to say goodbye?" she asks, again looking as if she's getting off on his discomfort.

"Fuck off," he mutters, swinging around her and practically jogging to the door.

"Fucking abusive piece of shit," I tell his stepmother in a sweet tone, which seems to throw her off, like her brain can't quite process the cruel words mixed with the sugary tone.

While her brain is short-circuiting, I hurry around her and rush out the entrance door after Hunter.

He's powerwalking toward his car parked in the back of the parking lot, and I jog until I catch up with him. I want to ask him so many things, like what she did to him, but as someone who has her own scars to bear, I know that words sometimes make things worse unless they're said perfectly. And I don't know perfection, so I don't trust myself to speak. I want to help him, though, help him work through that wave of pain and anxiety I know he's feeling right now. So, I do the only thing I can think of.

I reach over and take his hand, offering him a silent word of comfort, a quiet declaration that I know ... I *know* that fucking pain clawing at his mind and soul right now.

His fingers briefly stiffen in mine and, for a faltering moment, I think maybe I didn't offer what he needed. Then he latches on for dear life, slowing down and taking more calmer steps and more even breaths, even when it starts to rain.

Through the droplets weeping from the sky, we finish the rest of the walk to the car. He holds my door open, and I climb in. Then he rounds the car and gets into the driver's seat. Neither of us utters a word as he starts up the engine, but he doesn't drive forward. He just stares at the raindrops splattering against the window while I watch him, waiting for ... something. I'm not even sure what.

Then he finally looks at me. "You want to go with me somewhere?"

Maybe I should ask questions, like where are we going. Maybe I should say no. Instead, I say, "Yes."

He looks so relieved that I don't regret my decision ... at that moment, anyway.

But that's the thing about moments. When they exist in the present, you can't see much of the future in them, the catalysts they can become when they're no longer happening, when they've become a fading memory that gets wiped away by the disaster they've created.

Chapter 21
Raven

Hunter drives for a while. I'm not sure where he's heading, and I'm too afraid to ask. Not because I'm afraid of where we're going or him. I'm just afraid to shatter the silence between us. Again, it's like I have to find the right words, but I don't trust myself to dig them out of my mind.

Finally, the silence becomes maddening.

"Are you okay?" I ask.

He gives a dismissive nod as he continues to grip the steering wheel. "I always am." He flashes me a smile.

It reminds me of this string of fake pearls I had when I was a kid. They looked close to being the real thing, but eventually, the pearls got chipped and worn out, the surface quickly scratching off. And then they broke and made a mess all over the floor.

What should I do here? Call him out on it? Just let the pearls scatter and leave them there?

"It's okay if you're not," I try to offer some sort of comfort but realize I'm probably doing a pretty shitty job. "I ... I remember the scars you showed me and how you said your stepmom did that to you ... And I know ..." I place my hand against my scarred side. "Well, I know what it's like to see the person that caused that pain."

He grips the wheel tighter, not saying anything at first, and I start thinking of something else to say, maybe an apology since it doesn't seem like I'm saying anything right.

Then he looks at me, hesitancy written all over his face. But beneath the hesitancy, I detect a hint of fear.

"I hate her," he admits. "And I hate how small this damn town is so I have to see her everywhere. I hate that my father is married to her. I hate my father. I just ..." He quietly sighs. "I hate everything about her."

"That's understandable." I lean back in the seat and rotate my body toward him. "How long has your father been married to her? Because she looks really young." When he tenses, I add, "You know what? Forget I asked. You don't need to talk about her."

He rubs his lips together. "No, it's okay ... He's been married to her for seven years. She moved in with us when I was eleven. She looks young because she is young, but she's probably older than you think. She's basically addicted to Botox."

"My aunt is, too," I say, fiddling with the zipper on my jacket.

So, he's known her since he was eleven, which means she probably started abusing him when he was eleven. I was pretty young when my uncle started abusing me. It was confusing in the beginning. Still is, if I'm being honest with myself.

"I'm sorry," I find myself saying, "that you had to go through whatever you went through."

He glances at me again. "You don't need to be sorry. It's not your fault."

"I know, but sometimes it feels nice to have someone say that. At least, it is for me." I tuck a strand of hair behind my ear. "Like maybe someone actually understands it, or is at least aware that it's happening, so it's not like this secret between you and your abuser."

He wets his lip with his tongue, contemplating something. "Am I the only one who knows about your scars?" When I nod, he adds, "So, you've only had that feeling for like a day?"

"Pretty much."

"That's sad, baby."

"It's sad for you, too."

"I know." He carries my gaze for a bit longer before returning his attention to the road.

He grows quiet again as he steers toward a more rundown part of the town, a part that I haven't explored yet, filled with older homes, railroad tracks, and closed-down stores.

As I'm observing the area, wondering where we're going and also questioning what his silence is about, I feel fingers brush mine. I slightly startle, drifting my gaze to my hand. Or, more specifically, Hunter's hand over mine. He threads his fingers through mine, and it's kind of awkward the way our hands are positioned, so I turn mine over so they're palm to palm and rethread our fingers.

He doesn't look at me, but I detect a slight smile grace his lips.

I smash my lips together, my heart slamming against my chest. I don't know if it's because I'm stoned or because I'm just being ridiculously emotional, but it's a struggle to keep a smile from touching my lips. In the back of my mind, doubt is also plaguing me. It's based on years of being bullied and a darkness that's stemmed from it, one that feeds on my insecurities.

Maybe this is all a trick.

Maybe this is all in my head.

Maybe I'm still back in that padded room, doped up and delusional.

"Where are we going?" I decide to ask in an attempt to distract myself.

"There's this place I like to go to sometimes to hang," he tells me as he slows down to make a turn. "It's pretty chill, and we can either just hang or get high." He glances at me. "Whatever you feel like doing."

"What do you feel like doing?" I ask since he's the one who really looks like he could use the break.

He gives a half-shrug as he makes a turn down a side road that leads toward the foothills. "I'm not sure yet ... Maybe we can get high or something."

"I'm already still kind of high," I remind him as I sit back in the seat.

He casts a glance at me. "You don't want to get high with me?" His playful side returns as he juts out his lip.

Well, when he puts it that way ...

And looks at me that way ...

"Okay, we can get high."

"Yeah?"

"Yeah."

His smile remains as he focuses on the road, steering around a corner. The sides of the road are mainly fields and trees kissed with the taste of fall. A few houses are scattered here and there, and we end up pulling up to one of them. The driveway is narrow and bumpy, and his car doesn't do well getting up there. Eventually, though, we're pulling up to a two-story ... Well, I'm not really sure what to call the structure. An old barn? A really old house?

"What is this place?" I wonder as I unbuckle my seat belt.

"This is what the local cool kids call The Cabin," he tells me as he silences the engine. Then he flashes me a grin. "Which means we're officially cool."

I snort a laugh, but I don't know ... I'm getting a weird vibe from this place.

"Are you okay?" he asks as he slips the keys out of the ignition.

I nod. "Yeah, I'm good. This place is just giving me a *Cabin in the Woods* vibe."

"I get that." He pauses, assessing me. "We don't have to go in if you don't want to."

"No, it's fine," I assure him. "I'm just being weird."

"You sure?" he double-checks

"Yep." Then I open the door and climb out to prove that I mean what I say.

The second I climb out, thudding music hits my ears. It sounds like a party is going on inside and apprehension clips at the surface of my mind. I've been to a total of one party in my lifetime, and it turned out I was only invited as a prank, orchestrated by Dixie May.

Hunter follows suit, climbing out and meeting me at the front of his car. He glances from the house to me. "You sure you're okay with this?" he asks for like the umpteenth time, but I appreciate him checking and making sure I'm okay.

"I swear I am." Then I draw an X across my heart. "Cross my heart and hope to die, which FYI, that's such a weird saying."

"Yeah, it is." He studies me with this strange look on his face, like he can't quite figure me out.

Story of my life.

"Come on; let's go have some fun," he says, looking away from me as he hikes up the gravel path that leads to the building.

I trail after him, but that only goes on briefly. About a handful of steps in, he stops and waits for me to catch up. Then, when he starts forward again, he reaches over and takes my hand. He doesn't look at me or anything, just holds on my hand as we continue the walk to the building, and that gives me a drop of comfort in the panic soaring through me. I keep having to remind myself that Hunter brought me here, and he wouldn't set me up for a prank ... right?

I wish I could be one hundred percent sure. Wish I could fully trust someone. But that's the thing about trust—when you spend your entire life around people who abuse trust, the word itself becomes nonexistent.

By the time we reach the door to "The Cabin," my heart's a fucking mess of nerves.

Hunter wraps his fingers around the metal handle then looks

at me. "If you ever feel like leaving, just say the word and we'll go, okay?" He waits for me to nod before pushing the door open.

I imagine it creaks, because it looks like the kind of door that would, but the music is so loud inside that I can't hear anything else. I can't even hear the sound of my hammering heart.

Hunter gives my hand a squeeze before guiding me into the building, the worn wooden floorboards wobbly beneath my feet. The beamed ceiling is high, and the cloudy sky peeks in through the cracks in the wood. If it rains, it'll definitely drip in here.

I lower my gaze to the space in front of me. It's not entirely open, a few half-walls here and there. I can't see anyone around, but the area we're in is small. And I can hear laughter mixing in with the music, so someone has to be here.

Hunter pulls me in the direction that the voices are coming from. Eventually, we reach one of the half-walls, and he steers me around it, revealing an open room with a few tattered sofas and a table. About ten people are hanging out; some looking around our age, but others look older. It makes me wonder why older people are hanging out here. Just what are they doing that they can't do it in their own homes? I mean, some of them are drinking and a few are passing around a joint, but again, I don't see what the big deal is that they would need to hide. I mean, I smoked out back of the school. Something else has to be going on.

None of them notice us at first, probably because they're all too busy chatting, smoking, and drinking. Well, that and the music is loud as hell. But as we near one of the sofas, a girl spots us. She has purple hair that goes to her chin, a diamond stud ornaments her nose, and she's wearing torn jeans, an oversized T-shirt, and sneakers.

"Hey, Hunter's here!" she shouts drunkenly over the music.

And just like that, everyone looks up at us.

It takes all of my strength not to duck behind Hunter, but I loathe—let me stress *loathe*—being stared at. I also don't want to draw attention to myself by ducking behind him, so I stay put, even when eyes start to skim over me, noticing me.

I hate being noticed.

As if sensing an impending internal freakout, Hunter tightens his grip on my hand. I latch on, praying to all the demons—because I sure as hell don't think if a God exists that I'm going there—that I can keep my shit together.

Do not crumble, Ravenlee.

Do not look like the words that mark your flesh.

Do not become them.

Do not become what he thinks you are.

"Hey, man." A guy with a beanie stands up and greets Hunter with a chin nod. "What's up? We haven't seen you in a while."

"Yeah, I've been busy," Hunter replies evasively. "But I need a break from the business today and thought we could come hang here for a bit."

"Sure, yeah." The guy gives a quick glance at me then looks at Hunter with his brows raised. "But, *we*?"

"Oh, yeah, right. This is Raven," he introduces me by sort of lifting our interlocked hands, a move that results in us getting a few funny looks and the girl who shouted that Hunter was here gives me a dirty look.

Great? Is this another Katie conversation?

"Hey, Raven," the guy greets me with a smile that I don't trust. No offense to him. I don't trust anyone really.

"Hey." I offer him the best smile I can muster, but I'm sure I look like a freak.

His gaze quickly moves up and down me, and I try not to squirm, but for reals, what is he looking at? And then, to make things even weird, Hunter tugs me closer to him.

The guy looks intrigued, but all he says is, "Are you hanging out here? Or do you want to hang in the back?"

"Um ..." Hunter hesitates, looking at me like I have the answer. "The back?"

I shrug, because I have no clue what that means.

The guy must because he gets this little shit-eating smile on his face.

Hunter ignores him and moves past the sofas, heading toward a doorway that leads to what I'm guessing is "the back."

"Wait. You need anything?" the guy calls out after Hunter.

Hunter looks at me. "You still have your joint?" he asks, and I nod. "You mind sharing? Or is my BFF stingy and I need to get my own?" He cracks a smile.

I can't help giggling just a bit. "I guess I can share with my bestie."

That makes his smile broaden. "Nah, we're good, Ellis!" he calls back to the guy.

Hunter winces when one of the girls yells, "Hunter, can we talk for a minute?"

I turn to see who it is, but he just pulls me forward, ignoring her and hurrying through the doorway with me in tow.

On the other side is a curtained area. He heads toward that.

Okay, so I get a bit creeped out by it, especially when he pulls the curtain back and reveals what's on the other side—an air mattress on the floor.

"Um ..." *What the hell?* I mean, it's weird enough that there's an air mattress, but I'm not about to sit on it because who the hell knows what's on it?

"Don't worry; we'll just sit on the floor," he informs me, letting go of my hand to shuck off his jacket. Then he spreads it on the floor, sits down, and looks up at me with his brow arched. "You're not afraid of me, are you, pretty Raven?" A playful dare glints in his eyes.

"You know I'm not," I reply easily then sink down onto the floor beside him.

He smiles and shakes his head before twisting to face me, sitting cross-legged. I do the same, facing him. Then I reach into my pocket and take out the joint, along with a lighter.

"So, you and my sister were smoking this earlier, I'm guessing?" he says as I light up.

I take a hit and exhale before handing him the joint. "Yeah ... Does it bother you that she's smoking with me?"

"I'm not a fan of it, but I know she parties. And, while I've tried to talk her out of it, I can't force her not to." He lifts the joint toward his lips. "I will say, however, that I like her hanging out with you."

"Seriously?" I question. "With everything you know about me?"

He bobs his head up and down as he holds the smoke in before letting it out, a cloud of smoke circling his face. "You're not as bad as you think you are. In fact, I kind of like you." He offers me a teasing smile.

"I kind of like you, too," I admit, but probably only because I'm stoned.

He juts out his bottom lip, pouting. "Just *kind of*, huh?"

"Hey, you said the same thing first."

"True." He hands the joint back to me. "That was definitely the wrong word choice on my part." I take the joint as he continues with a smile, "I like you a fucking ton, Ravenlee Willowwynter."

Hearing him say my full name makes my heart do weird things.

"I like you a fucking ton, too, Hunter Hathingford."

His lips curve into a smile. "Yeah?"

I bob my head up and down. "Yeah." Then I take another hit, letting the smoke fog the truth of this moment a little bit more for me. "You know, Low's the first person I ever got high with. I mean, I've gotten high a ton of times, but always by myself."

"Really?" He appears only mildly surprised, probably because I've told him so much about my past.

I nod and pass the joint to him. "Yep. But it's okay. Sometimes I think I do better by myself."

He slowly raises the joint to his lips. "You're doing fine right now, baby."

"Maybe. But sometimes I feel like I'm out of step, like I have no clue what I'm doing."

"That'll fade the more time we spend together."

"You think so?"

"Yeah, experiences will change that for sure," he adds. Then he gives a short pause, considering something. "You want to experience something right now?"

"What?"

"I'd rather just show you," he says with an amused smile. "But I only will if you say it's okay."

"I don't even know what you're going to do, though," I point out.

"I know. I guess it all depends on how much you trust me."

I consider what he said, but not for long.

"Okay, Hunter Hathingford, give me an experience," I say with a smile. I'm nervous, though. And that nervousness grows as he slowly takes a hit from my joint while staring at me. He remains that way for a beat before leaning in.

Wait ... Is he going to kiss me?

The idea isn't too out there, since he's kissed me before. Then again, he did stress that he shouldn't have, so why is he—

His lips touch mine, but he doesn't kiss me. No, he exhales the smoke. It clicks a second too late of what he's trying to do, and instead of my inhaling the smoke, it just laces the air and makes me cough in his face.

Hunter slants back, his brows knit, and confused amusement glitters in his eyes. "You okay?"

"Yeah, I'm such a spazz," I mutter through a cough. "Sorry ... I didn't know what you were doing."

The confusion on his face dissolves and only amusement remains. "It's okay. It was kind of cute."

I arch a brow. "Me coughing in your face was cute?"

He gives a half-shrug, but his smile is all sorts of wicked amusement. "You want to try it again?"

Do I?

Yeah, I kind of do.

I nod, tucking a strand of hair behind my ear. "Yeah, let's do it again."

His lips quirk into a genuine smile, and then he lifts the joint to his lips, inhales, and leans in again. This time, I'm ready, and when he blows the smoke into my mouth, I suck it in. It burns down my throat, but it's a good kind of burn, the kind of burn that singes out anything else inside me. And leaves me *numb*.

Just the way I like it.

Chapter 22
Raven

"Do you ever get the feeling we're being watched?" I ask Hunter as I lay down on the air mattress, staring up at the ceiling of the cabin.

He's lying beside me, doing the same thing, our heads only inches apart. We've been this way for a while. For ... well, I'm not sure how much time has passed. My new phone has been buzzing beside me every so often, but I ignore it.

"Maybe ..." Hunter sounds high as hell. And he keeps playing with my fingers, tracing the folds with his fingertips. It's nice. Really, really nice. I didn't know things could be this nice.

I let out a quiet, sort of content sigh, a noise I've never really heard come out of my mouth before.

"What?" Hunter asks.

"What? What?" I reply confusedly.

He chuckles, turning his head, and our gazes collide. "I was just wondering what the sigh was for."

I shrug, an awkward move due to the fact that I'm lying down. "I'm just content; that's all."

"Really?" he asks, sounding a bit surprised.

I give a lazy nod. "Yeah ... It's a new feeling for me."

"Me, too," he agrees softly. "I mean, feeling content, because I am."

I smile, but he doesn't. No, he just looks at me for a moment then rolls over and props up onto his elbow.

"You're beautiful," he tells me as he sketches a path along my hairline with his fingertip.

I resist an eye roll. "You're always saying that."

"Because it's true."

I start to protest, but he silences me by putting a finger to my lips.

"No arguing. I may be wrong about a lot of things, but not this." He lowers his finger from my mouth and smiles.

I try to smile back, but my heart is beating way too swiftly in my chest.

Beautiful.

Beautiful.

Beautiful.

How can he say such a nice word to me?

It's too foreign.

Too much.

He traces my lips with the pad of his finger and starts to lean in. Maybe to kiss me, which is confusing since he keeps saying he shouldn't kiss me. And maybe I should stop him because of that. Maybe I would've. I never do find out, though, because his phone rings, distracting us.

Letting out a quiet sigh, he sits up and answers his phone. I sit up, too, raking my fingers through my hair, my heart still a mess in my chest. I'm flustered, and my emotions are all over the place. I need a distraction.

Remembering how many times my phone has vibrated, I decide to see who's been trying to get a hold of me. When I open the messages, I kind of wish I hadn't.

Unknown: You think you have friends now? A little boyfriend even? Well, you're wrong, Ravenlee. This guy, these people you think like you, are all liars. I know you can't remember things, so let me let you in on a little secret. The guy sitting beside you, the guy you think saved you the other day—they're lying to you. They know you, and they remember that. They're just lying to you.

My head snaps up, and I peer around, trying to figure out how in the hell this person knows I'm sitting by Hunter. I mean, they could've just guessed. Or it could be one of the people in the other room.

Or someone could be lurking in the shadows.

"Raven, are you okay?" Hunter's voice draws my attention to him.

He's off the phone and is looking at me with worry in his blue eyes. His blond hair is a mess, sticking up all over the place, and yet, somehow, he looks even more beautiful.

A beautiful little liar.

"Yeah, I'm fine," I lie. Until I know for sure if he knows me and is lying to me about it, I need to be careful. And I need to figure out what's going on. Maybe the sender is the one lying, but I can't stop thinking about those potential memories I have with the guys in them. *Maybe the sender is telling the truth.* "I was just thinking that maybe, if I can, I should try to get back to school."

"I'll have to sober up first," he tells me with a frown. "I can drive you in a bit."

"Okay. Thanks."

He searches my eyes with a pucker at his brow. "Are you sure you're okay?"

"Yep." I smile back.

It's plastic.

It's a lie.

But it's what I need to do until I find out the truth. And I will no matter what it takes.

Chapter 23
Raven

Sometimes, I wonder if lies will always be what my life is. At least, that's what it feels like most days. What sucks is that right as I believe things might change, shit like this happens.

Before I received the text, Hunter had been someone I could trust.

Now, he feels like another lie taunting me.

What makes it worse is that I'm stuck in this barn with him, and he's so stoned he can barely keep his eyes open. Me? I'm starting to come out of my self-induced haze, but that doesn't make it easier to get away from this place since I don't know how to drive.

I sigh heavily as I stare at the rotting wood of the barn's roof, wondering if my life will always be such a shit show. I want stability, but that seems completely implausible.

"Fuck." I drag my fingers through my hair as frustration builds through me.

Hunter mutters something in response, but it's totally undecipherable. I roll over to my side and gently shake him.

"Hunter," I say. "We need to get home."

He drapes his arm over his forehead. "The keys are in my pocket."

"Okay... But I don't know how to drive," I remind him, resisting another sigh.

"Give me... like... five... minutes or something," he murmurs, opening his bloodshot eyes.

More annoyance bites inside me. Honestly, I might not have been as irritated if I hadn't received that message.

I dig my phone out of my pocket and reread it. It could be a lie. I have no clue who's messaging me. And perhaps it is.

But I can't stop thinking about the possibility that it could be true. After all, whoever is sending me the messages has known accurate details about me.

What if it is true?

What if the guys do know things about me—

Ring.

I startle, nearly dropping my phone. When I glance at the screen, it doesn't show I have an incoming call.

Ring.

Okay, so it's Hunter's phone that's ringing.

"Hunter." I give him a gentle nudge. His phone rings again. "Hunter, your phone's ringing."

He manages to dig it out from his pocket, but then he hands it to me. "Answer it, please." He prattles off his passcode, something I wonder if he'd do if he weren't completely out of it.

Great. What if it's like his dad or something?

Still, I take the phone from him, and relief washes over me when I see *Jax* flash across the screen.

"Hello?" I answer.

A short pause, and then. "Raven?"

"Yeah, it's me." My gaze falls on Hunter. "Hunter told me to answer his phone." I chew on my thumbnail. "He's pretty stoned and basically passed out."

"Shit, really?" he asks but doesn't wait for me to respond. "Where are you?"

"At this old barn in the middle of nowhere." My gaze travels to the doorway as the people in the other room bust up laughing. I only saw them when we entered the barn, and Hunter briefly introduced us, but I got an unsettling feeling from them, but that might be due to my social anxiety. "There's some people in the other room... Should I ask them for a ride?"

"No," he responds quickly. "I know what barn you're talking about. I'll be there as soon as I can, okay? Don't go anywhere. Just stay by Hunter. And try to wake his ass up."

"Okay," I reply warily because seriously, how in the hell am I supposed to wake him up?

"And call me if you need anything," Jax adds. "You have your phone on you, right?"

"Yeah..." My thoughts travel back to the text message on my phone, and if what it says carries any truth, then that means Jax is lying to me too. The only one I'm not surprised about is Zay, but he's been an asshole to me from the moment we met.

"Raven, are you still there?" Jax asks, drawing me from my thoughts.

"Yep, I'm still here. Sorry, I was double-checking that my

phone was on," I lie. As the laughter grows louder, I add, "How far away are you?"

"Like twenty minutes. I'm actually getting in my car now. I'll drive fast."

"Don't drive recklessly. I can take care of myself for a while."

He falls silent for a beat, his truck engine roaring to life in the background. "I know you can, but considering what happened on the bridge...." Another pause and I swear I can feel him shiver through the phone. Or maybe that's just me. "I'll drive carefully, but quickly. See you soon. And call me if you need anything."

After I tell him I will, we say goodbye and hang up. Hunter has rolled onto his side and his head is resting on his hands. The dude practically smoked himself into a coma. I smoked a lot, too, but not as much as him.

But how much did he smoke—

His phone buzzes with an incoming message and I nearly piss myself. I move to set his phone beside him, but pause as a message banner flashes across the screen.

It's from someone on the basketball team, but that's not what has piqued my interest. I realize I have access to his phone. I could snoop and see if there are any clues as to if the unknown sender is telling me the truth. It feels weird, though, to do it.

But I want answers because what if they're lying?

However, what if I end up snooping only to find out that they're not? And then Hunter finds out I snooped?

I'll have no friends again.

Loser Raven, the girl no one wants.

"Goddammit," I grit through my teeth then set the phone down.

If I want answers, I'll have to approach this another way because I'm not about to risk ruining my only potential friendship I've had since I was a kid.

For the next ten minutes, I sit in the room, hugging my legs to my chest. My gaze remains fixed on the doorway as laughter filters through the air. I'm unsure why it makes me so nervous, but it does.

It's just laughter, I keep telling myself.

But I don't like not knowing what's going on in there. And what if someone comes in here? Then what the hell do I do? Talk to them? Ha, I suck at that normally, and am worse when I'm high.

Why would anyone come in here, though?

As if answering my thoughts, a guy steps through the doorway.

I can't tell if I met him when we entered the barn, since that meeting was brief, and I was nervous. He looks a bit older than me, has short brown hair, is tall, and lean. He's sporting a gray T-shirt and jeans with a tiny knee hole.

"Hey." He smiles at me as he rests his arm on the doorjamb. "You're Raven, right?"

I stare at him suspiciously and avoid his question. "Who are you?"

His lips kick up into a smirk. "I'm a friend of Hunter's." He nods his head in Hunter's direction. "My name's Jamison. He didn't mention me?"

I feel like he's toying with me, so I attempt to return the attitude.

"Oh yeah, he actually did," I lie, stretching out my legs. "Sorry, I didn't know what you looked like."

He looks me over then lowers his hand and steps further into the room, the floorboards creaking underneath his weight. "Since your boy's asleep, you should come party with us."

"No thanks," I reply.

Inside I'm a wreck. Something doesn't feel right. But maybe the paranoia stems from old memories, like when I was at a party and got locked in the closet. Or it could be the way he's smiling at me, all cocky and sure of himself with a trace of a taunting smile.

"You sure?" He moves closer to me. "We've got some E. You ever done that before, baby?"

Is this guy shitting me?

"No. And I don't plan on doing it, at least not with some rando I just met in a barn in the middle of fucking nowhere." I rise to my feet, resisting the need to stumble as the room spins ever so slightly. "And don't call me baby. You don't know me. And if you did, you wouldn't have called me that."

He drags his teeth along his bottom lip. "You and I are going to have some fun." He reaches for me, but I dodge away from his hand and slam my palms against his chest, shoving him back.

He stumbles, but laughs. "Fight all you want, but Hunter isn't waking up anytime soon, and we both know that if I fight back, I'll win." He smirks as he notes my confusion over his comment about Hunter not waking up. "He took a shot of what he thought was vodka just a bit ago. And it was vodka but with a side of rufi."

My attention snaps back to Hunter. No wonder he'd been so out of it. He was drugged.

Jamison laughs, and I swallow hard before turning back to him.

"Who are you?" I ask, thinking about the people who threw me off the bridge and how I have no clue who they were, which means this guy could be one of them.

Deciding I need to do something, I swipe my finger across my phone's screen, preparing to message Jax.

"I already told you my name, baby." He reduces the space between us with another step and then snatches my phone from my hand.

My breathing rushes out of me in waves. "I already told you to stop calling me baby." I lift my leg to kick him in the balls.

He jumps out of my way, then rushes toward me. I dodge to the side and try to swing back around to grab Hunter's phone from off the floor. But Jamison sidesteps in front of me. Growling in frustration, I reel around and hurry toward the doorway but pause, casting a glance at Hunter.

I can't leave him here. But as Jamison strides toward me, I realize all I can do is either stay here and fight—because clearly he's not giving up—or run and try to get some help. Sure, I'm all about holding my own in a fight, but this guy has me by at least sixty to seventy pounds and a handful of inches in height.

Why the hell have I not started carrying pepper spray with me at all times?

Making a mental note of that, I turn to face Jamison with my hands balled into fists. I may not be able to win this fight, but I can at least try to distract him until Jaxon arrives.

He stops short of me, his gaze falling to my fist, and then he busts up laughing. "You're seriously going to try to fight me?"

"Maybe. And maybe I'll lose." I tighten my fist. " But I have one thing that gives me a bit of an upper hand."

His gaze scrolls over me, and then he crosses his arms, amusement still prominent in his eyes. "Oh yeah, and what's that?"

"You underestimating me." With that, I crane my fist back and slam it into his jaw.

"Ah!" we cry out, him clutching his while I move my throbbing hand back.

The laughter from the other room dwindles, but I have a feeling the people in there aren't coming to my rescue.

"Bro, you okay in there?" a guy calls out. "Or do you need some help?"

Another guy from that room snickers, "Leave him alone. You know how loud he can get when he's fucking."

Jamison, who is currently hunched over and cradling his jaw, lifts his head and grits out, "No, I need help taking the bitch down." His gaze locks on me, and he charges.

My muscles stiffen, but I move to kick him. He slams his hand against my leg with so much force I fall to the floor. My palms scrape against the wood, and I'm pretty positive I have slivers lodged in my flesh, but I get up and spin around with my fist raised. But fear whips through me at the sight of another guy standing beside Jamison. This one is about twice my size, with shoulder-length brown hair and a scar running down his left cheek.

Jamison wipes sweat from his brow and says to his friend, "Hold her down so I can play with her."

"Screw you," I spat, the whirl around and run toward another doorway, hoping it leads to an exit.

I hate leaving Hunter, but taking on both of those guys will result in me getting knocked out, and who knows what after that. Plus, more people are in the other room, and what if they come in? Then I'll lose my chance of helping Hunter. No, what I need is to get to Jax so he can call for help.

I haul ass toward where I hope is the door we entered the barn in. Then I swing around beams and half walls, nearly tripping when I step onto a small clump of hay. I manage not to eat dirt and continue running until I make it out of the door and into the cool night air.

Footsteps are charging after me as I sprint out onto the dirt road stretching across the field between the main road and the barn.

"You don't even know, do you?" Jamison shouts, his voice echoing across the night. "You think you can trust them, but you can't!"

My stomach churns at how similar his words are to the unknown sender, but that doesn't mean I'm about to stop running.

"Like I can trust you!" I throw over my shoulder.

It's dark as hell, and I keep tripping and stumbling over rocks in the road. I can't even measure the distance left to the main road. And what in the heck am I even going to do when I get there?

I'm unsure, but stopping isn't an option.

Then, finally, headlights break against the darkness blanketing the land. Thank god, Jax is here.

Wait... What if it isn't Jax?

More panic floods my veins, and I start to slow to a stop. Could this car belong to someone else that wants to hurt me?

"Gotcha." Arms loop around my waist.

I lift my arm to elbow the person in the gut, but they swing me around and start dragging me back down the road. I dig my heels into the dirt and throw my head back, colliding it with their face. They scream a string of curses, their grip loosening. But then grab my shirt before I can make it even a handful of steps.

"Let her go!" A voice cuts through the moment.

I know that voice.

Jaxon.

The person holding me lets out a low chuckle, then jerks me against his body. "Jaxon, how nice of you to join us. "

"Let her go, Jamison," Jaxon warns over the sound of boots scuffing against the dirt.

He's the only one out here now, and I'm not sure why—what the others are doing.

"Or what?" Jamison laughs. "Dude, your boys passed out in the barn, and even if he were awake, you'd be outnumbered. So just let this go. I'll go have my fun with this one, and nothing else will have to happen—"

He's cut off as I slam my elbow straight into my nose. He

yelps in pain, and I take off toward Jaxon, who's a shadow of an outline as the headlights of his truck cast across his back.

Jaxon grabs my arms as I reach him, out of breath, exhausted, but I'm also fueled with rage.

"Are you okay?" he asks me, lowering his head just enough so I can make out the worried lines that crease his face.

I bob my head up and down. "I'm fine." I think... "But Hunter's passed out in the barn. I think someone drugged him."

Jamison releases a laugh. "Fuck yeah, he is, and you're not going anywhere near him."

"Wanna bet." Jax strides past me and straight toward Jamison.

Jamison releases another stupid laugh then raises his fists.

"Jax," I say worriedly as I jog after him.

Jax doesn't miss a beat, ducking as Jamison takes a swing at him. Then he pops right back up and slams his fist into Jamison's face so hard he collapses.

My eyes widen. Holy effing troll babies, I did not think Jax had this sort of side of him. But I'm so glad he does.

Jamison releases a groan as he lays in the dirt, clutching his face, and I'm sure it hurts like a bitch considering I bash my head into the same spot.

Jax crouches down beside Jamison and pats him on his injured cheek. "You fuck with me, Hunter, or Raven again, and I'm going to call my father and have him deal with you, do you understand? I may not be part of his circle, but he's still my father and he'll do anything to make sure his name stays powerful, you got it?"

Jamison doesn't respond, but he makes no effort to get up

either. Jax must take that as an agreement because he straightens and turns to me.

"Hunter's inside?" he asks, and I nod.

He dithers momentarily, then signals for me to follow him as he starts toward the barn.

I hurry to the side of him. "What're we going to do? Just walk in there? Because there's other people inside."

He shakes his head as he veers right, heading around the barn instead of through the doorway. "I may have been able to get Jamison to back down, but I doubt I can convince his lackeys. And if we don't hurry, Jamison will probably get up, get his buddies, and they'll outnumber us."

"Even with you threatening him, he'll still do that?"

"Yeah, he might be scared for a moment, but then he'll soon realize that there's a huge chance I can't make good on my threat." He stops in front of a section of the barn where the wood is gaped enough that the light from inside filters through.

"You can't?" I ask as I watch him grip one of the boards and pry it off fairly easily enough since the wood is rotting.

"Probably not. At least, I'd prefer not to because asking any of our fathers for a favor comes with strings attached." He grabs another board and tugs it off with a soft yank, leaving a gap wide enough for us to climb inside.

"I wish I would've thought to do this when Jamison had me cornered in the room," I grimace at my lack of creativity. "Although, I probably would've still ended up outside, running away from him."

He wipes his hands off on the sides of his pants. "Why didn't you call me when he cornered you?" he asks as he slips through the gap.

"Because like a dumbass, I left it on the floor when I ran out of the room." I duck my head through and then wiggle my body through. "I was holding it when Jamison came up to me, and at first, he was just trying to persuade me to come party with him and his friends. I was a little on edge, though, but I couldn't figure out why. Then he threatened me and I panicked, tried to call you, but he tossed my phone on the floor. So I fought and then ran." As I glance around the spot we're in, I realize we've climbed into the room where Hunter is.

He's still passed out on the mattress, too.

Jax puts his finger up to his lips, and I nod. Then he quietly pads over to Hunter and squats down beside him.

"Hunt," he whispers, lightly patting Hunter's cheek.

When Hunter makes no effort to open his eyes, Jaxon presses two fingers to Hunter's wrist and checks his pulse. That's when worry crashes into me.

"Is he okay?" I whisper as I crouch down beside Jax.

Jax frowns as he pulls his hand away. "I don't think he is. His heartbeat is slow." He looks at me with urgency in his eyes. "We need to get him out of here and take him to the hospital."

My heart slams against my chest. "Maybe we should call the cops."

He shakes his head. "It'll take too long for an ambulance to get out here, but we'll call the cops on our way." He shifts his weight then points to my phone that's on the floor. "Put that in your pocket while I try to pick him up."

I do what he says, rush over, pick up my phone, and stuff it into my pocket. By the time I face the guys again, Jax is carrying Hunter. But Jax's definitely struggling due to how limp Hunter's body is.

But ax manages to move him over to the gap in the barn wall and then starts to slip back through it.

"Make sure he doesn't hit his head," he whispers while maneuvering him through it.

I place my hand on Hunter's head to ensure it doesn't bump against the wall. Once he's safe though, I climb out myself. Then we start through the darkness and back up the road.

"Jamison's gone," I note aloud when I'm fairly certain we've reached the spot where we left him.

"Then we need to hurry because he's probably getting his friends to chase us down, and if they catch us, we're fucked—" He cuts himself off with a grunt as he trips over a rock in the road.

I grab the back of his shirt, steady him, and he breathes in relief. "Thanks, Ravenlee."

"You're welcome," I say as we hurry forward again toward the headlights beaming from the distance.

We're almost there when someone shouts, "There they are! Get them!"

Jax and I run. Jax is struggling, but he keeps going as quickly as he can. The sounds of footsteps fill the air, growing louder and louder. When I cast a glance over my shoulder, I spot figures in the distance running at us. It looks like at least five people, and if they catch us, it'll be so bad.

We need to do something.

I dig my phone out of my pocket, preparing to call the cops, even though they won't arrive in time. But at least they'll be on their way.

We're near Jax's truck at this point, though, and he tells me through his panting, "Can you open the back door of my truck?"

I put a pause on calling the cops and quicken my pace, running ahead to open the door for him. I move aside right as Jax reaches me, and as carefully as he can, he lies Hunter down in the backseat.

"Get in," he tells me as he slams the door shut.

I yank the passenger side door open and hoist myself inside. It takes some effort since Jax's truck is lifted, but I manage. Then I slam the door while Jax hops into the driver's seat.

The second he gets the door shut, he pushes the lock button and stares out the windshield, his chest rising and crashing as he breathes profusely.

I track his gaze, and my own breathing quickens.

Standing in front of the truck, directly in the glow of the headlights are Jamison and four of his friends.

We barely made it and it's terrifying to think what they would've caught us.

"Buckle your seatbelt," Jax tells me as he reaches to put on his own.

I grab mine, draw it over my shoulder, and buckle it in while Jax shoves the shifter into reverse.

Just outside, a tall guy with dark hair suddenly charges forward and tries to jump on the sidestep of the truck, But Jax slams on the gas, and the tires peel as we speed away, leaving everyone in a cloud of dust. He continues driving in reverse until he reaches the end of the dirt road, then he turns the wheel, shifts the truck into drive, then punches the gas as he pulls onto the asphalt road that leads to town.

"Fuck. Fuck. Fuck." Jax slams his hand against the steering wheel several times as we speed down the highway. Then his gaze flicks to me. "Sorry, I'm probably scaring the shit out of you."

"After what happened, you yelling is like a damn lullaby," I inform him, twisting around in the seat to look at Hunter.

It's terrifying how still he's lying, but his chest rises and falls, so he's still breathing.

"Can you check his pulse?" Jax asks.

Nodding, I lean over the console, gently grab his wrist, and press two fingers to his pulse.

The rhythm is slow and unsteady, and my stomach clenches. "Jax, it's really slow."

"Okay, just keep checking on him," he tells me as he shifts gears and speeds up.

I'm unsure how fast he's going—but it feels super fast. I give zero fucks, though, because we need to get to the hospital as quickly as we can. And we need to report Jamison and his friends.

"I'm going to call the police," I tell Jax as I swipe my finger across my phone screen.

"Yeah, you should. Nothing will probably happen to them, but at least the police will have to deal with drama for a bit." Rage bites into his tone, and when I glance at him, he's gripping the wheel tightly. "I'm getting so tired of this shit."

Me too. And I've only had to deal with it for a handful of days.

Still keeping one hand on Hunter, I dial the police to make a report. The operator tells me she'll send officers out to the barn and one to the hospital to speak to me. By the time I end the call, we're entering town. Minutes later, we're pulling up to the entrance of the hospital.

Jax parks near the front doors and hops out. "I need help!" he shouts as he yanks open the back door.

Everything happens so quickly after that. Nurses run out with a stretcher, and Hunter is put on it. Jax and I follow him into the hospital as they wheel him inside. Then we're told to stay back as they haul him through some doors. A doctor stays behind and asks us questions. Then everything stills as we're left in the waiting room.

We stand near the door for a while, completely silent, and I think Jax might be in shock. I'm unsure what to say or do. I've only known the guy for a few days, and while I've felt a connection to him, this is a major issue that I don't know how to handle.

Finally, Jax speaks. "I need to move my truck and call Zay and Low." His voice sounds so broken. "He should be here." He turns to look at me, and his eyes are watery with impending tears. "Can you stay in here in case the doctor comes out?"

I nod. "Of course."

He offers me a look of gratitude. "Thanks, Ravenlee."

He walks off before I can say anything while digging out his phone from his pocket. Once he steps out of the gliding glass doors, I move to the sitting area of the fluorescent-lit room and sink into a chair.

That's when the night's events come crashing down on me.

Hunter almost overdosed. Hunter, sweet Hunter, the guy

who's been nice to me since I moved here, almost overdosed. And I almost got... Well, I'm not positive what Jamison and his friends were planning on doing to me, but I can come up with a few ideas, once that make me feel both sick and furious. This game thing that's going on in this town is total bullshit. I don't want to be a part of it, and yet somehow I've gotten thrown into the middle of it. In fact, I seem to be the center target. Why? Because I'm hanging out with Hunter, Jax, and Zay?

My thoughts drift to the text I received right before shit hit the fan. Whoever sent it had implied that Jax and Hunter know me. How, though?

I keep thinking of these random slivers of forgotten memories... If that's what they are anyway. I honestly have no clue what's going on, including within my own mind. I think I might need some help, but the last time I saw a therapist, I was locked in a room and...

I shudder at the few memories I can recall during my time there, which was awful.

"Has the doctor come out yet?" Jax appears before me and I realize I've zoned out for several minutes.

I shake my head as I glance up at him and sweep strands of my hair out of my eyes. "Not yet."

He sighs, then slumps down into the chair beside me. "This is such a mess," he mumbles as he lowers his head into his hands. "I hate this town. I really do. We'll never be safe while we're living here."

"Are you guys moving when you graduate?" I ask in an attempt to distract him from his worry.

He bobs his head up and down, sits up straighter, and looks

at me. "We haven't decided where we were going yet, but yeah, me, Hunter, and Zay are getting the hell out of this town the moment we're handed our diplomas. The only problem is that Hunter doesn't want to leave Low, which I understand. He's a good big brother—he always has been."

"Yeah, I can tell." I pause. "Low has it lucky, doesn't she? I mean, to have someone always watching out for you like that."

With his lips pressed together, he looks at me and nods. "You know, I could look out for you like that." He pauses then begins to ramble. "Not like as your big brother or anything. I definitely wouldn't want to do that, but I mean, I could be your friend who watches out for you." He rolls his eyes at himself and rakes his fingers through his hair. "Jesus, I'm a babbling mess."

"You're not that bad." I lightly nudge him with my shoulder. "And you want to be my friend, Jaxon, you totally can. And you asking and getting embarrassed about it is kind of cute."

He rolls his tongue in his mouth, resisting a smile. "If you say so, but I don't agree with you." He reclines back in the chair and stretches his arm along the back of my chair, while propping his boot-clad foot onto his knee. Then he changes the subject as he grows serious again. "I'm not sure what to do about this game thing. Between them going after you and now Hunter..." A muscle in his jaw ticks. "I feel like we need to retaliate."

"I get what you're saying, but I think they may not have been going after Hunter," I confess. "I think they drugged him so they could get to me." I swallow hard at the reminder of tonight's event. "I'm not positive what they were going to do to me, but I have a few ideas." Fear clenches my throat.

"Hey." He fixes his finger underneath my chin and angles

my head to meet his gaze. "Nothing is going to happen to you. I promise. Hunter and I, and yes, even Zay, are going to make sure our family drama doesn't consume your life."

"What're you going to do?" I wonder. "To make that happen?"

He exhales slowly as he removes his finger from my chin. Then he faces forward again and bounces his knee up and down. "I'm not sure yet," he mumbles.

But I feel like he might know, and he just doesn't want to tell me. Like maybe they won't be friends with me anymore. And that... That's just as terrifying as being thrown off the bridge again.

I won't break, though, if that happens.

I'm strong.

I've been through a lot of shit.

But I'm starting to get tired of it. For once, I'd like to have a normal life.

Chapter 24
Raven

Jax is worried, but is attempting to conceal. His bouncing knee, though, is a dead giveaway. I'm unsure how to help him, and I'm almost relieved when Low runs into the hospital because it seems to distract Jax.

"How is he?" She asks us in a frenzy.

Her blonde hair is pulled into a ponytail, she's wearing torn jeans and an oversized shirt, and her puffy red eyes make it clear she's been crying.

"We're not sure yet." Jaxon rises to his feet and wraps his arms around her, hugging her. "But it'll be okay. He'll pull through—I know he will."

"How do you know?" she whispers. "You don't know that, Jax. Something could—"

"Shhh...." He cuts her off. "I may not know it for sure, but Hunter is strong and he's survived a lot of shit."

I release a slow breath as the reign over my emotions starts to slip away from me. I feel like a wreck on the inside, my thoughts bouncing back and forth between my worry about Hunter.

While Low and Jax are hugging, I dig my phone out and distract myself by rechecking the message again, like maybe it'll somehow disappear. It doesn't. I consider sending them a reply to see if maybe they'll explain what they meant.

But right as I'm about to, a uniformed officer enters the hospital. He peers around as if searching for someone, and assuming it's me, I get up, stuff my phone into my pocket, and make my way over to him.

"Are you Ravenlee Willowwynter?" he asks as I approach him.

I nod and raise my hand like a freak. "Yeah, that's me."

"And you made the call to the police tonight?" he asks, glancing down at his handheld device. "Concerning your friend's overdose?"

The muscle in my jaw ticks. "It wasn't an overdose. He was drugged."

"I see." He pushes a few buttons on the device, and it lets out a series of beeps. "So allegedly your friend was drugged. What's his name?"

"Not allegedly," I reply with annoyance. "He was drugged. I know that for a fact because the person who did it told me he did, so no, not allegedly."

The officer's gaze lifts to me and irritation flickers in his eyes. "There's no need to get an attitude."

"Hey, is everything okay?" Jax steps beside me and brushes his fingers along the small of my back.

I cross my arms and glare at the officer. "This kind officer was just writing down that Hunter was drugged."

The officer glares back at me. "Watch your tone." He pushes a few buttons. "What's your friend's full name?"

Jax is the one to answer, "Hunter Hathingford."

The officer freezes, his back stiffening. "Oh, I didn't realize it was Mr. Hathingford's son." He stops pushing buttons for a moment, but then shakes it off. "I need a complete detailed recap of what happened tonight."

I do my best to do that and Jax chimes in with what he knows about it. I hate that I have to tell the officer Hunter and I were getting stoned because I know he'll be annoying about it, but weirdly he breezes over that. I wonder what he'll do about this, if anything. I wonder if he works for my uncle.

I eye him over. He looks frumpy, short and stocky with thin hair. What does he do when there's a crime committed and he has to chase down someone? Does he win—

"Ravenlee?" Jax saying my name with concern pulls me from my daze.

I blink at him. "Hmmm?"

His worry deepens. "The officer wants to know if there's anything else you can think of."

I shake my head. "No, that's about it."

The officer eyes me over with skepticism, but he can do that all he wants—I'm not lying about anything.

"All right, well, I'll make an official report and if we have more questions, we'll call you," he tells me as he tucks the hand-held underneath his arm.

Then he walks off and leaves through the sliding glass doors.

"He's not going to do anything," Jax mutters. "I could tell when he recognized Hunter's last name. He's more than likely going to tell Hunter's father."

I meet Jax's gaze. "Will he do anything about it?"

Jax shakes his head and shrugs. "I don't know. It depends on what role his father is playing in this stupid game. But honestly, I doubt it. If Hunter is okay, his father will likely call him into his office and discuss his failure of the game." He smashes his lips together. "When Hunter is okay, I mean."

"Yes, *when*," I stress while looking him in the eye. "Because he's going to be okay."

"Come on, let's go sit by Low." He threads his fingers through mine, startling me.

But he appears not to notice as he leads me toward the chairs, then pulls me down with him as he sits in a chair two spaces down from Low, leaving me to sit beside her.

Her arms are propped on her legs and her head is lowered in her hands.

"Are you okay?" I ask, crossing my arms as Jax lets go of my hand.

She shakes her head. "I can't lose him, Raven. He's all I've got." Then she leans into me and starts to cry, her shoulders heaving.

I do my best to console her, patting her back. She continues to cry for a handful of minutes before excusing herself to go to the bathroom.

I watch her go and then it's just Jax and I. The hospital is quiet, the lights are too bright, and the air smells awful, like too much cleaner has been used to mask the stench of death..

"Do you think death's scary?" the little blond boy asks me.

"I don't think so," I reply. *"In fact, I bet it's better than this."*

He looks up at me, his eyes shiny with tears. "But what if we're not together."

"We will be," I assure him. *"I promise, Hunter."*

I gasp so loudly I startle the hell out of Jax, enough that he jolts.

"What's wrong?" he asks, buzzing with anxiety as he yanks his fingers through the wisps of his inky black hair.

"It's nothing," I sputter as I leap to my feet. "I think I need some fresh air."

I practically run out of the hospital and burst outside, gulping the cool night air in. The parking lot is quiet, so no one is around to witness my meltdown because yes, I'm about to have one.

In the memory, I said Hunter—a memory of when I was a child. Which means, I knew him once. But does he know that? Does Jax?

"Ravenlee." Jax's voice floats over my shoulder. "What's going on?"

"Nothing," I say, wrapping myself around me.

Tears are burning in my eyes, partly from being overwhelmed by the memory and partly because of what's happening with Hunter. Maybe they're lying to me and they've known me this entire time, but that doesn't mean I want Hunter to be hurt.

In fact, it aches deep inside my chest.

Just who was Hunter to me whenever I knew him—

A hand lands on my shoulder, causing me to jolt and glance behind me.

Jax is standing behind me, his black attire and hair nearly matching the midnight sky. The moment he spots the tears streaming down my face, he frowns.

"Sweetheart, you don't need to cry. Hunter will be okay," he assures me. "I know he will. I can feel it." He rotates me around and wipes the tears away from my cheeks with his fingers. "I have an intuition about these things."

"And your intuition is saying he'll be okay?" I question, searching his shadowy eyes, wondering if he can feel that spark of connection with me like I do with him and Hunter and sometimes Zay.

He nods, then cups my cheeks with his hands. "I can feel it. Trust me, if I didn't, I'd be a total basket case right now." He offers me a sad smile. "I have anxiety, in case you didn't notice."

I did, but...

"I do, too," I mumble. "I usually handle it better when I'm stoned."

"I usually handle it better when nothing is happening," he tries to joke.

I start to smile, but it falters, and my eyes pool with tears again.

"Come here." He pulls me against his chest.

It's not as shaky of a hug as last time, but it's equally as intense.

And for a moment, I forget about everything—

"I hate to break up this moment, but Jax, I need to talk to you." Zay's voice slices through the moment.

Jax pulls back and glances at Zay who gestures for him to come inside. Jax looks back at me. "I'll be right back, okay?"

I nod. "Take your time. I need to call my aunt anyway and tell her where I am before she sends my uncle after me."

Jax hesitates. "I don't think it's a good idea for you to be out here by yourself."

"I'll be fine," I assure him. "We're at the hospital. And I'll make sure to stand near the door. I just need to talk to her privately."

He remains reluctant but ultimately gives in and starts toward the door.

I dig my phone out of my pocket, and dial my aunt's number as him and Zay go into the hospital.

The phone only rings two times before I'm sent to voicemail. Odd, but not totally out of the ordinary, so I pocket my phone and move to go inside when a vehicle rolls up to the curb.

And not just any vehicle. My uncle's patrol car.

I tense as he climbs out of the car and shuts the door. He's in uniform, and at first, I think maybe he's here for another reason.

But then his eyes fix on me, and he rounds the front of the car as he says, "I received a call from an officer, informing me that my niece was at the hospital because she had to bring in some junkie that almost overdosed."

"What?" My lips part in shock. "That's not what happened—"

He holds up his hand. "Be careful what you say. The more you lie, the worse your punishment will be."

My fingers curl into fists. "I wasn't going to lie, but I'm also not going to just stand here and let you believe a lie about what I was doing because I didn't bring a junkie here. I brought a friend of mine that was drugged."

His heavy boots scuff against the concrete as he starts towards me, the keys clipped to his belt jingling with each step he takes. Each sound causes my heart to painfully skip a beat, and the scars on my side burn. The awareness that no one else is out here is heavy, like thick fog; so thick, I can barely breathe.

"Bullshit." He stops in front of me. "We both know you're a liar. A dirty little whore who needs to be punished." He hooks his thumbs in his belt loop. "And I'm not going to go around having people think my flesh and blood are spending time with drug addicts."

"I'm not hanging out with drug addicts." My tone is low and full of anger. Usually, I don't fight back this much, but he's insulting Hunter. Sweet Hunter, who's currently in the hospital, struggling to stay alive. "And your officer who told you that lied."

His eyes darken, his muscles tightening. Then he grabs my arm.

"You're such a goddamn liar—you always have been." He begins to drag me toward the trees that encompass the parking lot. "What I want to know is if you actually believe them or if you just lie to yourself so you don't have to deal with the truth." He yanks on my arm harder as I try to dig my heels into the ground. "Because if you admitted them to yourself, you'd have to accept that you killed your parents."

"Let me go!" I shout, yanking on my arm.

I move to kick him, and nail him in the shin, hard enough that his hand slips off of me.

"Fuck," he curses as I take off running.

But a split second later, his arms are wrapped around me. I go wild as he lifts me up and hauls me toward the trees, kicking, screaming, and digging my fingernails into his flesh.

He curses but never lets me go until the forest is swallowing us up whole. "You're going to regret fighting me," he snaps the moment the hospital is out of view. Then he throws me on the ground so roughly that my teeth clank together, and I bite my tongue.

"Ow," I groan as I roll to the side in the dirt and leaves.

I need to get up, but the world is spinning around me. I think I may have hit my head, which would explain the warm liquid trickling down my temple.

I groan again as I lift my hand and touch the tender spot.

"I think it's time you were properly punished," my uncle says as he looms above me, unfastening his belt.

"No," I whisper, struggling to get to my feet, but I barely push up before he kicks me in the ribs.

I cough as the window gets knocked out of me.

"Stay the fuck down, and this'll be over more quickly," he growls out as he undoes the button on his pants and then climbs on top of me, pinning me down on my back.

"No!" I shout, but he slaps his hand down on my mouth.

Between his weight and the concussion that I'm pretty sure I have, I feel like I'm being crushed alive.

Help! Help! Help!

"You want to know a secret," he whispers as he flicks the button of my shorts undone. "Your entire life is a lie, Ravenlee. Or should I say Willow?" He slides the zipper of my shorts down. "You don't even have a damn clue who you are. And you want to know why? Because everyone hates you so much they tried to make you disappear. But no, it ended up falling on me. And what do I get out of it? Nothing. And I'm tired of that shit—I'm tired of taking care of a worthless loser."

His words barely register as I feel around for anything that will help me get him off of me.

I can't let this happen.

I can't.

I need to fight.

My fingers brush against something hard and round. I don't think. I just grab it and slam it against his head as hard as I can.

I expect him to scream.

I expect to hit me.

What I don't expect is for silence to follow.

The kind of silence that only follows death.

About the Author

Jessica Sorensen is a *New York Times* and *USA Today* bestselling author who lives in the snowy mountains of Wyoming. When she's not writing, she spends her time reading and hanging out with her family.

For more info:

Facebook: Jessica.Sorensen.Author

Facebook group: Sorensen's Stars

Instagram: jessica_sorensenauthor

jessicasorensen.com

Other books by Jessica Sorensen:

The Royal Academy:
The Royal Academy
The Royal Promises
The Royal Flame
The Royal Rose (coming soon)

The Art of Being Friends:
The Art of Being Friends
The Rules of Being Friends
The Art of Kissing (coming soon)

-
The Heartbreaker Society:
The Opposite of Ordinary
The Simplicity in Unordinary (coming soon)

-
Capturing Magic:
Chasing Wishes

Other books by Jessica Sorensen:

Untitled (coming soon)

-
Broken City Series:
Nameless

Forsaken (coming soon)

Cursed Moon Series:
Wishes Upon a Cursed Moon (coming soon)

Monsters of Madness:
Monsters of Madness

Monsters of Darkness (coming soon)

-
Enchanted Chaos Series:
Enchanted Chaos

Shimmering Chaos

Iridescent Chaos (coming soon)

Forever Violet:
Forever Violet

Forever Stardust (coming soon)

-
Tangled Realms:
Forever Violet

Forever Stardust (coming soon)

-
Curse of the Vampire Queen:
Tempting Raven

Alluring Raven

Other books by Jessica Sorensen:

Untitled (coming soon)

-

Mystic Willow Bay Witches Series:
The Secret Life of a Witch
Untitled (coming soon)

Guardian Academy Series:
Entranced
Entangled
Enchanted
Enitce (coming soon)

Forget Me Not:
Forget Me Not
Fall With Me (coming soon)

The Honeyton Mysteries:
Chasing Hadley
Falling for Hadley
Holding onto Hadley
The Mystery of Hadley
The Secret of Hadley (coming soon)

-

Other Books:
The Forgotten Girl
The Illusion of Annabella
Confessions of Luna & Grey
Rules of a Rebel and a Shy Girl

-

Other books by Jessica Sorensen:

Shadow Cove Series:
What Lies in the Darkness

What Hides in the Darkness (coming soon)

-

Sunnyvale Series:
The Year I Became Isabella Anders

The Year of Falling in Love

The Year of Second Chances

The Year of Us (coming soon)

Unraveling You Series:
Unraveling You

Raveling You

Awakening You

Inspiring You

Finding You (coming soon)

The Coincidence Series:
The Coincidence of Callie and Kayden

The Redemption of Callie and Kayden

The Destiny of Violet and Luke

The Probability of Violet and Luke

The Certainty of Violet and Luke

The Resolution of Callie and Kayden

The Secret Series:
The Prelude of Ella and Micha

The Secret of Ella and Micha

The Forever of Ella and Micha

Other books by Jessica Sorensen:

The Temptation of Lila and Ethan
The Ever After of Ella and Micha
Lila and Ethan: Forever and Always
Ella and Micha: Infinitely and Always

The Shattered Promises Series:

Shattered Promises
Fractured Souls
Unbroken
Broken Visions
Scattered Ashes

Breaking Nova Series:

Breaking Nova
Saving Quinton
Delilah: The Making of Red
Nova and Quinton: No Regrets
Tristan: Finding Hope
Wreck Me
Ruin Me

The Fallen Star Series:

The Fallen Star
The Underworld
The Vision
The Promise
The Lost Soul
The Evanescence

The Darkness Falls Series:
Darkness Falls
Darkness Breaks
Darkness Fades

The Death Collectors X Series (NA version):
Ember X
Cinder X
Spark X
-

Death Collects Series (YA version):
Ember
Cinder
Spark
-

Unbeautiful Series:
Unbeautiful
Untamed